Deck *the* Donuts

Books by Ginger Bolton

SURVIVAL OF THE FRITTERS

GOODBYE CRULLER WORLD

JEALOUSY FILLED DONUTS

BOSTON SCREAM MURDER

BEYOND A REASONABLE DONUT

DECK THE DONUTS

Published by Kensington Publishing Corp.

Deck *the* Donuts

GINGER BOLTON

KENSINGTON
PUBLISHING CORP.

www.kensingtonbooks.com

KENSINGTON BOOKS are published by

Kensington Publishing Corp.
119 West 40th Street
New York, NY 10018

ISBN-13: 978-1-4967-2561-5 (ebook)

ISBN-13: 978-1-4967-2560-8

First Kensington Trade Paperback Printing: November 2021

10 9 8 7 6 5 4 3 2

Printed in the United States of America

ACKNOWLEDGMENTS

Thanks to my agent, John Talbot, and my editor, John Scognamiglio, I can do what I dreamed of doing since I was a little girl. I love creating worlds using words. I couldn't do it without the backing of the entire team at Kensington Publishing Corp. Special thanks to Larissa Ackerman, Carly Sommerstein, and Kristine Mills. Mary Ann Lasher, your paintings bring the book covers to life. Thank you!

Many thanks also to the unsung heroes who keep things running even during the most difficult and heartbreaking times—workers in pharmacies and grocery stores, farm workers, and the people who keep our means of communication open. What would we have done without the Internet and virtual meetings?

Thanks to my friends and critique group members who used to meet in person for lunch—Cathy Astolfo, Alison Bruce, Melodie Campbell, Joan O'Callaghan, and Nancy O'Neill. May we soon be able to go back to our potlucks! And thanks go also to the friends and colleagues who have always met online and occasionally at conferences—Allison Brook, Laurie Cass, Krista Davis, Kaye George, and Daryl Wood Gerber. In addition, there is a wide network of supportive writers. Thanks to all of you.

Sgt. Michael Boothby, Toronto Police Service (Retired) has kept me from straying too far from what real investigators do, and I owe him many thanks.

My friends and family have always put up with me and my quirks. Thank you.

Most of all, I want to thank you, the reader. Without your imagination, my books would be only so many squiggles. Your collaboration brings them to life.

Chapter 1

How could a blizzard be on the way to this part of northern Wisconsin? Puffy white clouds dotted a blue sky, and even though I was wearing ski goggles with dark, mirrored lenses, the snow seemed brighter than white in the sunlight.

I latched my boots into the bindings of my cross-country skis and pulled on my red, green, and white striped stocking cap and my leather-palmed gloves. I slipped my hands into the straps of my poles and grasped the handgrips. The blade-like tips on the ends of my poles would help propel me along the snow-packed driveway where Brent and I had parked our SUVs. My black wind-resistant nylon pants and matching jacket, worn over leggings and a long sweater, would be enough to keep me warm when we really started moving.

Brent and I had once rented the equipment for skate-skiing and had decided we preferred the more classic form, keeping our skis parallel except while turning, slowing, stopping, or herringboning up steep hills. The flat, mostly plowed driveway was snowy enough for us to ski along it to a groomed trail crossing the front yard of a gorgeous natural wood chalet nestled among pines. Snow from the previous week's storm covered the building's steeply pitched roof and drooped in scallops below its eaves, not quite covering holly-bedecked cedar garlands and Christmas lights. Wreaths and candles decorated windows.

When Brent had invited me on the afternoon's ski outing, I had asked who owned the property where we were going, but he had only answered that we could ski there that afternoon and again in three days when he was hosting a Saturday-before-Christmas party.

The trail curved to the left. The chalet's front yard ended at the brink of a forested hill where the trail headed abruptly into a valley. I clamped my poles to my sides with the ends sticking out behind me, crouched, and swooped downward. Wind whipped past my cheeks and ruffled the curls sticking out beneath my cap. I couldn't help a huge, teeth-chilling smile. Slowing, I navigated a tricky S curve, first right and then left. The trail became less steep and ran beside a creek where miniature waterfalls flowed around rocks mounded with snow.

In the valley, a lake was mostly covered in thin sheets of shifting, grumbling ice. The trail widened around a sharp left turn and then passed a small boathouse and what might have been a beach underneath the snow.

Above me, clouds gathered and blue patches shrank. Inhaling the exhilarating, clean, and piney air, I settled into a comfortable rhythm of push, glide, push, glide. I skied up short slopes and down shallow dips.

The predicted blizzard began to seem possible. The clouds became dappled with gray and darker than the white of the snow-laden pine branches beside the trail. My skis sang against hard-packed snow. Behind me, Brent's did, too.

At almost six feet, he was about nine inches taller than I was and could easily have skied faster than I did, but he always stayed far enough back to avoid ramming the tips of his skis into the tails of mine and sending me tumbling into soft snow beside the harder groomed trail. The previous winter, I'd learned that climbing out of deep, fluffy snow while wearing skis wasn't as easy as it sounded, even with the help of a big, strong man. To his credit, he had tried not to laugh.

In a way, I was relieved that, on this first outing in a long time with the big, strong man, skiing prevented us from talking or even looking at each other. Brent had been my late husband's best friend and his partner in the Fallingbrook Police Department. After Alec was shot and killed, Brent's and my grief had kept us apart. About three years later, we'd finally begun doing things together like eating at my house where he could play with my cat, kayaking in the summer, and cross-country skiing in the winter. Our shared grief had drawn us closer than we'd been when Alec was alive, but it had also kept a barrier between us.

Now I thought I might want to destroy that barrier.

I had a problem. I didn't know how.

Alec had told me that if anything ever happened to him, I should find happiness with another man. At first, I hadn't been able to imagine being with anyone besides Alec. Now I felt almost ready to begin thinking about dating again.

The trouble was that Brent was the only man I wanted to be with. Worse, I really wanted to be with him. Back in August, I had finally admitted to myself how much I cared about the tall detective who was always available when I needed someone, and here it was almost Christmas, and I still hadn't given him a hint about my feelings.

I was scared. What if merely being my dining, kayaking, and cross-country skiing buddy was enough for Brent and was all he wanted in a relationship with me? What if he felt, as I had at first, that a romance between us would be disloyal to Alec? What if he preferred to date other women?

Skiing through the elegantly lacy woods, I wondered who owned this property with its freshly groomed trail. I was skiing in grooves made by weighted skis towed behind a snowmobile. The tracks of its treads were still visible. In the short time we'd been in this snowy wonderland, I hadn't seen or heard anyone else. No other vehicles had been in the driveway, but there could have been some behind the closed doors of the double garage I'd glimpsed at the rear of the chalet.

Brent's eyes had held a teasing glint earlier that afternoon when he'd told me to follow him in my car to a ski trail. At the time, I'd figured he'd found a fun new place to ski. That was true, but I could also imagine that he might have bought the chalet and these acres of woods, complete with a stream emptying into a lake where we could go kayaking in the summer. I could also imagine that he might have decided to surprise me by showing me his exciting purchase instead of telling me about it first.

All of this imagining gave me a new worry. Had I waited too long to let Brent know how I felt about him? If he had bought this place, would he think I had suddenly become interested in him only because I wanted to spend time kayaking and skiing here?

But even if that thought wasn't about to occur to him, I still didn't know how to show him how I felt.

I pictured throwing myself into his arms. That warmed me even more than skiing had.

But what if he pushed me away?

I was overthinking it. Maybe I should take a chance.

The trail turned left again and started up a series of hills. None of them were steep, and I didn't have to spoil the tracks by herringboning. Pushing hard with my poles, I skied to the top of the final hill. I kept going on the flat trail beside the long driveway and stopped beside our SUVs. Mine was medium sized and white. Brent's was huge and black.

Behind me, he asked, "Do you want to go around again, Emily?" He usually called me "Em" unless other police officers were around and an investigation was going on. Then he became more formal and used my full name. But the way he'd said Emily just then had sounded more friendly than formal.

Without lifting my skis, which faced forward, I twisted my body around to look at him.

Smiling, he leaned casually on his poles. He wasn't wearing a hat and had pushed his mirrored goggles up onto his head. Breezes had tossed his light brown hair. He looked relaxed and happy. And kind and caring. And extremely attractive. His unzipped black jacket showed off muscles that his tight black sweater accentuated.

Above us, the sky was now a heavy, sullen lead. If we skied around the trail again, I risked having to drive home through a blizzard.

"It's a beautiful trail, and I'd love to ski down that first hill again." I pointed a pole toward an ominous charcoal mass of clouds to the southwest. "But . . ."

"There will be other times. Like Saturday."

"Okay." I unsnapped my skis and thrust them and my poles into my car. The first flakes of snow landed on my face.

Brent took off his skis and held them and his poles in one hand. He glanced toward the chalet. "Would you like to go inside for hot chocolate?"

Would I be able to drive home before the roads became impassible even for my SUV? What if Brent and I became snowbound out here in the country?

Maybe that wasn't a bad idea. . . .

Not quite knowing how to respond to his invitation, I asked, "Who owns this place?"

He pulled keys out of his pocket. "Guess."

"You?"

Grinning, he nodded.

"Since when?"

"Last week. Like it?"

I waved toward the snowy woods we'd just skied through. "Do you own all of that, too?"

"Yep. The woods, the stream, a beach, and a boathouse

big enough for a couple of kayaks and not much else. And a dock that can be put in for summer."

"You didn't tell me." I hoped I hadn't sounded accusing.

"I wasn't sure the deal would close, and I wanted to surprise you."

"You did."

He gave me an enigmatic look similar to the neutral expression he wore when he was on duty as a detective, but this was different. It was cautious and maybe a little hesitant.

"I like it," I answered belatedly. "It's perfect. It's so . . . so you!"

He looked down toward the evergreens on the slope below us. "We can ski and kayak other places, but this will always be available."

"You'll be a half hour from work." The police station was near Fallingbrook's village square. So was Deputy Donut, the café that Alec's father and I owned. My home was also near downtown Fallingbrook.

Brent conceded, "It's a long commute, but this place is worth it."

"I see that." I took a deep breath, braced my shoulders, and looked up into his face. "Thank you for bringing me here."

"My pleasure." He gazed into my eyes for a couple of seconds and then dropped his skis and poles into the snow. He leaned toward me. A question lurked in those kind and caring gray eyes.

With my eyes locked on his, I tilted my face up.

His phone rang.

Chapter 2

✺

Pulling his phone from a pocket, Brent backed a step away from me. "Sorry, I'll have to answer. It's dispatch." I couldn't help hearing his side of the conversation. "County Road C five miles north of Fallingbrook? Right, I'm at my new place now. I'll be there in a few minutes." He put his phone away. His face had taken on his grimmest police detective look. "A tour bus went into a ditch. I'm closer than other Fallingbrook first responders. I'll head there now." He held out his keys. "Would you like to warm up inside? I might be awhile."

I refused the keys. "I'll come, too. I'll follow you."

"You're not a first responder."

Knowing he wanted to protect me from the sorts of situations that he and our other first responder friends encountered much too frequently, I put on my toughest expression. "I've kept up with my first aid training." I'd been a 911 dispatcher until shortly after Alec was killed, but after his death, I hadn't been able to stand working at 911 where we couldn't rescue everyone.

Where I hadn't been able to rescue Alec.

A new dispatcher had filled in for me that night. Brent had been only grazed. He had told me he had radioed for help for Alec before a citizen called 911, but I would probably never get over my feelings of guilt about taking that evening off work to go to dinner with out-of-town friends.

And Brent would always wonder if he could have done more to save Alec, who had been not only his partner, but his best friend.

Wretchedly, I grated out, "Those poor people . . . I could make a difference. I have to go."

Brent slung one arm around my shoulders and described the turns he would take to reach the wrecked bus. "Don't try to keep up with me. Someone might pull you over."

"You're the only police officer for miles around, and you'll be busy."

He let me go and said in faked ominous tones, "Don't count on it." He threw his skis and poles into his own SUV, got in, and raced down the driveway.

Feeling hollowed out and also dreading what we would find at the scene, I sped after him. I didn't like wearing gloves while driving and threw them onto the passenger seat. Dark gray clouds now covered the sky, bringing with them an early dusk. Snow began falling heavily. Turning onto County Road C, I caught a glimpse of the plain gold wedding band I'd worn since the day, ten and a half years before, that Alec had slipped it on my finger. He'd been thirty-two. I'd been twenty-one, barely more than a kid. I missed his quick wit, his joy, his kindness, and his warmth, but maybe it was time to stop wearing that ring as a shield against other men.

Against one other man, anyway.

Sunshine had been warming the pavement only an hour or so before, and at the moment, the snow was melting. Ahead, the pinpricks of Brent's taillights disappeared into the storm. I drove as quickly as possible considering that I could see only bits of the yellow line in the center of the road and white snow pounding toward my windshield. On the radio, a chorus sang cheerfully about dashing through the snow.

The onslaught of icy flakes rapidly cooled the road. Snow

accumulated and deepened. Gripping the wheel more tightly, biting my lip, and afraid I would accidentally pass the crash, I slowed. Finally, in the blur of the snowstorm ahead of me, a pinkish glow blinked off and on. I slowed more.

Its hazard lights flashing, Brent's SUV was on the road's right shoulder. I parked a car's length behind him and turned on my own hazard lights.

I grabbed the first-aid kit I kept on board and ran along the road to Brent's SUV. He wasn't in it. Ahead and to the right, wide tire tracks veered off through a lumpy ridge of the previous week's plowed snow.

The bus faced away from me in a ditch. I followed Brent's tracks over the piled-up snow next to the road. He had preserved clues about the cause of the crash by staying far from the marks the bus had made. In places, his feet and legs must have sunk into the snow, and mine did, too, sometimes up to my knees. Finally I made it beyond the plowed clumps of snow and ice, and walking became slightly easier. With the words of "Jingle Bells" echoing inside my head, I slipped and slid down the slope on a crusty base of old snow. I was still wearing my cross-country ski boots. Apparently, Brent hadn't taken time to change out of his, either. The quickly falling snow hadn't completely covered their prints. I followed them. The closer I got to the bus, the more blinding its taillights became.

The left front of the bus was crumpled against a massive tree trunk. The bus's remaining working headlight illuminated the woods beyond the ditch. I walked past the back of the bus and between the bus and trees at the edge of the woods. I heard subdued voices but couldn't make out what anyone was saying. Branches whispered across my nylon pants and jacket.

The door of the bus hung open. Reassured because Brent was already on the bus, but apprehensive about what we might need to cope with, I reached for handholds and climbed the crazily slanted steps.

The inside of the bus reeked of booze, and the only light was reflected from that one headlight shining into the whitening woods. It was enough to let me see what I should have expected on a bus tour ten days before Christmas—children. I gasped in shock, but far from appearing injured, the children seemed excited about their unexpected ride down into a ditch in a bus. One boy near the front swooped his hand from above his head to below his shoulder. "It was like a roller coaster!"

The boy beside him bounced in his seat. "Yeah!"

Out on the road, something roared and scraped. The noises stopped and were replaced by the sound of a rumbling diesel engine. Amber light swung past the bus windows.

Passengers seemed to be buckled into their seats except for a woman standing beside the driver. She was wearing a dark green nylon jacket with TOUR GUIDE printed in white on the back. Actually, all I could read was TOUR G IDE. The strap of her shiny black tote bag crossed over her body from her right shoulder and hid the U. Tears running down her face, she grasped the driver by the shoulders as if to keep him from tumbling out of his seat. "I don't know what happened," she wailed to Brent. He was helping her hold the driver, who didn't appear to be wearing a seat belt. "Suddenly, we went off the road." Her long hair fell over her eyes. She rubbed her shoulder against her chin and dislodged some of the hair from her face. I saw fright in her pale eyes.

Beyond Brent's arm, I caught a glimpse of the bus driver's bloodied face. His eyes were open, zigzagging back and forth, and his head wobbled. His eyebrows seemed stuck in one position, high over his nose and lower toward the outer corners of his eyes, as if he couldn't get over astonishment at the bus's having left the road. In front of him, snow was coating the cobwebby rays of the fractured windshield.

Metal jingled. A burly man ran up the bus steps behind me. The front of the bus was lower than the back. I moved up the slanted aisle to let the man inside.

"How can I help?" he asked. "I've got a snowplow." He wore a stocking cap over a baseball cap, both covered in snow. He squinted at the driver and aimed an index finger at him. "Travis Tarriston." I heard a sneer in his tone. "What are you doing around here again?"

Travis Tarriston, if that was his name, asked in a creaky voice, "Where are we?"

The tour guide answered, "We're on our way to the Fallingbrook Ice and Lights Festival, Travis, and the bus just went off the road." She turned her head toward the snowplow operator. "Can you pull us back up?"

"No, ma'am."

In the distance, a siren wailed, coming closer.

The snowplow operator stared toward the people still buckled into their seats. "Don't the inside lights work?"

The tour guide snapped, "I don't want to run the battery down."

The snowplow operator grunted. "You aren't going to need that anytime soon. This thing's a write-off." Readjusting his hat duo, he knocked snow onto the shoulders of his bulky parka.

Still hanging on to the driver, the tour guide clamped her elbow against the huge tote bag, pulling it closer to her body. "It's freezing in here. We need to start the engine so we can turn on the heater." She wasn't dressed warmly. Still in our cross-country ski clothes, Brent and I weren't, either.

Gently, Brent told the tour guide, "I don't advise starting the engine." He flipped a switch in front of the driver. Dim greenish lights came on inside the bus.

Travis Tarriston rasped out, "How did I get here?"

A siren whooped outside and stopped.

Chapter 3

✄

Kids aboard the bus shouted, "Here's an ambulance!" More pinkish lights flashed through the whiteness.

Brent turned to the snowplow operator. "Thanks, Ronald. Can you keep the road between here and Fallingbrook as clear as possible for emergency vehicles and until we get everyone transported to safety?"

"Sure thing, Detective Fyne." With a final glare toward the injured bus driver, Ronald clomped out of the bus.

Corey Ides, an emergency medical technician I'd met a few times, dashed up the stairs into the bus. He sniffed audibly and grimaced as if the whiskey-like smells hit him as hard as they'd hit me. At first, I didn't see Samantha Houlihan, the petite EMT behind her younger, taller partner. Samantha was one of my two best friends from ever since junior high. She and Corey were in their winter uniforms—black stocking caps and heavy black parkas and matching pants crisscrossed with reflective stripes. Some of Samantha's brown curls, streaked with red and green, showed beneath her cap. She and Corey took over Travis's care.

Travis told them, "I must have driven here." He sounded more confident than he had moments before.

Brent and I moved farther up the slope of the aisle. Brent

called out, "Some of the rest of you said you were slightly injured. Raise your hands, please."

I was relieved that none of the children were among the few injured people. Brent held up his first-aid kit where I could see it. "I'll take this side, Emily. Can you take the other one?"

I showed him the first-aid kit that he'd probably already noticed in my hand. "Sure."

Brent and I asked people about injuries. One mother had an undoubtedly broken arm and one man thought he had whiplash.

Corey left and returned with a rescue sled. He and Samantha strapped Travis, with his neck now stabilized, into the sled. I ran to the front of the bus and told them about the broken arm and the possible whiplash. Samantha said, "I'll help Corey maneuver the sled out of the bus, and then while Corey's pulling the sled up to the ambulance, I'll check on the other victims. Don't move them." She and Corey carried Travis out.

Brent carefully wrapped a thin, silvery emergency blanket around the man with the sore neck. A man and a little boy who looked about seven helped me wrap another emergency blanket around the woman with the broken arm. The little boy told me, "Mommy's hurt. Daddy and I are taking care of her."

Samantha returned and fastened a cervical collar on the possible whiplash victim and guided him down the sloping aisle toward the front of the bus. Brent helped the woman with the broken arm down the aisle.

The tour guide announced, "I'm coming, too."

Samantha gave her an assessing look. "Are you injured?"

"No."

"We can only fit the man we already took out and these two people, one in the back with your bus driver and my partner, and the other up front with me."

Brent added, "We'll transport the rest of you as quickly as possible."

The tour guide sobbed, "I need to be with Travis. He's confused. He's not usually like that."

Brent assured her, "He'll be looked after, and we'll get you to the hospital." He went to the front of the bus, removed a small black object from an open compartment near the steering wheel, and helped Samantha take the injured people down the oddly canted stairs.

The injured woman's husband assured their son that everything would be fine, his mother's arm would stop hurting, and they would both see her soon. The boy's lower lip trembled, but he didn't cry.

I wrapped an emergency blanket around the tour guide. She asked me, "What can I do? I'm Paige, by the way."

"I'm Emily." I gave her a fistful of adhesive bandages printed with Santas, elves, and candy canes. "Let's see if any of the children need these."

One boy shouted, "I want a superhero cape, too."

"They're only for sick people," his mother told him.

He wailed, "I'm sick!"

His mother held a hand toward me. "He'll need one if we want any peace." I gave her a survival blanket from my first-aid kit.

The boy's two older brothers clamored for them, too. "You'll have to share," their mother told them. "The lady doesn't have any more."

That wasn't true, but I didn't admit that I had another one, and Brent probably had more, too. Other passengers might need them more than the obviously uninjured boys did, and we definitely didn't have enough for all of the children on the bus.

Outside, the siren on the ambulance started up. Kids on the bus cheered. The sound of the siren dwindled. Brent came back, talked to adults, and gave kids his special brand of heartwarming smile.

Still carrying her tote bag as if she feared that someone might steal it, Paige started up the sloping aisle ahead of me. She had to turn sideways to slip the bag past elbows and knees sticking out into the aisle.

Fortunately, none of the children were hurt. Paige and I put bandages on many of them anyway, and Paige started singing "Frosty the Snowman." Unlike me, she had a great voice. Children chimed in.

The father of the boy wearing the superhero cape was un-injured, but his face was red. His mouth contorting, he announced, "The driver was speeding and drinking and needs to be arrested."

Paige stopped singing. "He was not!"

Pointing at Brent, I told the angry father, "That man is a detective. He'll want statements from all of the adults."

Paige claimed, "It was totally an accident." Singing again, falteringly, she moved farther up the slope toward the back of the bus.

The man might have thought that I was also a police officer. He muttered to me, "The road was clear. No ice, no snow, no animals, no reason to leave the road. And we got a much later start than we were supposed to, thanks to him, so he was speeding so he could fit in the Ice and Lights Festival. We were supposed to tour that and then go to Duluth and have dinner in our hotel in time to put the kids to bed. That's not going to happen." He unbuckled his seat belt and turned in his seat as if to make certain that Paige wasn't near enough to hear him. "She distracted him. She was talking to him almost all the way. And I suspect she was drinking, too. They both were." He held up his phone. "And no one at the tour company is answering the phone. They need to send another bus."

Maybe, from inside, he didn't realize how much snow was piling up. Now that lights were on, we couldn't see outside unless we imitated some of the kids and put our noses up to the windows, shielded our faces with our hands, and then rubbed off the condensation from our breath.

I asked, "Where are the tour company's headquarters?"

"Green Bay, but they could send a bus from somewhere closer. There must be cities nearby."

I made a face. "Not really."

"Then I'll keep calling." He focused on his phone.

More sirens sounded. Colored lights strobed past the windows. Kids hollered, "Fire trucks! Police cars!"

I slithered in my icy-soled cross-country boots down the slanted aisle to the front of the bus and clambered down the steps in time to allow firefighters in full gear and uniformed police officers in thick parkas to swarm into the bus. "Brent's in there," I told the other of my best friends since junior high, police officer Misty Ossler.

She raised an eyebrow. "What are you wearing, Emily? You're shivering."

She was right. "We were skiing." The wind-resistant pants and jacket over my leggings and long sweater had been fine for skiing, but not for standing around in a blizzard. "I have a warmer jacket in the car."

In addition to the police-issue parka, she wore gloves and a woolly hat. "Go put it on." She spoke with the authority of a police officer and the concern of a friend. Tall and elegant as always, she climbed into the bus, followed by her patrol partner, the boyishly freckled Hooligan Houlihan, Samantha's husband. He waved and winked at me.

Another friend, fire chief Scott Ritsorf, who was dating Misty, scrambled to me through the snow. He was even taller than Misty. He also told me to go put on a warmer coat.

I tramped up out of the ditch to my car. I couldn't hear much besides wind and snowflakes buffeting me. I took off the wet jacket, put on my parka, cinched the hood around my face, wallowed back to the bus, and waited outside in case anyone needed me. I brushed and shook snow off, but it kept attempting to turn me into a snowman. Voices on the bus were louder than they'd been when I first arrived.

Brent had come outside. Still in cross-country ski clothes, but with his jacket now zipped, he tramped around in the snow, making notes and taking pictures of the bus and the tracks it had made.

With amber lights flashing and blades clattering and scraping, a snowplow cleared the road from the direction of Fallingbrook. A stream of vehicles followed it.

Scott came out of the bus and looked toward the vehicles. "Good."

I was still shivering, probably not entirely from having become chilled. "What's going on?" It looked like a parade, but that wasn't likely.

"Brent called your father-in-law. Tom called a few other people. They organized a convoy to take the stranded passengers to Frisky Pomegranate. The restaurant is gearing up to feed them all. While the passengers are eating, we'll find people to take them in. Cindy made the arrangements with Frisky Pomegranate and now she's working on accommodations." The passengers wouldn't be able to stay in hotels even if they could get there. Most of the local resorts and motels were closed for the winter or booked solid with skiers, snowboarders, and snowmobilers. Scott commented, "With parents like Cindy and Tom, it's not surprising that Alec was so all-around good."

I agreed. "They're the best in-laws anyone could have. They still treat me like a daughter." Before I could get teary, I changed the subject. "One of the passengers told me they began their trip today later than planned. Why did they start out, especially late? This storm was predicted."

Scott must have recognized that my question was mostly rhetorical. He answered, "Yeah, why?"

I stabbed at a guess. "People don't like to change plans?"

He looked up at the falling snowflakes. "They don't, do they?" He squeezed my shoulder.

He and other firefighters spread a tarp beside the bus, and then they helped Paige retrieve luggage from the compartments underneath the bus. We set the luggage on the tarp. The firefighters spread another tarp over it all, and then they helped the passengers out of the bus and guided them to our improvised baggage claim. I shined a flashlight and did whatever I could to help Paige and the firefighters reunite people with their bags.

I felt sorry for Paige when the angry man from the bus rudely grabbed his and his wife's and children's suitcases as if he suspected that Paige might abscond with the suitcases or dump them out.

We helped the passengers carry bags and children through the deepening snow. Tom and the other drivers filled their cars, vans, and SUVs with passengers and luggage. The snowplow turned around and began plowing its way back to town. The other vehicles followed.

I found Brent examining the bus's crumpled hood. In the glow from that one headlight, he looked strained. "I've made collision reconstruction notes and taken photos. Misty and Hooligan will wait for the tow truck to haul the bus to the forensics lab. You and I should go while the road is being cleared. I'll follow you."

I said, "You don't have to. You could go home." I thought, *If we both went to your place, we could warm up there and maybe pick up where we left off.*

"I'll have to file reports and orchestrate the investigation. I'll probably be at headquarters all night or most of it."

A hesitant female voice behind us called out, "Excuse me?"

I jumped and turned around.

Paige.

Where had she been? She should have joined the passengers in Tom's convoy. Even with the silvery blanket she was clutching with one hand below her chin, she couldn't have been dressed warmly enough in her lightweight jacket and thin leggings. She waded through the snow to us. Unlike me, she was wearing knee-high boots. She asked Brent, "Should I stay with the bus?"

Brent frowned. "The police officers who are here will remain until the bus is removed. I didn't realize you hadn't left with the volunteers."

Paige peered into the snow where the last of the taillights had disappeared. The reek of alcohol seemed to be coming from her. Had she been drinking too much to understand what had been going on during the past quarter hour? She held up one hand and showed us two small duffel bags, a dark one and one that appeared in the dimming light to be pink. "I had to get Travis's and my bags. They were way back behind the others."

Brent asked, "Which bag is Travis's? I'll take it to the hospital and give it to him."

"The brown one. I . . . I could take it."

Brent's answer was terse. "I need to talk to him."

I thought, *Probably while you're testing his blood alcohol level.* I didn't want to add to Paige's worries, so I didn't say it.

Instead, I suggested, "You can ride with me, Paige. I'd like company on the drive."

She handed Brent the brown duffel bag. "Okay. Can you take me to the hospital so I can be with Travis?"

Before I could answer, Brent told her, "He's going to be busy for awhile. You're probably cold, tired, and hungry. Emily can take you to Frisky Pomegranate where everyone from your bus will eat dinner. You can go to the hospital later." He gave me one of his lowered-eyebrow looks. "Let's go so we can take advantage of the plowed road before it fills up again. I'll be right behind you."

Chapter 4

✤

Paige and I shuffled through the snow to my SUV. I set her duffel bag in the back and offered to let her put her enormous tote bag there, too.

She opened the passenger door. "I'll keep it with me." She placed the tote on the floor in front of the seat, but she didn't get into the car. She closed the door. Grasping the silvery survival blanket at her neck with one hand, she started sweeping snow off the windshield with her free arm.

I took the brush out of the back and handed it to her. We needed to get on the road before it became choked with snow. Telling myself to invest in a second brush, I swept snow off the windows with my gloved hands. The snow was light and fluffy.

We hopped into the car, and I drove past Brent's SUV. His windows were mostly cleared, also.

He pulled onto the road behind us. Glad that the right lane had been plowed recently, I drove as quickly as I dared, but I didn't see a sign of Tom's convoy. Brent stayed a cautious distance behind us. I knew he wouldn't let my car out of sight if he could help it.

Paige still smelled strongly of alcohol, but she didn't seem drunk. Did that mean that only Travis had been drinking? I hadn't seen any bottles on that bus, but maybe passengers had tucked empties underneath their seats. Misty and Hooligan would look for clues like that.

Paige must have noticed how tense I was. "You're doing great, Emily."

"I learned a lot about defensive driving from my late husband. He was a detective."

She turned to look out the back. Her blanket crackled. "Like that guy behind us?"

"They were partners on the force, and best friends."

"I'm sorry for your loss."

I failed to relax my tight grip on the steering wheel. "Thank you. It's been just over seven years."

"It must still hurt."

"It does."

She heaved a sigh.

I asked, "Is Travis your husband?" She seemed to be in her early twenties. I hadn't gotten a good look at Travis, but I guessed he was in his middle thirties. It was approximately the difference between Alec's and my ages. And between Brent's and mine.

"My boyfriend. I hope he's okay."

"The hospital is a good one." I risked a quick glance at her. Like an experienced driver, she stared ahead at the road. I asked, "Do you drive a lot?"

"I don't have a commercial license, so I couldn't help Travis drive the bus. I'm working on getting a commercial license. Was working on it . . ."

"You still can."

Another sigh. "I guess."

My headlights showed little besides wind-driven snow pelting toward us. I told Paige, "Yelp if you see something in the road that I might be missing."

That got me a tiny breath of a laugh. "Okay, but I can't see very far ahead, either."

Certain that she was cold, I turned the heat all the way up. "Do you live in Green Bay?"

"Yes. Do you live around here?"

"In Fallingbrook."

"It's supposed to be a pretty town."

"It is, especially now. Everything's decorated for Christmas. We go all out, and it looks like this year, we'll have a gloriously white Christmas."

"Lucky! I was hoping to see the Ice and Lights Festival, but now I'll miss it."

"You'll be spending at least one night in Fallingbrook. I don't know if you heard about the arrangements people are making for you and the other passengers. As Brent said, we're delivering everyone who doesn't need hospital care to one of Fallingbrook's fun restaurants, Frisky Pomegranate. People are calling around to find families you can stay with."

This time, her sigh sounded almost like a sob. "That's very nice."

I tried to be encouraging. "You'll like Frisky Pomegranate. It's an upscale pub with really good food."

"I suppose. How far is it from the hospital?"

"About a dozen blocks."

"Could I walk?"

"You could in nice weather. Tonight's snow might make it difficult."

"Oh." It came out barely above a whisper.

"I could drop you off at the hospital but from what Brent said, you'll have a long wait before you get to see Travis. And except at lunchtime, the hospital has only vending machines."

"That's okay. I don't want to eat with the people from the bus. They were giving me hostile vibes, like they thought Travis made the bus go off the road on purpose, or I did it somehow."

"What do you think happened?"

"Are the police going to investigate it?"

Why had she asked that question instead of answering mine? I explained, "Brent already started. They'll also take the bus to a forensics lab and check it for mechanical malfunctions."

"The steering broke."

"What makes you think that?" If the investigators found out that Travis knew the steering was faulty before he set out with a load of passengers, Travis could be in legal as well as medical trouble. If he'd been drinking or speeding, he would be in legal trouble, anyway.

Paige leaned forward and peered toward the windshield. "That's about the only thing it could be. Travis didn't slam on the brakes or anything. I don't think he braked at all before the bus went into the ditch. And there was nothing on the road. I was watching. If there was ice it was that black kind, that you can't really see, you know? It wasn't snowing when the accident happened. That started shortly before you got there, but I wasn't paying attention to much besides keeping Travis from falling out of his seat."

"Who called Emergency?"

"I don't know. Passengers were shouting about doing it, so one of them must have."

Watching the road beyond my windshield wipers, which were slapping back and forth at their fastest, I thought back to the scene. The bus had gone off the road on an unusually straight stretch of County Road C. Investigators might be able to discover black ice underneath the accumulating snow. Between Brent's notes and photos, they'd be able to determine the approximate speed the bus had been going to rocket through those piles of ice chunks and plowed-up snow.

At the outskirts of Fallingbrook, streetlights illuminated snow cascading around them. We passed homes and businesses where swaths of snow softened multicolored Christmas lights. Brent's SUV was still a safe distance behind me.

"You're right. It's pretty here." Paige sounded wistful.

"See that brightness ahead? That should be the Ice and Lights Festival."

To go home, I would ordinarily stay on Wisconsin Street and drive down the west side of the village square, and then several blocks past Deputy Donut before going west into my neighborhood. Instead, I turned east and drove slowly along the north end of the square to let Paige see as much of the lit ice sculptures as possible. Brent followed me. I stopped across the street from Frisky Pomegranate, gloriously decorated with strings of Christmas lights. The dancing pomegranate on the sign above the door and windows was wearing its usual happy grin and a new Santa hat. Brent probably expected me to drop Paige off at Frisky Pomegranate, and he probably thought I would eat there also. He knew that if the snow became too deep for my SUV, I could leave it beside the square and ski home. He tooted his horn, drove past, waved, and turned south toward the police station, across the street from the south end of the square.

Paige gazed out her window toward the ice sculptures. I told her, "The restaurant is across the street. Are you sure you don't want to go in?"

"I'm sure." Her voice was tentative, as if she feared I would force her to party among the stranded passengers.

Tom and Cindy's SUV was parked beside Frisky Pomegranate's decorated, snow-covered patio. "Okay. I'll take you to the hospital, but first, I'll call my in-laws. They're organizing where you folks are staying tonight. They'll tell me where you should go after you leave the hospital."

Cindy answered on the first ring. "Where are you, Emily? Are you okay?" She sounded breathless with worry.

"I'm fine. I'm in my car across the street from Frisky Pomegranate. Paige, the tour guide from the bus, is with me. She doesn't want to eat at Frisky Pomegranate, but do you know where she's going to spend the night?"

"Let me see." I heard pages flipping. "Oh, dear. None of the others mentioned her. I'll find someone who can fit her in."

An idea had been bubbling in the back of my mind ever since Paige implied that she preferred going without dinner to joining the rest of the tour at Frisky Pomegranate. "She can stay with me."

"That would be great, Emily. Thank you! We now have everyone looked after, including everyone we expect to be released from the hospital."

"Does that include the bus driver, Travis?"

"Travis Tarriston is the only one being admitted. For observation, they said."

"I'll tell Paige. Take care, Cindy. Drive safely."

"You, too. After dinner, Tom and I will take our houseguests home with us. There's a three-year-old! And her parents."

Remembering the cute, curly-headed girl staring in awe at the candy-cane bandage I'd smoothed onto the dimpled back of her hand, I smiled. "Have fun."

"We will. We'll borrow books and toys from the kids next door and set up playdates."

I disconnected and turned to Paige. "The hospital is keeping Travis overnight for observation."

"I was hoping they would let him go."

"They'll want to take the best care of him. Do you mind staying with me at my place until the roads are clear enough for you to go home?"

"Thank you, Emily. That's very kind. I'd be glad to. You people are wonderful."

"Fallingbrook's a great town. We like cooperating with each other and accomplishing a lot."

I would have preferred to drive south on Wisconsin Street, which had been plowed recently, but I didn't want to turn around in the snowy road. Instead, I followed the rapidly filling tracks that Brent's car had made down the east side of the square. Falling snow softened the scenery, making the square and the trees and the colorfully lit sculptures on it look even more magical. We saw ice Christmas trees, angels, stars, intricate ice snowflakes, and a miniature sleigh with eight tiny reindeer, nine counting Rudolph and his red bulb nose. I turned west at the south end of the square and drove slowly past the police department, the town hall, and the fire department on the left side, and ice sculptures of wreathes, Christmas elves, and heaped-up wrapped packages on the right. At Wisconsin Street, I stopped and pointed at the nearest ice sculpture, a snowman made of three ice "donuts" with a carved ice top hat on the snowman's head. Lights outlined the sculpture. "My father-law-and I own a donut shop. That's our display, Frosty the Donut."

"Cute. I hope Travis gets out of the hospital in the morning and we can come up here and walk through the entire festival. Where's the hospital from here?"

I turned south on Wisconsin Street. "About six blocks ahead and then one block to the right. Would you like me to drop you off there? You can call me when you're ready to come home, and if driving's impossible, I'll walk or ski over and walk back with you."

"I wouldn't ask you to do that."

"It wouldn't be a problem."

"I just couldn't. I'll go home with you now if that's okay."

"Sure. We can have dinner and then play it by ear."

"I'm sorry. Maybe you'd have preferred to eat at that pub back there."

"Not really. On a night like this, it will be good to be home."

"But you shouldn't have to dig up supper for an extra person at the last minute. Not during a blizzard."

"I'd planned dinner for two, but Brent's not going to be able to make it. How does pasta with pesto sound?"

"Wonderful."

I pointed to the right. "There's our donut shop, Deputy Donut."

"That's a cute name. Did your detective husband name it?"

"Good guess. In a way, he helped. Before he was shot, we adopted a kitten with circles on her sides that resemble donuts. Alec laughed and called her Deputy Donut. Alec's father and I didn't open our shop until later, after Alec was gone. Tom's a retired detective and police chief, so we borrowed my cat's name for the shop. I usually just call her Dep."

"Aww, sweet."

"I hope you're not allergic."

"I'm not." She opened the front of the blanket draped around her and held the sides of it toward the vent as if to funnel hot air toward herself. "I don't know about Travis, though. Do you have room for him, too, if he isn't allergic and if we still need a place to stay after he's released?"

"Sure. The guest room has a pull-out couch that makes a double bed, or one of you could sleep on the living room couch. There's a love seat in the sunroom, but it's too short, even for you or me."

"How far is the hospital from your house?"

"About seven blocks."

"Maybe if you give me directions, I could walk to the hospital in the morning. Maybe the storm will have let up by then."

"It's not expected to." She'd brought only that one duffel bag. I asked, "Is the jacket you have on underneath that blanket the warmest jacket you have with you?"

"Yeah, but I have a sweater."

"We're about the same size. I have warm clothes I can lend you."

"Okay." She wrapped the blanket more tightly around herself.

I glanced at her and couldn't help a smile. I told her, "The Christmas lights from the shops and the lights on the dashboard are reflecting on that silver blanket. You look like you're sitting inside a Christmas ornament."

"Maybe I'll wear this all season." Hearing the smile in her voice, I was glad that, after everything she'd been through that afternoon and evening, she was able to joke.

"Maybe we all should. It would be fun to give out those blankets for everyone to wear while they're walking around the Ice and Lights Festival." I turned right on my street. At the next intersection, I pointed south. "The hospital is four blocks down this street. We're almost home. That is, if my all-wheel drive can make it through this stuff."

Chapter 5

❧

Again, Paige reassured me, "You're doing fine."

Maybe partly because of her encouragement, I made it through the last three blocks of drifting snow and parked in front of my yellow brick Victorian cottage.

Paige stared out her window. "Wow, is that yours?"

I wasn't sure if she was talking about the house or the cat inside it on the windowsill in front of the Christmas tree. "Yes."

"It's so pretty! I love Victorian houses, especially when they still have their gingerbread woodwork."

"The gingerbread is kind of hidden by snow."

"It's peeking out. It's adorable, especially with all those Christmas lights."

Brent had helped me hang the lights and cedar ropes with holly decorations. I should have realized that the chalet in the woods where we'd skied—it felt like days ago instead of hours—was his, and that he'd decorated it more or less like he and I had decorated mine. But he didn't have giant Christmas stockings topped with equally giant fake candy canes hanging from his porch railing like I did.

Still pinching the corners of her blanket together at her neck, Paige hauled her oversized shiny black tote bag out of my SUV and turned to stare at my house again. "Is that cat in the window the one you told me about, Dep?"

I opened the back hatch and pulled out Paige's duffel bag. "Yes."

She took the bag from me. "I always wanted a cat."

"Come meet her." Carrying my skis and poles, I tramped a path through snowdrifts to the porch. I leaned the skis and poles beside a couple of snow shovels in the corner between the brick wall and the wooden railing, opened the front door, and grabbed Dep before she could run out into deep snow that I knew she would loathe. Hanging on to the wiggly cat, I let Paige precede me into the living room. I set Dep down.

We took off our boots and put them on the mat beside the front door. Paige wadded up the silvery blanket and tucked it between her boots. "There. The noises that blanket made were probably scaring Dep. She's so cute! It was like she couldn't decide whether to be a tabby cat or a tortoiseshell. Look at that darling orange stripey patch on her forehead! And I see what you mean about those circles on her sides. They do look like donuts."

Our jackets had mostly dried during the ride home. I put them in the closet on the landing, two steps up from the living room.

Dep slunk close to the crackly blanket. With her mouth open slightly, she sniffed Paige's boots.

Paige and I were dressed almost alike in black leggings and tunic-length sweaters. My sweater was red and scoop necked, and hers was a thinner black turtleneck. We both wore Christmas socks, too. Mine were green with black cats wearing Santa hats. Hers were red with green Christmas trees. One had an uncomfortable-looking hole in the toe. She gazed around at the living room. Before Brent had helped me carry the Christmas tree inside, I'd rearranged the seating to give everyone at least a sideways view of both the Christmas tree and the fireplace. Paige clasped her hands together below her chin. "Everything's so pretty! I love the old-fashioned red velvet couch and matching chair. And that dark blue wing chair looks really comfy."

"Thank you. They were my grandmother's. I figured they belonged in a Victorian home."

"They do, and your oriental rug is in the same jewel tones! I love it." I turned on the tree's lights, and Paige praised the tree, too. "I always wanted high ceilings so I could have a tall tree. And I love how fat that tree is. Where did you get so many ornaments?"

"My grandparents and my parents."

"I'm sorry. Are they gone?"

"My grandparents are. My parents downsized to an RV and spend their winters in Florida. They come back for most of July and August every year. Meanwhile I've been adding my own ornaments to the collection."

"Are you going to Florida for Christmas?"

"No, and they're not coming here, either. After weather canceled flights three years in a row, we decided that traveling to or from Wisconsin at this time of year is too iffy, so we enjoy Christmas with friends and wait until summer to get together. Do you spend Christmas with your folks?"

Her face closed. "Travis and I will probably spend it with friends." She again gazed at the tree. "Putting all those decorations on must have taken a long time."

"It was fun. Friends helped. I had a tree-trimming and cookie-baking party."

She looked longingly at the tree. "What a great idea."

Figuring that she was probably still cold, I set the thermostat to a warmer temperature. "Come up to the guest room, and let's get you settled."

Dep led the way. In the guest room, Paige set her duffel bag on the floor near the closet. "What a pretty room! I like the white walls and the blue accents in the rug and furniture."

"One of these years, I'm going to decide what artwork to hang. Since the house has only two bedrooms, I use this one as an office." I went over to the desk, turned on the computer, and showed her how to log in. "You can check your email."

She thanked me. "You think of everything."

I laughed. "Maybe not, but please ask for anything you need."

I was afraid that my playful cat would attempt to help open the pull-out couch and make the bed, but she hopped to my desk and from there to the windowsill. Streaks of white snow streaming past the streetlight and onto my car seemed to intrigue her. Paige and I made the bed quickly and smoothed a quilt that my grandmother had made, calico squares in shades of blue and white, over it. I showed Paige the extra blankets on the closet shelf and asked her, "Do you think you might be hungry in about fifteen minutes?"

"Sure. Do you know the hospital's phone number?"

"It's on my phone." I pressed the number and handed my phone to her.

She stayed upstairs. Dep and I trotted downstairs. The cottage-like home didn't have a hallway on the ground floor. I went through the kitchen and into the dining room. Alec and I had decorated it in mostly white because the room's only windows were stained glass, and they were small and high on the wall beside the fireplace. In the kitchen, I filled a pot with water and turned the gas on underneath it.

Paige joined me. Her eyes were red. She placed my phone on the island. "They wouldn't tell me much. I'm supposed to call in the morning around ten to see if the doctor is going to discharge him."

"That could be a good sign."

"I hope so." She gazed around and commented in wistful tones, "This is a huge kitchen for one person."

"There were two of us when we designed it."

She closed her eyes briefly as if in pain. "I'm sorry. I should have realized. It's just—that huge stove and fridge and those deep sinks. It's all beautiful."

"Thank you." I opened the freezer and pulled out a packet of pesto I'd made during the summer.

Paige asked, "What can I do?"

I gave her a chunk of Parmesan cheese and a grater. She grated the cheese energetically, as if she were trying to work out her frustration and fear for Travis.

I fetched a package of bow-tie pasta from the pantry.

Dep was being surprisingly standoffish. Usually, by the time visitors had been in the house for a few minutes, Dep was rubbing against their ankles and begging to be cuddled. She was in the house's back room, the sunroom, which, rather strangely, faced north. The room was surrounded by windows looking out into the rear yard and separated from the kitchen by a half-height wall. I couldn't see anything outside those back windows, though, because of the lights in the kitchen and the darkness outside. Dep probably couldn't see much, either. Paige no longer smelled like alcohol, but I offered only sparkling water to go with our meal, and she didn't ask for anything else.

She and I sat at the counter and ate deliciously garlicky pesto-coated pasta and a tomato and green pepper salad. Dep dashed into the kitchen and jumped onto the empty stool beside me, the one farthest from Paige. "Meow." She settled down, tucked her paws underneath her chest, and closed her eyes.

Paige told me how much she liked the pine cabinets, the terra-cotta floor tiles, and the granite countertops. She stroked a finger along the rim of her pasta bowl. "And your dishes, too. I love this chocolate brown color."

"My mother-in-law teaches high school art. She's also a potter. She made them."

"Is that the woman who looked after finding accommodations for everyone from the bus?"

"Yes. Cindy."

"You're lucky to have such nice in-laws."

"I am!"

We feasted on some of the Christmas cookies that my friends and I had baked at my party—buttery sugar cookies shaped like bells, stars, and snowmen and decorated with colorful lemony icing and sprinkles.

After we tidied the kitchen, I stretched and looked through the dining room to the living room and the window beyond the Christmas tree. "I'll leave you with a book in front of the fireplace while I tackle the shoveling."

"I'll help."

"You're a guest."

"That's why I should help. I saw two shovels on the front porch."

"Yes, but you really don't have to. I'm in shape from shoveling last week." Brent had helped me, and the extra shovel was still on my porch.

"I want to. There's too much snow out there for one person. It could take you half the night by yourself. Besides, there's no hope of walking to the hospital if people don't shovel their walks. We can at least do yours."

We put on our winter boots. Rustling, the silvery rescue blanket unwadded itself. Dep stared for a second with her ears twitching, and then she skittered sideways, her back arched, toward the dining room. I considered throwing the apparently menacing blanket out, but I'd given it to Paige. If she didn't take it with her when she went home, I would discard it.

I offered her a parka, but she pointed out that we would warm up shoveling. She wore her nylon jacket with Tour Guide written the back, and I put on the lightweight jacket I'd worn while skiing. The snow was still light and fluffy. With Dep watching us from the windowsill inside, we cleared the porch, the steps, the path to the sidewalk, and the sidewalk beside the street. Neighbors were shoveling, too. We called out greetings and joking complaints about the white Christmas coming too early and going beyond the call of duty, besides. Paige and I shoveled only enough of the driveway for my SUV, and then Paige went back inside while I brushed snow off the SUV and parked it in the driveway. I promised myself for about the millionth time that I would have a garage built.

When I returned inside, Paige was sitting in my wing chair and Dep was purring on her lap. Lights on the Christmas tree cast a warm glow in the otherwise dark room.

I touched a match to the knot of newspaper underneath kindling and logs in the fireplace. "Dep finally made friends!"

"I sat here quietly, and she crept up and joined me." She cooed baby talk to Dep, who raised her chin to be scratched. Paige looked up at me. "We can't expect everyone to shovel this quickly, and that snow's too deep for walking. You wouldn't happen to own a snowmobile, would you, that I could borrow to drive to the hospital? Maybe if I go in person, they'll let me visit Travis for a few minutes."

"No, but I can try some friends who might know of someone who does."

I sat on the couch facing the Christmas tree and called several people, but the only snowmobiles they knew of were rescuing people from cars, transporting patients to the hospital, or picking up prescriptions and other supplies for people who couldn't get out. I asked Paige, "Do you know how to cross-country ski?"

"Yes."

Our shoe sizes were close enough that she could borrow my boots. And because we were about the same height, my skis and poles would be the right lengths for her, too.

Pointing, she repeated what I'd told her earlier about the

route to the hospital. "I turn left at the street, go four blocks, turn right, and then keep going down that street until I come to it." She yawned and rolled her shoulders as if shoveling snow had tensed them. "But Travis could be sleeping now. Maybe I'll wait until morning. Maybe the snow will have stopped by then."

I didn't tell her that the snow was predicted to go on until at least noon the next day, and in the meantime, the wind was supposed to pick up and we'd be in a full-fledged blizzard. I silently thanked Alec for ensuring that our home would be cozy and snug no matter what the weather was like.

Paige's eyebrows lowered in a frown, giving her wrinkles above her nose. "Do your skis need to be waxed?"

"No. I don't mind sacrificing speed to the convenience of throwing them into the car and going skiing whenever I feel like it."

Her face relaxed. "Good, because I wouldn't know how to wax them."

"They're on the front porch in case you get a call in the night or get up early and go visit Travis." I pointed at the landing near the front door. "If you need a warmer jacket or some scarves, hats, or mittens, look in that closet and borrow whatever you like."

"Thank you. I like everything you have."

Cindy had made me a cute little brown pottery pitcher and a matching tumbler that fit, overturned, on the pitcher as a lid. I gave them to Paige so she could have drinking water on her bedside table during the night, and then we went up to our bedrooms. I shut Dep in with me and fell asleep.

I woke up to the sound of my front door slamming.

Chapter 6

I turned on the bedside lamp. Dep stood with her nose against my closed bedroom door. Her tail twitched back and forth, and the fur along her spine stood up in a way that made my own hackles rise.

It was one thirty in the morning.

Who had closed the front door? Had Paige left, or had someone arrived? I always locked the door, but maybe seeing Dep on Paige's lap after I came in from parking the car had distracted me and I'd forgotten.

I flung the covers back, slid my feet into slippers, opened my bedroom door, and listened.

Across the hall, the guest bedroom door stood open, and the room was dark. I had turned off the lights downstairs before I went to bed, but now, light from the living room shined through the stair railing and lit the wall in ornate stripes between shadows of Victorian spindles.

I tiptoed downstairs. Dep trotted down more quickly but more quietly. Paige's and my winter boots were on the mat beside the door. My ski boots were missing.

The front door was unlocked. I picked Dep up, hugged her against my nightgown, and cautiously opened the front door.

Wind blew snow in on us.

"Meow!" Dep wriggled out of my arms and raced toward the stairs.

Both snow shovels were on the porch, but my skis and poles were gone. Because of blowing snow, I couldn't see as far as the street or my driveway. I could barely tell that we had shoveled. I closed the door. I almost locked it, but I hadn't thought of giving Paige a key, so I merely latched it and hoped the wind wouldn't blow it open.

I realized I'd half expected that rescue blanket to make crinkling noises when the wind was blowing in through the open doorway, but it hadn't.

The blanket was gone.

Dep was partway up the stairs, sitting on a step and holding one paw up as if she'd suddenly stopped licking snow off it. As soon as she saw me heading toward her, she meowed and bounded to the second floor.

I followed her and listened outside the guest room. I heard no snoring or other breathing sounds. "Paige?"

No one answered. I reached into the room and snapped on the overhead light. My late grandmother's quilt was pulled up over the pillows, and no one was in the bed. The rescue blanket had been folded and smoothed across the foot of the bed. Had Paige been too cold to sleep but hadn't wanted to use the spare blankets I'd offered her?

I turned out the light and went downstairs. With Dep trotting ahead of me, I padded through the living room, dining room, kitchen, and sunroom. Paige wasn't in any of them. I even turned on a light in the back, but my walled garden was solid white, and so was the air above it. I'd read too many scary stories about basements to go down there, but I opened the door, turned on the light, and looked down the stairs. "Paige?" No answer. Reassured that Paige had gone somewhere on skis and that no one else had come in, I shut the basement door and turned out all of the lights downstairs except the one that Paige had left on, the overhead fixture near the front door.

Upstairs again, I closed Dep into my bedroom with me and crawled into bed. Had Paige received a call from the hospital that made her rush over there?

Chilled and feeling sorry for her, I didn't expect to sleep, but I must have. I didn't hear the front door open and close, but I did hear the click of the guest room door as it latched. It was almost three. I considered getting up and asking her where she'd been and if Travis was all right, but if she had received bad news, I didn't want to upset her more with piercing questions. I also didn't want to leave my warm cocoon or the cat curled on my pillow next to my face.

Besides, I needed to get up in a couple of hours. Tom lived farther from Deputy Donut than I did and drove to and from work. He might not be able to make it there at the time we usually started making donuts, six thirty, but I could ski to the shop and open it for anyone who needed to come in out of the blizzard and enjoy fresh donuts and a hot drink. If Paige needed my skis again, I could walk.

The moment my alarm went off, I silenced it. The guest room door was closed, and I heard faint snoring. I took a quick shower. As usual, Dep accompanied me downstairs and into the kitchen. I fed her, ate a quick breakfast, and left Paige a note with my phone number and suggestions for breakfast and lunch. I added, *I should be back before six this evening.*

Ordinarily, Dep went to work with me. In warm weather, she wore a halter and walked very nicely, well, mostly, on a leash. In cold or rainy weather, I tucked her into a carrying pouch inside my parka or rain jacket. She usually positioned herself near the front door when it was time to leave.

Now, with her eyes half closed, she was sitting on the couch as if she had decided not to go near the door where wind and snow had blown in on her at one thirty in the morning. I stage-whispered, "Sorry, Dep, you're not coming today."

She didn't open her eyes. "Mew."

I put my cross-country ski pants and jacket over my work uniform of black jeans and white long-sleeved shirt. I attached a broom to the backpack I carried as a purse and slipped the backpack's straps over my shoulders. The broom's bristles stuck up above my head. From a distance in the snow, I might look like a tall person with a skinny neck and hair standing on end. My ski boots were wet, but my thick wool socks would insulate my feet and keep them toasty.

The front door was locked. I bent to prevent the broom's bristles from hitting the doorjamb, let myself out, and turned the dead bolt with my key. Except for streetlights and the Christmas lights on my porch, it was dark outside. I didn't want to take time to shovel, and besides, snow was still falling. The temperature had risen to only slightly below freezing. Although the snow was wetter and heavier than it had been when Paige and I shoveled, it was still blowing around in strong gusts of wind and heaping itself into drifts. Feeling with my feet for the stairs underneath the snow, I carried my skis and poles down to the sidewalk. The deep, wet snow on sidewalks would make skiing difficult. Still carrying my skis and poles, I trudged through a bank of plowed snow to the street. Enough snow had accumulated since the plow had passed to create a reasonable although slightly slushy base for skiing. I snapped my boots into the latches on my skis.

Pushing with my poles and gliding on my skis, I warmed up. The snow wasn't coming down as furiously as it had been when I'd looked outside after hearing Paige leave, and I could actually see the houses I skied past.

I wasn't the only one whose Christmas lights were shining before dawn. Between those lights and the decorated Christmas trees brightening front windows, the neighborhood resembled a Christmas village covered in a soft white blanket.

Farther along, on Wisconsin Street, streetlights were closer together, their brightness softened by falling snow. Tinsel garlands and lights outlined shop windows. Construction paper ornaments and cards that kids had made covered most of the inside of the library's front windows. Battery-powered but realistic candles flickered on stacks of Christmas books in the windows of the bookstore.

A man in a pickup truck was plowing the driveway to the parking lot behind Deputy Donut and other shops. I waved and skied past our sweet little donut shop. The dim lights we always left on during the night inside Deputy Donut and the streetlights outside glittered off tinsel on the big Christmas trees we'd set up in the twin front windows. Even though I couldn't see much of the shop's interior, and the lights on the trees were dark, the shop gave me a feeling of warmth and Christmas cheer.

After a long block of skiing in the street, I reached the village square. The ice sculptures were covered with heaps of snow, turning the landscape into a miniature mountain range. Although the festival's lights weren't on underneath the snow, flashlights were moving around the square, and people were calling to each other and laughing while cleaning snow off their ice sculptures.

Which was what I'd planned to do.

But I couldn't.

Frosty the Donut had disappeared.

I twisted to look all around me. My first impression had been correct. Frosty the Donut was gone.

How could a giant ice sculpture vanish during the night? Frosty the Donut had been important to Tom and me as a whimsical method of advertising our shop during the holiday season, and we'd been proud of the sculpture we'd designed. Besides, although the festival still had many fun and exciting sculptures, the loss of one of them would be a blow to everyone in our close-knit community. At least one busload of tourists had set out to see our inaugural Ice and Lights Festival, and if all went well, more visitors might come other years.

But all was obviously not going well.

In a sort of disappointed shock, I forced my skis through deep snow close to where I'd seen our ice sculpture the night before when I'd pointed it out to Paige. From the ice block at its base to the crown of its crystalline top hat, Frosty the Donut had been about seven feet high. Except for towering old oaks, nothing nearby was anywhere near that tall, but mounds of snow where Frosty had been, if stacked end-to-end, might have reached that height.

The wind swirling snow around me was not as strong as it had been during the night, but I didn't think that even at its fiercest it could have toppled Frosty the Donut. It would not have had enough surface to push against. It would have whistled through the holes in the middle of the three ice donuts representing snowballs.

I pulled my broom up and over one shoulder and used it almost like a shovel to push the uppermost layer of snow off the nearest mound of snow. The next layer was lighter and fluffier.

Sure enough, snow had been hiding Frosty's base. Surrounding Frosty's carved name on the Wisconsin Street side of the base, snow was imbedded in cracks and dents that hadn't been in that ice before the storm.

A vehicle must have slid into this corner of the square and

knocked Frosty the Donut onto its back. Since then, the vehicle must have driven away or been towed, and snow had covered its tracks. The furrows my skis had made between the street and the fallen sculpture were already filling.

I pushed snow off the miniature hill beyond Frosty's base and found the edge of the largest of the three ice donuts.

It and the other two donuts were on top of something.

Chapter 7

❧

I swept at a small mound of heavy snow sticking out below the largest ice donut.

And uncovered a bare foot and ankle.

A bare human foot and ankle.

I could hardly hear my scream over the wind whipping snow around me. Fingers shaking, I called 911 and told them where I was and what I'd found.

Voices of other people on the square became fainter, as if a cave of spinning snow tightened around me, shutting me in with the human lying in the snow underneath our ice sculpture. If I hadn't been leaning on my poles and the broom, I might have tumbled down into cold white fluff.

The cave of snow shifted around me, and a streetlight illuminated a shadowy figure dashing toward me through the storm. He was tall and powerful. His unzipped parka flapped as he ran.

Brent. Underneath the parka, he was wearing the black pants and turtleneck he'd had on the afternoon before when we'd been skiing.

He stopped in deep snow beside me and grasped my shoulders. "Are you okay?"

Barely nodding, I gasped an irrelevant question, "How did you get here so fast?"

He waved back toward the police station. "I didn't go home last night. You called about someone buried in snow?"

I pointed at the foot.

Brent knelt, felt underneath the fallen ice sculpture, and then rose and steadied me with one hand on my shoulder. In the darkness, I couldn't read his expression. He bent toward me. "I'm afraid he's beyond hope." His grim statement was almost lost in the moaning wind.

"I figured, but an ambulance is coming, just in case, right?"

"Right."

Across the street, one of the fire station's big overhead doors rumbled up, revealing a yellowy interior and the snow-blurred shapes of fire trucks. I heard raised voices but couldn't make out what they were saying.

Using my phone's flashlight, I showed Brent the cracks and dents on the front of Frosty the Donut's base. "It looks like something crashed into this and knocked the rest of the sculpture onto the victim." My words came out separated by choppy attempts to breathe.

Brent leaned into the wind as if to protect me from it. "I see."

I held my broom toward him. "Need this?" I was too rattled to think.

"The investigators will have their own brooms and brushes." I appreciated his calm way of coping with everything, including a hysterical friend.

Calling to one another, firefighters ran toward us.

Brent asked me, "Where can I find you later?"

"Deputy Donut."

He squeezed my shoulder. "I'll come talk to you as soon as I can."

"Okay." Still on skis, I backed away. As soon as I could safely turn around without ramming Brent's ankles with the curved-up tips of my skis, I pushed myself down Wisconsin

Street, quickly, as if I could leave behind the memory of what I'd found underneath heavy snow and even heavier ice. More snow accumulated on the pavement.

I was disappointed but not surprised that Deputy Donut was still lit only by our dim overnight lights. It was too early for anyone else to arrive, but I really wanted human company. I skied up the driveway to the rear of the shop, left my skis, poles, and the broom on our back porch, and unlocked the door into our office. Skiing had warmed me, but I was shivering. I turned on lights and the gas fireplace and then shed my boots and outer garments, put on comfy shoes, and tucked my backpack into a lockable drawer in the desk. The fireplace was already warming me.

The room's charming quirkiness helped. Tom and I, with suggestions from Cindy, had designed and decorated our office to provide a safe place for Dep to sleep, eat, and play when she came to work with me. It was her own little apartment where her presence wouldn't violate health regulations. I already missed her. I knew that even though she wasn't in Deputy Donut, I would automatically look through the windows into the office many times that day. I would expect to see her sleeping on the back of the couch or sitting up and watching our dining area or kitchen. I would look for her sitting on our desk and staring through the side windows to the driveway or through the back windows to the parking lot. I would catch myself checking her playground of kitty ramps, staircases, and carpeted columns leading to catwalks and tunnels near the ceiling. She even had a few small but comfy beds up there.

Hoping that she and Paige were enjoying each other's company, I turned on all of the lights in the dining area and kitchen.

I wished that Brent didn't have to cope with a tragedy and could be in Deputy Donut with me, a mug of hot coffee, and a fresh donut or two. How soon would he be able to come over?

I walked into the dining room, went behind our serving corner and then around the half-height wall into our kitchen. I started the oil heating in the deep fryers and returned to the dining room. The ornament-covered Christmas trees in the big front windows and the fairy-lit garlands high on the walls made me smile for the first time since I'd swept snow off Frosty the Donut and made that heart-wrenching discovery.

Our tables were round, sized for two, four, six, or in a couple of cases, eight diners. Tom, Cindy, and I had painted the tops to resemble donuts. Each one was different, and we'd covered them with glass to protect the paintings and make cleanups easy. For the holiday season, we'd placed miniature Christmas trees on the glass above the "holes" in the table-top donuts. I flicked switches on the bases of the tiny trees. More lights twinkled and sparkled.

Cheerful voices and foot-stomping came from the office. I glanced through the window between the office and the dining room. Tom and I had needed to replace our former full-time assistant, Nina, and had hired Olivia Kentsen in late August when our part-time assistant, Jocelyn, was heading back to college. Jocelyn was home for the holidays. She and Olivia were in the office. They waved.

A few moments later, dressed in black jeans and long-sleeved white shirts, they burst out of the office. Although only about average height, Olivia was taller than Jocelyn and I were, and she covered the distance to me quickly. "What's going on up the street near the square?" she demanded. "Lights are flashing near the corner where Frosty the Donut is, and they don't look like the twinkly lights of the Ice and Lights Festival."

I answered in a deliberately flattened voice. "It's exactly at the corner where Frosty the Donut was. I went there to clean the snow off Frosty, but he had fallen over. On top of someone. A man, I think."

Now that Jocelyn was in college and studying to become a teacher, she'd stopped competing in gymnastic events, but she stayed fit. She was right behind Olivia. Eyeing me, she shook her head slightly as if she knew the answer but had to ask, "Is he okay?"

My mouth twisted. "I don't think so."

"Who is it?" Olivia asked. She was in her late twenties, but her lustrous and wavy ponytail in mahogany-touched deep brown and her fine-grained skin made her look younger, especially when her eyes opened as wide as they did at the moment.

"I don't know." I shuddered. "Brent responded to my 911 call and sent me away." While the other two asked questions and I answered, we went into the storeroom. I plopped my fake police hat, embellished with a fuzzy donut where a police badge would be, onto my head and added, "We'll find out more when Brent comes over for my statement." Remembering how discreet police officers were about their investigations, I muttered, "Well, maybe."

Jocelyn settled her own Deputy Donut hat on her head, carefully avoiding the low bun she wore to work.

We all tied on fresh white aprons. Our Deputy Donut logo, the black silhouette of a cat wearing a Deputy Donut hat, was embroidered on them. Olivia strode toward the coffee grinder. "Brent's going to need some decent coffee when he gets here, not that cop-shop stuff the others complain about." She'd met Brent only once when he came to pick up Dep and me after work, but other police officers, especially Misty and Hooligan, were regulars at Deputy Donut.

I admitted, "I could use about a quart of it."

Jocelyn hid a yawn. "Me, too. I didn't get much sleep last night, thanks to our sudden houseguests."

Olivia's hand halted near the coffee grinder's ON button. She turned and stared at Jocelyn. "Sudden houseguests?"

Jocelyn explained that she and her parents were hosting a mother, father, and three boys who had been in a bus crash the night before.

I added that as far as I knew, only the bus driver had been seriously injured, and his girlfriend was staying with Dep and me.

Olivia's hand still hovered near the ON button. "How did you two end up having people from a bus crash stay in your houses?"

Jocelyn poured cream into tiny pitchers with our Deputy Donut logo on them. "The people on the tour were supposed to go to Duluth for the night, but they couldn't, even if there had been another bus available, because of the blizzard. Tom's wife, Cindy, called around and found accommodations for everyone. The man staying in our house, Dustin, was absolutely livid. I mean, he was grateful for a roof over his head and beds for his family, but he was really mad at the bus driver. Dustin said there was no reason, other than drinking, for the driver to go off the road, through a pile of plowed-up snow, and into a ditch. Dustin's wife, Ashley, took him aside, and she must have convinced him not to display so much anger around their sons and my parents and me."

Removing a bowl of dough from the proofing cabinet where it had risen in the ideal temperature and humidity overnight, I asked Jocelyn, "Did one of the boys have a survival blanket he was using as a superhero cape?"

She rolled her eyes. "I wasn't sure which boy had it. There were fights, and Dustin took it away. Then there was a lot of weeping and wailing." She grinned. "I think Ashley was about to give in to them, but you know my mom. She's hardly bigger than the boys, but when she ordered them off to bed, they went."

I laughed. I'd met Jocelyn's mom and could easily picture her keeping those three boys in line. Their parents, too.

Olivia started the coffee grinder.

Over its crunching roar, I heard thumps and men's voices in the office. I turned from rolling dough to look through the window between the kitchen and office. Tom and Brent removed their coats. Brent was unusually tired-looking and his black turtleneck and pants were rumpled, but the smile he shot toward me was as warm as ever.

I waved, lifted a pretend mug to my lips, raised my eyebrows in question, and mouthed, "Coffee?"

His eyes opening with exaggerated anticipation, he nodded.

Tom came into the kitchen.

Olivia shut off the coffee grinder and smiled at Tom. She still seemed a little more formal around him than around me.

Although she had been able to fake it during gymnastic competitions, formality was not one of Jocelyn's traits. She demanded, "Did you pick up a hitchhiker, Tom?"

"I stopped to see what was going on, and Brent was about to come over, so I gave him a ride."

I set the rolling pin on the counter carefully so it wouldn't roll off. "You're as bad as I am, Tom, snooping around."

"I could never be as bad as you are. It wasn't that long ago that I was a police officer myself, so you need to give me some leeway for asking questions." He turned serious. "I should have been the one to attempt to brush the snow off Frosty the Donut, though, not you, Emily."

"I've seen bodies before. He was dead, wasn't he?"

"Very. Go talk to Brent. I'll bring you each a mug of good strong coffee and some donuts when they're ready. What's our special coffee today, Olivia?"

"That dark organic roast from Sumatra."

I took a deep breath. "The freshly ground beans smell delicious. Thanks, Tom. Thanks, all of you."

I went into the office. Perhaps as aware as I was of the

window from the kitchen and of my three coworkers possibly watching us, Brent shook my hand instead of giving me one of his usual hugs.

Only yesterday, he and I had been skiing together in the sunshine. Now that carefree outing felt like months ago, and the possible promise of a new understanding between us seemed as fleeting as the snowflakes destroying themselves against our office windows. Would my unintended involvement in yet another of Brent's cases destroy any possibility of our ever becoming more than friends? His hand was still cold from being outdoors. I let it go and asked him, "Did you get any sleep last night?"

"Enough. We have couches at the police station."

Without thinking, I blurted, "You could have come to my place."

He tilted his head.

Feeling myself flush, I hastily added, "Paige, the tour guide from the bus, was in the guest room. The love seat in the sunroom is too short for you, but the couch in the living room is velvet, not vinyl like that uncomfortable one I sat on in an interview room in the police station." That day had been hot, I'd been wearing shorts, and the backs of my thighs had stuck to the vinyl. Besides, the situation had been upsetting.

Brent seemed to be trying not to laugh, but he managed to sound almost serious. "Your living room couch is probably too short for me, too. I was fine. I'm used to sleeping in the office when I need to. It's almost like home."

"Too bad you didn't get to spend last night in your new place." My face heated even more. "It looks like a great house."

"There will be other times."

My flush did not subside, but Tom provided a distraction by coming into the office with a mug of coffee for each of us and a plate of warm, old-fashioned donuts. He set them on the coffee table. "Olivia waylaid the donuts to add Christmas cheer." She'd sprinkled red sugar on some of the donuts and green sugar on the others.

Smiling through the window at Olivia, I gave her a thumbs-up.

Tom left the office and shut us in. Brent and I sat on the couch. Beyond the windows facing the outdoors, dawn was delayed by the storm, but it was finally beginning to get lighter out there.

Brent opened his notebook. "Tell me everything you saw and heard this morning before you found the deceased."

I didn't have much to tell Brent that he didn't already know. While I talked and he wrote, we sipped the hot, bracing coffee and ate the soothing, nutmeg-flavored donuts. He closed his notebook.

I asked, "Do you know who it was?"

"Tom didn't say?"

I made a phonily pouty frown. "Of course not."

Brent stared down into his coffee. "I recognized him from his bandages. We'll need someone to formally identify him, but I'm almost positive he was the driver from last night's bus crash, Travis Tarriston."

Chapter 8

I was sure my face showed my bewilderment. "I thought Travis was in the hospital."

Brent's lips tightened.

I recognized the expression. He had to be careful about divulging the details of an investigation into an unexpected death, but it was more than that—he didn't want to make me uncomfortable.

But I was strong. I prompted, "Why were his foot and ankle bare?"

Again, a short silence, and then a quiet response. "He might have come straight from the hospital without getting fully dressed. He was wearing a hospital gown and a lightweight robe. His coat and a pair of paper slippers were nearby."

"That's horrible!" I couldn't help shivering. "Why did he leave the hospital without boots or socks, and how did he end up in the village square underneath Frosty the Donut?"

Those gray eyes warmed with compassion. "I'm asking the same questions."

Beyond the window into the kitchen, Tom watched us from where he stood frying donuts. His thick eyebrows lowered in obvious consternation.

The coffee began making me feel less like I was trapped in

a nightmare, and I thought of another question. "Do you have any idea when it happened?"

"Several hours before you found him."

I covered my mouth with one hand.

"What, Em?"

"Paige, the tour guide, spent the night at my place. At one thirty, I heard the front door slam shut. Paige was gone."

"In the storm?"

"I had offered to lend her my skis if she wanted to ski to the hospital to visit Travis, and my skis and boots were gone, too. I heard her close her bedroom door when she came back. It was around three."

Brent put down his donut and wrote in his notebook. "Unusual time to visit a hospital. I'll find out if they called her." Without looking up, he asked, "Did she say where she'd been?"

"I didn't get up or ask her, and she was still sleeping when I left this morning."

He finished writing and looked at me again. His eyes were bleak. "I'd better talk to her."

"She wouldn't have harmed Travis. For one thing, he was her boyfriend."

Brent tilted his head as if to remind me that the victims of murderers were often their supposedly nearest and dearest.

I argued, "She was very worried about him last night."

"Could she have been acting?"

"I guess so. But even if she took off the skis to get near enough to the sculpture to give herself some leverage, I doubt that she could have shoved it hard enough to knock it over. And you and I both saw the marks where a vehicle must have hit the base. I'm guessing that the vehicle hit the sculpture higher, also, on the donuts carved to look like a snowman, since that's the part that fell."

Brent nodded as if he agreed with everything I'd said, and

I silently congratulated myself for successfully arguing Paige's case. Then he told me gently, "A snowmobile was reported stolen in your neighborhood around one forty-five this morning. It was found later, shortly before six, on a nearby street."

I felt my shoulders droop. "Last night, Paige asked me if I had a snowmobile she could borrow, but what did she do with my skis while she was driving a snowmobile?"

"My snowmobile has a rack for skis."

"Does the stolen one?"

"I don't think so, but even if it doesn't, there are ways to stow things like that. Or she could have left them behind and picked them up later."

"Was the snowmobile returned to where it had been stolen?"

"It was only a few blocks away. Most likely, she took your skis and poles with her on the snowmobile." He pushed his empty mug away from the edge of the coffee table. "At the very least, she sounds like a likely candidate to make a positive identification and also to tell me who else we should notify. Is she at your place now?"

"Probably, unless she decided to walk to the hospital. I gave her my phone number, but she hasn't called me. I didn't ask for hers."

"Would you mind coming along? She might not open your door for me."

"Of course not. I don't think we'll be swamped with customers today." I picked up the empty plate and mugs. "I'll ask the others if they can cover for me."

They said they could. Tom gave me the key to his SUV. "I know Brent likes to walk when his calls are near the police station, but trudging through two feet of snow might be too much even for him." Tom was barely exaggerating about the depth of the snow.

Knowing that police officers weren't fond of riding with civilians, I offered to let Brent drive.

"No, thanks. Tom's my friend, but you're his daughter-in-law, and he trusts your driving. If I close my eyes, it won't be because your driving scares me. I'll be taking a nap."

I punched his elbow. He probably barely felt it through his heavy parka.

Outside, it was still cloudy and snowing, but at least it was finally daylight. We cleared the snow from Tom's car and stowed my skis, poles, and the broom in the back.

Plows had kept up, mostly, with the snow, and driving was easier than it had been the night before. Exactly as he'd threatened, Brent closed his eyes.

I pulled up to the curb in front of my house. Brent opened his eyes.

Paige was outside with one of my snow shovels. Despite the heaviness of the most recently fallen snow, she had already cleared the porch, the steps, and the path to the sidewalk. She stopped shoveling, straightened, rested an arm on the handle of the shovel, and stared at Tom's SUV. I wondered if she'd tried to zip her TOUR GUIDE jacket and had given up without realizing that the jacket was inside out. Like the night before, she wasn't wearing a hat, but the amount of shoveling she'd done had probably kept her warm. Her long brown hair was damp, possibly from perspiration as well as from falling snow.

"She's very nice," I told Brent.

He grunted and got out.

I walked around the SUV, and called, "Thank you, Paige! You didn't have to shovel. I was going to do it after work."

"More could pile up by then. Besides, I had to do something while I . . ." She broke off and brushed her hair out of her face with the sleeve of her jacket. "Did you close your donut shop for the day already?"

I reintroduced her to Brent and told her, "You've done a lot. Let's go inside for a break." My non-answer sounded extremely lame.

Paige gave Brent a frightened look. She knew he was a police officer. Was she afraid of what he might do or say? She lowered her head.

I couldn't see her expression.

Beside me, Brent wouldn't be able to, either.

I wanted to believe that someone who shoveled my snow and got along with my cat could not be a murderer. I had trouble imagining this petite woman stealing a snowmobile, kidnapping the man she was dating, ramming the snowmobile into an ice sculpture until it fell on him, and then driving away, leaving him helpless in below-freezing temperatures while snow poured down.

Brent gently took the shovel from her and started toward the porch. Dep watched from the windowsill inside. When she saw me looking at her, she stood up and pawed at the window as if she could dig her way out through the glass.

I considered grabbing one of the shovels, staying outside, and clearing the sidewalk, leaving Brent by himself to inform Paige about her boyfriend's death.

I could hardly bear to think about the time that Brent had, despite his own injury, insisted on being the one to tell me that Alec had been fatally shot. I was still embarrassed about the way I'd pushed Brent, who was in shock about the loss of his best friend, out of my life for three years. During the past four years, Brent and I had become close friends again. I felt like I needed to apologize to him about the way I'd acted, but I knew he understood.

Now, although I would have liked to avoid being present when he gave Paige possibly the worst news of her life, she needed friendly support.

Besides, I couldn't hide outside. I wanted to hear Brent's questions and her answers. Could she convince him—and me—that she had not stolen a snowmobile and used it to murder her boyfriend?

I followed Paige and Brent up the porch steps. Brent put the shovel beside the other one.

Inside, Dep meowed and wound around our ankles, slowing us down while we removed our boots. I offered to hang Paige's wet jacket in the closet near the kitchen. "Alec and I designed it with a drain in the floor and vents to circulate the air. Things in there dry quickly."

She hugged herself. "No, thanks, I'll just keep it on for now."

I didn't argue, and I didn't tell her that it was inside out. She was wearing her black leggings and matching tunic. Brent's and my jackets were dry enough for me to hang them in the closet on the landing.

Dep planted herself in front of Brent and meowed up at him until he picked her up. She rubbed her face against his chin. He hadn't shaved yet that morning. She purred. Cat hairs stuck to his black sweater.

I asked, "Can I get anyone coffee?"

Paige looked toward the kitchen. "I helped myself, so not right now. But it was the best coffee I ever tasted. And I helped myself to cereal, too. And juice."

I smiled. "I'm glad you found everything. Brent?"

"I'm caffeinated enough at the moment, thanks."

I waved toward the living room's comfy furniture. "Have a seat."

Brent eased into the wing chair, the chair closest to the front door. Paige perched on the edge of the couch across from him. She sat with her hands grasping each other in her lap, her back stiff and straight, and her feet flat on the floor.

Feeling protective, I was relieved for the sake of her pride that this morning's cheerful Christmas socks, green with red and white candy canes on them, were new-looking with no holes. Not that Brent was judgmental about clothing. Like me, he had probably discovered that traveling light, as she had, increased the possibility that the outfits we'd packed would end up torn or stained.

I sat at the other end of the couch from Paige, closer to the fireplace. I wanted to lean back and look relaxed. I couldn't.

On Brent's lap, Dep went almost perfectly limp, closed her eyes, and purred. "Paige," Brent said softly, "I'm afraid I have bad news."

Her hands flew to her cheeks. "Travis? Is he worse? I haven't gotten any information from the hospital." She lowered her hands and darted a glance at me, and I realized that I had dialed the hospital for her and hadn't given her the number. She could have found it herself, though. I had shown her how to log into my computer.

Maybe she hadn't gone to the hospital after I left for work that morning because I'd taken my skis. Or maybe she knew that the hospital would not be able to update her on Travis's condition because she herself had taken Travis—on a snowmobile—from the hospital sometime between one thirty and three that morning.

Brent gazed steadily and kindly at her. "A man we believe to be Travis Tarriston has died."

She shook her head, flinging her long hair across her face. "No!" she cried. "Noooooo. It can't be. Not Travis."

Brent offered her a glimmer of hope. "We still need to make a positive ID."

She scraped wisps of hair off her mouth and chin. "Then it's not him. It can't be. He wasn't that badly injured." Her voice dwindled. "At least, I didn't think he was. But with concussions, you never know, right?"

I scooted closer on the velvet couch cushions and placed my hand on her arm. She pulled her arm away and wrapped both arms around herself again.

Brent asked her, "Where were you during the night?" The abrupt change of subject felt harsh.

Paige's mouth fell open. She drew in a quick breath and then firmly closed her mouth. Tensely staring toward Dep on Brent's lap, she finally whispered, "Last night?"

Brent answered, "Yes."

"Here. I was here, in bed in Emily's guest room."

Chapter 9

✻

I wanted to respond to Paige's obvious lie, but I left the questioning to Brent.

He asked her, "Were you in Emily's guest room all night?"

"Except to go to the bathroom." Again, it was only a whisper.

"Are you sure?" He sounded calm and gentle, but his eyelids were lower than usual, a sign that he was intent on drawing the truth from her.

She wiped her cheeks with the backs of her hands. "Yes." The answer was shaky.

Brent persisted. "All night?"

Paige twisted her fingers in her lap. "Well, I guess I did go out for a little while before I actually went to bed. I'm a night owl, so to me, night begins at, like, two or three in the morning. I knew I wouldn't sleep, and the hospital wouldn't give me information when I talked to them before dinner." She glanced at me. "Emily said I could borrow her skis if I wanted to go out, and she told me where the hospital was, and I thought the storm was letting up, so I decided to just go there and find out whatever I could. But that was before what I think of as night, so I was here after that, asleep in bed, for what is night to me. That's why I said I was here in bed all night." After that suspiciously long and involved justification for her questionable statement, she turned to me. "I hope your door didn't wake you up, Emily. When I was leaving, the wind slammed it shut."

"It wasn't a problem. I went downstairs to make sure that it hadn't blown open or that we didn't have an intruder. My skis were gone, so I realized you must have gone out." Considering all the shoveling Paige had done, she must have gotten up shortly after I left home around quarter to six that morning. It was now only about eight thirty. I commented, "You must not have slept long."

"I don't, always, especially in a new place."

"I'm sorry. Did Dep wake you?"

"It's not your fault. I was worrying about Travis, and . . . everything. And Dep didn't wake me up. She's a good kitty. I just woke up and felt like I needed exercise. That's the good thing about shoveling snow. It's a workout."

I asked her, "Did the hospital call you in the night? Is that why you went out?"

Watching me but not interfering in my "good cop" line of questioning, Brent buried his fingers in Dep's fur.

Paige shook her head. "They didn't call."

Still playing the part of a friendly hostess but also trying to dig out the truth, I asked, "What did you find out at the hospital?"

Paige's knuckles were white. "Nothing. I never made it to the hospital. I was wrong about the storm. It was still going strong. I've skied before, but on, like, a trail. It was impossible in such deep snow. I made it a couple of blocks and fell. Snow was pouring down, and I couldn't get up. I twisted my ankle. It's okay now, but for a few seconds, I wondered what was going to happen to me, especially when I heard an angel's voice." She flicked half a smile at my undoubtedly dumbfounded expression. "It wasn't a real angel. Well, I mean it was, but it was a real woman who was like an angel. This lady came flapping down from her porch in her nightgown, bathrobe, and boots. She helped me out of the snow. Then she invited me inside to warm up, and we talked and talked. She was really nice. When I did finally leave, she told me to try skiing in the road where the snow wasn't so deep. She even came out and helped me over the pile of snow near her curb."

I asked, "Why didn't you go to the hospital then, by skiing in the streets?"

"Skiing was such a struggle, like swimming through mud or something, and the wind and snow were even worse. I wasn't sure I'd make it all the way to the hospital and all the way back, and I thought it was too late for the hospital to let me in, anyway, after all that talking with the nice lady, so I just came here. I shouldn't have gone out at all. I hope I didn't break your skis, Emily."

"You didn't. I skied to work this morning." I added encouragingly, "I might have met that woman a couple of times. What did she look like?"

"She was tall and thin with white curly hair and wrinkles from smiling a lot."

That described the woman I'd met. The first time I'd seen her, back in August, she'd been carrying pruning shears, and ever since, I'd thought of her as the pruning shears lady. I asked, "Which side of the street was her house on?"

"This side." Paige's answer was firm.

I leaned toward her. "How many blocks from here?"

"Two. Or was it three? Maybe four? It took forever to get there in the soft snow, so it probably felt farther than it was, and then, coming back, I was in the street and there was no traffic, so I didn't notice how many streets I crossed."

I thought about the house where the pruning shears lady lived. "Did you notice anything about her house?"

"The kitchen was yellow, the ceiling, too, and there were daisies on the wallpaper."

I smiled. "I meant the outside of the house."

She held her palms up in an I-don't-know gesture. "It was too dark and snowy outside to get a good look. There were steps up to the porch like you have, but more of them, I think, and they were covered with snow except where she flew down them. And the door was dark green or blue with a wreath. That's all I noticed, besides snow everywhere." A hint of a pained smile crossed her face.

"Did the woman tell you her name?"

Paige scrunched her mouth to one side and gazed toward the Christmas tree. "I don't remember if she told me."

Even if she had, it wouldn't have helped me, since I didn't know the pruning shears lady's name. Maybe I would have to change my secret nickname for her to the snow angel.

Brent stroked Dep. "Paige, I know this is a lot to ask, but can you go with me to identify the . . . the deceased person?"

Biting her lip, Paige looked down. A teardrop fell onto one of her fists. She brushed it off against her leggings.

Brent asked gently, "Do you know of anyone else who knows Travis well enough to say that it is or isn't him?"

She seemed to be studying her fists, clenched in her lap. "His parents are dead, and he lost track of his sister and brother years ago. We have friends in Green Bay, but you probably don't want to wait for someone to come all the way from there to identify . . . to tell you that it's not Travis."

Brent scratched Dep's upraised chin. "That could take a while."

She shuddered. "I don't know of anyone here. I mean, except the bus passengers."

I suggested, "The snowplow operator seemed to know him."

Hunching her shoulders, Paige tugged at the front panels of her unzipped jacket until one side overlapped the other. "But maybe he didn't know Travis, like, not well. That man might say it was Travis when it wasn't." She raised her head like someone grasping for new hope. "Was the person carrying ID?"

"No." Brent didn't tell her that Travis hadn't been completely dressed.

Paige gazed straight ahead toward the window beyond the Christmas tree, but she couldn't have seen much outside except the almost solid white of falling snow. "There's this little shelf near the steering wheel on the bus. I think that's where his wallet was."

Brent nodded. "I made certain it went with him to the hospital."

She sat up straighter. "So, he must have had it, and the person you need to identify isn't him."

Neither Brent nor I said anything.

Paige asked, more tentatively, "And you took him his duffel bag, too, didn't you?"

Brent's answer was terse. "Yes."

Paige's spread-out fingers were pale against the thighs of her leggings. She brushed at her knees and stood up. "I can go with you to see this . . . this person. I had to do it when my . . . for my sister."

I couldn't help repeating, "Your sister?"

Tears welled in her eyes. "I can't talk about it." She pinched her lips together.

I quickly became businesslike. "You can't wear that light jacket. It's not warm enough, and it's wet. You can borrow a spare parka."

Bowing her head, she wiped her eyes. "Thank you."

Brent stood and put Dep on the floor. "I'll get your skis and poles out of Tom's car, Emily." He removed his coat from the closet. "See you in a few minutes, Paige." He went outside.

Her tail quivering, Dep crept toward the tree. She was obviously on another mission to chew ribbons and bows off packages. She always seemed to think I might have changed the rules since the last time I told her not to do it.

I warned, "Dep . . ."

With a show of disdain, she skirted the tree and hopped up onto the windowsill.

"Good girl," I said.

She lifted a paw and washed it.

Since Paige wouldn't need to carry a cat underneath her coat, I got her one of my smaller parkas, a red one. The fuzzy white scarf and hat I wore with the parka were in a sleeve where I usually left them, but the matching mittens weren't. I checked the closet floor. No mittens. Finally, I found them in the front pockets. Either I'd put them there the last time I'd worn the parka, or Paige had accepted my offer last night and had looked in my closet for warmer clothes. These didn't seem damp, but they could have dried during the six or seven hours since I'd heard her return from her trip out on skis. She took off the green nylon jacket. Smiling, I told her, "You had it on inside out."

"Did I?"

"Yes. I'll hang it in the closet near the kitchen to finish drying." I took it from her and handed her the parka, hat, scarf, and mittens.

She thanked me. "Are you sure you don't mind if I wear these? Your things are all so nice." I half expected her to say that she'd already borrowed them during the night, but she didn't.

"I'm sure." I handed her my house key. "I'm going to work. Here's a key in case I'm not here when you get back. I have another one upstairs."

She shoved the key into one of the parka's pockets. "Thanks for being so sweet."

I teased, "It must be from all the donuts." I added more seriously, "You'd do the same for me or for anyone visiting you."

"I guess. Listen, Emily, you're a nice person, so I don't like to, um, you know, ask too big of a favor, but do you think your friend the detective actually believes I went to the hospital in the night and . . . and killed Travis? Because I didn't."

"He has to do his job, and he's a good detective. He'll keep an open mind, and he'll find out the truth."

She wound the scarf around her mouth and chin. "I hope so, but I don't trust policemen. They arrest people falsely."

"Brent's a good person." I didn't tell her that for serious crimes, the Fallingbrook Police Department brought in the Wisconsin Division of Criminal Investigation. The state had more forensics tools and equipment than small towns did. A DCI agent would probably arrive soon to supervise the case. Brent would report to that detective, who might not be as honest, thorough, and caring as Brent was.

Paige pulled on the hat and shoved most of her long hair up underneath it. "Can you help me prove that I didn't hurt Travis? Like, maybe go talk to the woman who helped me out of the snowdrift? She'll tell you I was with her while I was gone from here."

It seemed to me that if Paige were guilty, she wouldn't have asked for that particular favor. "I'll try, but I can only help in ways that are legal and safe for both you and me."

"Fair enough."

A little voice in my head said that Paige could have stolen the snowmobile and taken Travis out of the hospital either before or after she talked to the snow angel.

Brent stomped his feet on the porch and then opened the front door. "Ready, Paige?" Cold breezes whooshed inside along with a mini-tornado of snowflakes.

"Just my boots." She zipped them and then joined him outside. When I shut the door, she was putting on the mittens.

The little voice in my head babbled at me. *You shouldn't have told Paige you'd try to help her prove she didn't hurt her boyfriend. Brent won't want you interfering.*

I answered, *I'll be helping with the investigation. And all I'm going to try to do is find the snow angel and see if she corroborates Paige's story.*

The relentless voice asked, *Are you sure that's all you're going to do? You could destroy your friendship with Brent.*

Silently, I grumbled, *I've helped his investigations before without destroying our friendship. He knows I'm always on the side of justice.*

And then the voice reminded me, *You've been imagining a relationship closer than friendship. Are you sure you want to jeopardize that?*

I folded my arms over Paige's green nylon jacket and said, forcefully and loudly, "I don't know what you're talking about."

Chapter 10

With her tail draped in a stylish curve over the sill, Dep gazed out the front window. I flung Paige's jacket over the newel post and sidled past the Christmas tree. Ornaments and pine needles rustled. I stroked Dep's warm, furry back, and looked out, too. Paige was in the passenger seat of Tom's SUV.

Brent drove it away from the curb, and then they were gone and I was staring at a blank void of white, swirling snow. My sigh must have been too loud for Dep. She stopped purring.

Brent loved his job and was good at it, but days like this had to be tough, and the pain he had to face hurt me, too.

And then there was Paige. I knew too well what she was about to go through. She was going to be devastated.

I edged past the festively lit and decorated tree, grabbed Paige's jacket, marched into the kitchen, and hung it up.

Back in the living room, I asked Dep, "Would you like to go to work with me for the rest of the day?"

She jumped down from the windowsill. "Mew."

"You can stay here if you prefer. You have kibble, water, toys, and kitty litter."

She strutted to the door. "Mew."

I couldn't help smiling at the way she appeared to be answering my questions, but I knew what she really wanted, and I had to tell her, "Sorry, he's not coming right back."

Obviously not about to give up hoping for Brent's immediate return, she sat facing the door and swishing her tail back and forth on the wood plank floor.

I ran up to my bedroom, fetched my spare house key, trotted downstairs, and slid my feet into snow boots. As soon as I strapped Dep's carrying pouch over my shirt, she dashed to me and rubbed against my pantlegs. This time, she was answering my question. She wanted to go to work, or at least she wanted to snuggle with me and be taken places. I tucked her into her carrier, put on my parka, and zipped it up to her chin so she could keep track of the scenery.

Brent must have cleared the sidewalk in front of my house while he was waiting for Paige to come outside, and neighbors were shoveling, but snow was still pouring down. I didn't see or hear any vehicles nearby. I shuffled through one of the canyons that Brent, Paige, and I had trampled in the heap of snow near the curb and then walked in the street. Dep snuggled deeper into my coat. I couldn't hear her purring, but I felt the vibrations. And the warmth.

I stopped in front of the home where I thought Paige's snow angel lived. Snow frosted the hedge the woman had pruned in August. It was impossible to tell if the woman and Paige had come and gone from that house between approximately one thirty and three in the morning. Snow had drifted over the porch steps and the path between the house and the sidewalk. Paige had said that the front door was dark green or blue, with a wreath. I brushed snowflakes off my eyelashes. In the snowy, clouded-over daylight, the door appeared to be dark teal. A quilted red and white wreath with a big red bow trailing ribbons decorated it. I made a mental note of the house number. Giving it to Brent so he could talk to the woman was probably better than questioning her myself. For one thing, he would get the information directly from her, and for another, I wouldn't be interfering in his investigation.

Dep poked her head out above the zipper. I started walking again. Dep settled down.

Inside our office at work, she dashed to the highest catwalk and stared down at me while I took off my boots, hung up my parka, and stowed her carrying pouch and my backpack. Her pupils were at their widest and most mischievous. I blew her a kiss, went out into the dining room, and shut her into the office.

Smelling of cinnamon, nutmeg, and coffee, the dining room was still almost empty. From their regular table beside one front window, a group of retired men traded jokes with the women who called themselves the Knitpickers and sat at the big table beside the other front window. In the middle of the room, a bunch of firefighters talked and laughed.

Waving, I called out, "Season's greetings!" Everyone waved back. The good-natured and affectionate cheer gave me back some of the Christmas spirit that the morning's tragedy had stolen, and so did the soft Christmas music coming from speakers in the ceiling and the twinkly lights decorating the garlands on the walls, the big Christmas trees in the front windows, and the miniature Christmas trees on the tables.

I went through the kitchen to the storeroom, washed my hands, and put on my Deputy Donut hat and a clean apron. In the kitchen, Jocelyn and Olivia were pouring coffee for the firefighters and putting donuts on their plates. The Knitpickers and retired men had already been served.

Jocelyn and I took the plates and mugs to the firefighters. Eyes twinkling, one of them advised her to stop taking courses that would lead to becoming a teacher, and to train as a firefighter, instead. "Your gymnastic skills would come in handy," he added.

She was as sassy as ever. "Hey, some of you are volunteers,

right? You have day jobs. I could be a teacher and a volunteer firefighter at the same time. If I wanted to."

A fireman pointed at Scott. "Not him. Our chief and some of these other guys work at firefighting full-time. They have it easy, sitting around all day and night, waiting for a call."

Jocelyn gave the firefighter a side-eye. "And not that I mind, but why do volunteer firefighters take a break with the chief? Shouldn't you be working hard at your day jobs?"

Scott flexed his biceps. "We're building up our strength before we go out with off-duty cops and EMTs to shovel snow for seniors and others who need help." I suspected that he and the other firefighters were also taking a much-needed sanity break after following police investigators' instructions and, being careful not to destroy evidence, lifting Frosty the Donut off Travis.

I set Scott's coffee and his chocolate-and-candied-ginger donut on the table in front of him. He turned partway in his seat, facing me but not the other firefighters who were still teasing Jocelyn. Concern in those blue eyes, he examined my face. "Brent told me you were first at the scene. Are you getting over the shock of finding Travis?"

I slid into an empty chair next to him. The snowplow operator had known Travis's name. Did other municipal employees, like our fire chief, know Travis, too? I pinched my fingers together in my lap. "Does one ever quite get over that sort of shock?"

His lips thinned. "Not really. But I signed up for danger and disturbing scenes. You didn't."

Shrugging in an attempt to show that I could be almost as emotionally strong as my first responder friends, I asked, "Has a positive ID been made already? The tour guide, Paige, is staying with me. Travis was her boyfriend. Brent took her to identify him only about fifteen minutes ago."

Scott winced. "That poor girl. Woman, I guess, but she seems awfully young and fragile, especially to cope with the death of her boyfriend. The ID is not official, as far as I know, but I recognized Travis in Emergency last night and again this morning in the snow. We were in the same grade in school. He went to Gooseleg High, though, not Fallingbrook. He was one of Gooseleg's star football players. Maybe you, Misty, and Samantha were too young to remember Travis Tarriston. He was Fallingbrook High's Football Enemy Number One even before you started high school, but we still thought of him that way when you three were freshmen and I was a senior." Scott bit into the donut. "Delicious, as always."

"I was too overwhelmed by everything else at high school to pay much attention to football my freshman year. I don't remember him."

"Did Paige tell you where Travis has been living?" Drinking coffee, he watched me over the rim of his mug.

"She said they had friends in Green Bay, and that's where their tour began."

He set the mug down. "That strong coffee is just what I need, thanks. I think Travis left Gooseleg shortly after high school. Maybe he's been returning to Gooseleg from time to time. I don't know. We're seldom called to help with fires up there."

"Paige said that Travis's parents are dead, and he didn't know where his sister and brother were."

Scott stared down into his mug. "I think his sister and brother were older. I remember something about that family having problems. Maybe the brother dropped out and the sister disappeared, or they were jailed for various crimes. Or they wanted to distance themselves from Travis and the trouble he got into."

"What sort of trouble?" I glanced toward Tom. From where I was sitting, I could see only his shoulders and head. He was hovering over the deep fryers in the kitchen. He'd been a patrol cop, then a detective, and finally police chief in Fallingbrook, but he must have known officers in Gooseleg.

He might remember if Travis or his brother or sister had been arrested.

Scott answered, "Mostly fighting whenever he showed his face in Fallingbrook. None of the kids in my class liked him, mainly because of football, but also because he acted like he was untouchable, like he knew people in high places and could do whatever he wanted and never get into real trouble. Also . . . I probably shouldn't tell you this, but it wasn't exactly a secret. I'm sure lots of other people remember. There was another reason no one liked Travis. He dated one of the girls in our class and then dropped her, and she took it really hard."

Remembering the heightened joys and despairs of being a teen, I smiled and said gently, "Kids do that."

"In this case, everyone said he had stolen her from her boyfriend just to show that he could, and then dropped her. She ended up marrying the first boyfriend. He was in our class, too. She and her husband are living happily ever after. . . ." Scott's voice trailed off and he frowned.

I prodded, "I think I heard a 'but' at the end of that sentence."

"You did. You see, there might still be a connection between the three of them. The girl was Whitney, the woman who organized the Ice and Lights Festival."

"Whitney Valcriffe? That means that the original high school sweetheart is Leo Valcriffe, the electrician who designed the lighting for the festival and put it all together."

Scott lifted his mug to his lips. His nod was so slight that if I hadn't been watching him carefully, I might have missed it.

I asked him, "Do you think Travis was bringing tourists to the Ice and Lights Festival because Whitney and Leo created it?"

Scott drained his coffee and set down the mug. "I don't know, but it's not like busloads of people come from Green Bay or even closer for events in Fallingbrook. I wonder how

Travis found out about the Ice and Lights Festival, and why he decided to bring tourists to it. He used to love stirring up trouble, but maybe he matured after high school." Scott sounded skeptical.

I guessed, "Maybe he wanted to show off his much-younger girlfriend to Whitney and Leo."

"Which would mean that he could still have been trying to cause trouble, at least until late last night or early this morning when someone forced him to stop." Scott bit into his donut again and made an appreciative noise.

I scrunched up my face. "Whitney is really sweet, and Leo is a big teddy bear. I can't imagine either of them harming anyone."

"I can't, either."

The other firefighters pushed their chairs back and stood. "We have to go clear snow," one told me, "not like this bum." He slapped at Scott's shoulder.

Scott tossed more than enough cash onto the table to cover his and the other firefighters' bills. He picked up the rest of his donut. "I'm coming."

They called out cheerful goodbyes. Scott's was muffled by the quarter donut in his mouth. Jostling one another like high school boys, they trooped out.

In the kitchen, Olivia and Jocelyn were giggling at the Long John donuts they were decorating to look like Santas. "They're a little skinny," Olivia admitted.

I told Tom, "Brent and Scott think that the man who died early this morning was Travis Tarriston. Scott just told me that Travis and his brother and sister might have gotten into trouble with the law. They lived in Gooseleg when Scott was in high school. Scott graduated three years ahead of me, so that would be about seventeen years ago. Do you remember anything about them being arrested?"

Tom lifted a basket of donuts out of the hot oil and shook it. "Tarriston . . ." He hooked the basket over the edge of the deep fryer. "There was a congressman named Tarriston, and there were rumors that members of his family got away with things that other people might not have. Maybe this Travis Tarriston was related to him." Tom gave me a stern look. "But we'll leave it to Brent to investigate, won't we." It wasn't a question. He added, "Brent and whoever the DCI sends."

I agreed, maybe too readily. Tom threw me a suspicious glance.

Chapter 11

At about ten, Brent came in through the front door. He was still wearing his cross-country ski clothes from the day before underneath his unzipped parka.

Tom and I left Jocelyn and Olivia in the kitchen and met Brent at the end of the serving counter nearest the office. Brent thanked Tom and handed him his car key.

I asked, "How's Paige?"

Brent looked tired and defeated. "Crying. She identified the deceased as her boyfriend, Travis Tarriston. Misty and I took her back to your place."

I knew too much about holding on to every last crumb of hope and then being shattered by the finality of inescapable truth. I asked, "Do you think she'll be okay by herself?"

"Misty offered to stay. Paige said she wanted to be alone."

I stared straight into Brent's eyes. "I know the feeling."

He glanced toward Tom and then back at me.

The air seemed to vibrate with the memory of Alec's death and the grief the three of us shared. Tom and Brent had been required, too many times, to inform other people of their loved ones' deaths. Tom had retired from the police force, but did Brent relive the loss of his best friend whenever he had to give someone terrible news? The three of us, four including Cindy, had never discussed it. Maybe we needed to.

But not at the moment. I mentally shook myself back to the present and gave Brent the address of the woman who might have helped Paige. I added, "When I skied past there this morning, snow covered their footprints, if there were any."

"Thanks, Em. I'll talk to her."

"And talk to Scott. Travis was at Gooseleg High when Scott was at Fallingbrook. They're the same age. Scott can tell you about some of the kinds of trouble Travis got into."

Brent quirked up an eyebrow. "Like . . . ?"

Tom folded his arms and didn't say anything.

I answered, "Fights, and 'stealing' a girl from another boy and then dropping her. She's okay now. She's married to the first guy. But here's the thing. I know that couple. They're Whitney and Leo Valcriffe, the organizer of the Fallingbrook Ice and Lights Festival and her husband, who did the electricity."

Brent stood as still as a sculpture made of ice. I looked up at him questioningly.

Jocelyn breezed past, heading into the dining room with a carafe of fresh coffee. "Hey, Brent!"

Brent sounded normal when he returned her greeting. Then he turned back to Tom and me, and his face was serious. "I've met Leo and Whitney Valcriffe," he told us quietly. "They owned the place I just bought."

I tightened my apron strings. "They seem very nice."

Brent gave a slight nod. "Very. They loved that place and hated letting it go."

I asked him, "Why did they?"

"To be closer to downtown."

I wondered if Brent questioned that reasoning. I didn't say anything, but could Whitney and Leo have been in financial difficulties? And if they had been, could that have given them a motive to kill Travis?

Tom must have been considering similar ideas. He asked Brent, "Have you located Tarriston's will?"

Brent frowned at his former boss. "No."

Behind us, Olivia hummed along with the Christmas music coming from our speakers. In front of us, Jocelyn was refilling the retired men's mugs. And laughing and joking with them.

Tom said, "A high school kid doesn't usually write a will, let alone leave everything to a girlfriend he dumps shortly afterward, so it's unlikely that the beneficiary would be Whitney."

Brent glanced at me. He must have decided it was okay to tell us, "Travis had a tattoo on his left bicep. A heart with the name Whitney inside it."

I cringed. "Did Paige see that?"

Brent's face became even grimmer. "She recognized it. That tattoo eliminated any doubts she might have had about the identity of the deceased."

I took a deep, shaky breath. "Poor Paige."

Tom asked Brent if he wanted a ride back to work.

"No, thanks. I'll think while I walk."

A teasing glint lit Tom's eyes. "And do you have proper detective clothes in your locker? And a razor?"

Brent saluted. "Yes, sir. I'll shower and become presentable before interviewing anyone else, like Emily's 'snow angel.'"

I walked with Brent to the front door. He told me, "Call us if Usinor gives you any trouble."

"Who?"

"Paige. Her last name's Usinor."

I offered, "If you're worried about me or if the roads are impassable, you can stay on my couch tonight."

He examined my face as if wondering why it had suddenly heated. "I think I can make it home." He gave me a brief smile. "I need to get ready for Saturday's party."

Knowing how hard he worked on his cases, I wondered if

the investigation would allow him much time. "Has a DCI agent arrived yet?" I'd met three of them. Yvonne Passenmath, the negligent one, was no longer with the DCI. Rex Clobar had been stern but competent. Kimberly Gartborg was also stern and competent, but she was a single mom who was possibly a little too distracted by Brent to focus properly on a case. This close to Christmas, Detective Gartborg should be able to stay home with her twin teenage boys and their big fluffy puppy, who had probably grown a lot since our clamorous meeting in August. I wondered if the puppy had calmed down.

Brent told me, "One should arrive tomorrow."

"Do you know who they're sending?" With luck, it would be Rex Clobar or someone like him.

"No."

"Having another detective take charge of the case should free you to spend more time getting ready for your party." That might be true if the DCI agent did not expect Brent to spend the next few days explaining everything he'd already done.

"I hope so." He made an amusingly rueful face. "You'll never guess who I invited."

"Paige?"

"No. Whitney and Leo. They loved skiing there and the skiing should be great on Saturday, so I told them to come along."

"I can't see either one of them harming anyone."

"You probably know them better than I do, but I'm not worried even if they are murderers. Cops and an ex-cop are coming to the party. Leo and Whitney wouldn't dare try anything."

I merely shook my head.

He opened the front door. "Talk to you later, Em." I watched him walk away between our snowy twin patios. At the sidewalk, he turned and waved. His parka was still unzipped. He headed north toward the village square and the police station.

Jocelyn was back in the kitchen. After I was sure that no one in the dining room needed anything, I went there, too. Tom was frying donuts. Jocelyn, Olivia, and I piped Santa hats, white beards, noses, mouths, and coal-black eyes on jelly-filled donuts. Jocelyn deadpanned, "Let's call them jolly-filled donuts." Chuckling over the adorable and chubby jolly-filled Santas and the equally adorable but skinny Long John Santas distracted me from my concerns about Paige.

At noon, the Knitpickers and retired men called their goodbyes. We all told one another to be careful out there. While I enjoyed their company, I didn't want any of them falling and breaking bones. They could have used the weather as an excuse to stay home, but almost nothing would keep those two groups from their weekday morning meetings—and the opportunity to call out to the other table and offer teasing suggestions and friendly gibes.

Tom and I shooed Jocelyn and Olivia out for a break. They said they were going for a walk together and would eat later. I was happy but not surprised that they got along so well. After only fifteen minutes, they were back, bringing with them fresh smiles and fresh air. Jocelyn explained, "We were afraid you'd be swamped in here."

I liked their dedication, but I shook my head. "We aren't."

Tom went into the office to take a call. Through the window, we could see him holding his phone in one hand and petting Dep with the other. He was grinning when he returned to the kitchen. "Cindy is a wonder. She has arranged for the stranded passengers to spend the early afternoon at the library. The librarians are planning entertainment for the kids. I said we'd bring over some donuts and coffee at one thirty."

Olivia clapped her hands. "Great idea! The kids from the bus can probably use some extra care and attention."

Jocelyn offered, "I'll take them over there. Our walk was too short." She threw Olivia a teasing smile.

Olivia retorted, "You wanted to come back. You were hungry for one of Tom's deep-fried lunches."

Jocelyn put her fists on her hips. "So were you!"

I suggested, "It might take two of you. One to carry the urn and the other to carry the nice, lightweight donuts and the paper plates, cups, and napkins."

Olivia shook her head. "It's all yours, Emily. I have this idea, and if you all like it, I should stay here and get ready. What if we hold a kids' donut-decorating party this afternoon after the library party? It would help entertain the kids who were on that bus. They can walk here from the library."

"Let's!" Jocelyn said.

Tom agreed. "And they can walk from here to Frisky Pomegranate for dinner afterward."

Jocelyn rolled her eyes. "If they're still hungry."

Olivia came up with another idea. "Let's make invitations for you two to hand out at the library. We can write the details on business cards. That way, everyone will have our address, and you won't have to write it out every time."

I started toward the office. "I'm glad we hired you!"

Olivia blushed.

In the office, Dep was snoozing in a tunnel high above the desk. She stretched her front legs out straight but didn't otherwise move. I retrieved a stack of business cards. Olivia, Jocelyn, and I sat at the table in our dining area closest to the kitchen and began transforming business cards into invitations.

Tom asked us, "What would you all like for lunch? I was planning French fries, mozzarella-stuffed onion rings, and beer-battered pickles."

"All of the above," Jocelyn said. Olivia and I nodded.

They were, as always, delicious, and the customers who made it through the blizzard for lunch praised them.

After we ate, we packed Christmasy donuts into boxes and brewed a smallish urn of coffee. Tom and Olivia told us that since we had very few customers in Deputy Donut, we should take our time in the library and enjoy the party. We said we would.

Jocelyn looked at me. "I thought you were going to do your Christmas shopping today during your lunch hour, but you didn't go out."

Olivia asked in a joking voice, "You haven't finished your shopping yet, Emily?"

"No, have you?"

She pretended to flick dust off one shoulder. "Weeks ago."

I made a fake pout. "I don't think I should take more time off today after going with Brent when he talked to Paige. When we're done at the library, we'll need to get ready for our party here."

"You can finish your Christmas shopping before our party," Olivia offered. "I'll wait tables and help Tom make donuts while you're gone."

I argued, "But you might need me."

Tom shook his head. "We're not going to be busy today. Take your time." He gave me a look over Jocelyn's head that I interpreted to mean that he always wanted Olivia and Jocelyn to feel needed. He added, "You've had a stressful day, Emily. Cindy would say you can use some retail therapy."

The kindness of my colleagues made me swallow hard. I pretended to complain. "I'm outnumbered."

"You sure are," Olivia said.

When it was time for Jocelyn and me to go, Olivia came into the office with us to prevent Dep from escaping when we opened the back door. Outside, the snow had let up a little, the temperature was still only slightly below freezing, the driveway had been plowed again, and shopkeepers had been shoveling. Walking with Jocelyn was always fun. Although carrying an urn of coffee, she twirled for a panoramic view of Fallingbrook's picturesque downtown. "It's like a Christmas card out here, with the snow and the decorations!" She slowed down and commented, "Olivia might be too shy to cope with all the people who might be at the library, but I'm glad she came up with the idea for the donut-decorating party. She can hide in our kitchen during that, if she likes, but the fact that she suggested it shows that she's definitely coming out of her shell."

"With your help."

"And yours. I don't think she's taken time for a life of her own. On our walk today, she told me some of her story. Her parents died when she was eighteen. Her little sister was eight. Olivia decided not to go to college. Instead, she threw herself into looking after Hannah."

"How did their parents die?"

"Mountain climbing or rock climbing. Olivia didn't say, exactly, but she thinks that almost any physical exertion is dangerous. Even gymnastics."

"Hard to believe," I deadpanned. "You always make it look easy."

"It is."

"If you've worked at it ever since you were a toddler, yes, probably. Did you know Hannah in high school?"

"She's three years younger. I knew who she was, but that's about all. I had the impression that she was quiet and studious. I hardly did anything in high school except schoolwork and gymnastics, and I don't think our paths often crossed."

"Except on the honor roll."

Looking startled, she turned toward me. "How'd you know about that?"

I smiled. "Just a guess."

"Hannah ended up with huge scholarships, but I'm surprised she felt comfortable enough to leave town and go away to college. She and Olivia are closer than most sisters, I think, and closer than most mothers and daughters, too, but now, other than coming to work at Deputy Donut, I don't think Olivia knows how to start living for herself, making friends except for us, and just relaxing and enjoying life."

"Maybe an eligible police officer or fireman will come into Deputy Donut and fall for her."

"You and your matchmaking! I'm glad I already had a boyfriend before I started working at Deputy Donut."

"Is Parker coming home for Christmas?"

"Yes, in time for Brent's party."

The library's front windows were now almost completely covered in children's construction-paper Christmas ornaments. We opened the door and heard children laughing, shouting, and singing a gleeful version of "Rudolph the Red-Nosed Reindeer."

Irma, the head librarian, welcomed us and handed our coffee urn and packages to an assistant. Jocelyn and I removed our boots, coats, hats, and mittens. Irma gave us disposable paper booties to slip over our socks. I had a sickening feeling that the paper booties could have been almost like the slippers that Travis had worn when he left the hospital.

We walked farther into the library. Near the front windows, Fallingbrook children were giggling with children I'd seen on the bus. They worked together creating more ornaments and cards from construction paper, markers, and glitter.

Beyond that busy space, older children were browsing bookshelves or nestling into oversized cushions and reading. In one room father back, the tiniest tots were having stories read to them. In another, kids were galloping in a circle, singing "Jingle Bells," and shaking bracelets made of actual jingle bells. I hoped that song wouldn't get stuck in my head again.

Irma and her assistant took us down a hallway and opened the door to a meeting room. At the far end, red-covered tables were decorated with "candles" that children had made by wrapping red and green tissue paper around the cardboard rolls from paper towels. The candles spouted flames cut from red, orange, and yellow tissue paper. Some of the flames were bigger than the candles and trailed down their sides.

The library had supplied boxes of juice. The four of us arranged them, the coffee urn, and the donuts, cups, plates, and napkins on the tables. Telling us she was going to call the partygoers to come into the room for refreshments, Irma took her assistant and left.

Jocelyn and I sat at a green-covered table near the door where we could invite library patrons to our donut-decorating party.

Footsteps approached in the hallway outside the meeting room. Ready to welcome everyone, Jocelyn and I started to push back our chairs.

The footsteps stopped before anyone appeared in the doorway. Out in the hall, a man said in a low, angry voice, "I wanted you to come with me, back here where my wife can't hear me and interfere with her goody-goody, let's-all-get-along nonsense. I call it like it is. I'm glad that man is dead. He deserved to die for what he did to us. Many of us were injured, and it could have been a lot worse. And to add insult to injury, we're holed up in this backwater that no one wanted to visit for more than a few minutes while we wait for rescue that never comes."

Chapter 12

꙰

Jocelyn and I looked at each other. She placed a forefinger against her lips. We quietly eased down into our chairs. She leaned forward and cupped her hands behind her ears. Although I knew I shouldn't encourage her to be snoopy, I imitated her.

Out in the hallway, a second man asked in milder tones, "Are they still not answering your calls?"

"They're probably afraid to. They need to send another bus and another driver immediately. But we're perfectly within our rights to demand full refunds. Don't you agree?"

The other man said, "Probably. There's no phone reception back here, though. I'm going to the front door. Maybe if we both keep trying to reach them, one of us will get through."

Footsteps receded down the hallway.

Jocelyn and I placed our hands on the table as if we were perfectly innocent of eavesdropping. Her eyes wide and looking darker than ever, she whispered, "I recognized the voice of the first man, the really angry one. That was Dustin Loyvens, the man who's staying at our house with his wife and their three boys."

"He was really angry at the crash site, too, and rude to

Paige. He blamed her. She doesn't want to go near the people from the bus, probably because of him. You and your parents have taken on a lot."

"We don't mind."

"Is he like that at your house?"

"Not exactly, but—" She broke off. Footsteps, lots of them, pounded toward us down the hallway. "Tell you later," Jocelyn said.

Irma popped her head around the doorway and winked at us. "Here they come!"

Kids erupted into the room and dashed toward the table of food. Within seconds, Irma and the parents were limiting the kids to one donut apiece and encouraging them to sit down on the carpet to open their juice boxes and eat their donuts. One craggily handsome father with dark hair that kept falling over his eyes snapped at a boy for spilling juice on the man's jeans. Jocelyn nudged me and muttered, "That's Dustin." A slight and pretty blonde who was bending over and helping another boy straightened, gave Dustin a serious look, and gestured with her head toward the doorway. Dustin apologized to the boy, helped him clean up the juice, and then followed the blonde into the hallway. Jocelyn whispered to me, "That's his wife, Ashley."

I heard Dustin and Ashley murmuring out there, but I couldn't tell what they were saying. Ashley returned by herself and thanked us for providing the coffee and donuts and helping transform what she called a "disaster" to fun events for the kids.

Jocelyn introduced us. Ashley praised Jocelyn and her parents for their hospitality.

During the party, we gave Ashley and the other adults our hastily created invitations to our donut-decorating party. Nearly everyone said they'd be there, and they would also attend the Christmas caroling that night.

"What Christmas caroling?" Jocelyn asked.

A mother answered, "We're meeting outside Frisky Pomegranate at seven, and we'll sing as we walk through the Ice and Lights Festival. We'll serenade the police station and the fire station. Then we'll wend our way to the hospital and carol in the lobby. Before that, anyone who wants to eat at Frisky Pomegranate at five thirty is welcome to join us, but you'll have to make your own reservations."

Certain that, in her grief, Paige would be even less likely to want to eat at Frisky Pomegranate with the stranded passengers than she had been the night before, I said I'd join the carolers at seven. "Though I can't say much for my singing."

The mother told me I was being modest.

Jocelyn tossed me a wicked smile. "No, she's not. Neither of us can carry a decent tune."

After every crumb had been eaten, every juice box had been sucked dry, noisily in many cases, and most of the coffee was gone, Jocelyn told me she'd clean up. "It doesn't require two of us, and you can go do your Christmas shopping. I'll take the urn back."

"That's very nice, but . . ."

"Go on," she urged. "I'd hate for you not to finish your shopping. I mean, what if you don't have a present for me yet?" Her eyes glinted.

I stretched my neck up and attempted to look haughty. "What makes you think you're getting a present from me?"

She made shooing motions. "Go!"

Out at the main desk, I thanked Irma for letting us show off our donuts and coffee. She returned the thanks. "From what I've overheard, you'll have a lot of people at your party."

"Are you going to join us?"

She gestured toward rows of bookshelves. "Thanks, but I have to work whether patrons are here or not."

I put on my cozy parka and boots and went outside. Snow was still falling, but the flakes had become fatter and were drifting down lazily. I stuck out my tongue and caught one.

The Craft Croft was one of my favorite shops. Just inside the door of the warm and welcoming shop, I took a deep, appreciative breath. Summer Peabody-Smith, the manager of the artisans' co-op, had apparently been mulling cider. Customers were walking around carrying mugs of the spice-laden brew. Carefully.

Summer spotted me and rushed over. "Leave your boots on, Emily. This tile floor is a breeze to mop. Would you like mulled cider?"

I stamped as much snow as I could onto the mat beside the door. "I'd love some."

She grasped the bottom of her tunic-length sweater and pulled it away from her leggings. "How do you like my ugly Christmas sweater?"

"It's not ugly!" Obviously hand-knit, the sweater was tunic length but Scandinavian style at the top, with a knit design around the shoulders like a wide circular collar. The design was a string of Christmas balls knit from many colors of fun yarns featuring fuzzy, shiny, and sparkly strands. The rest of the sweater was a pretty shade of deep green. "Did you knit it yourself?"

"Yes, and I even found leggings in the same shade of green."

"And earrings to match. Did you make those?"

She fingered one of the pearlescent Christmas ornaments dangling from an ear below the red curls piled on top of her head. "A member did. Come, get some cider, and look around. Are you still Christmas shopping?"

"Yep, and it's not last minute. Today's only the sixteenth."

Summer was nearly six feet tall, and her laugh was sized to

match. It was also contagious. Smiling, I accepted a mug of cider from her. She went off to let me browse.

The Craft Croft's décor was sleek—white walls, gleaming glass, and brushed stainless steel, all of it understated and allowing the colorful artwork, jewelry, and other crafts to shine. The Craft Croft, with its selection of beautiful gifts, was always inspiring. Someday, I might try making gifts, but for now The Craft Croft merely inspired me to buy them.

Tom had been right about the retail therapy he'd said Cindy would advise. I wanted to gaze at everything. The shop was jam-packed with beautiful handmade objects. I didn't know where to start.

Tom and Cindy always invited me to their place for Christmas Eve, and then I always stayed overnight and spent Christmas Day with them. I had made them plum pudding and a fruitcake and had bought them a gift card to a great restaurant in a ritzy year-round resort. We always filled one another's stockings, so I needed to find small gifts in addition to the homemade cookies and candies I planned to slip into their stockings.

In the jewelry case, I found darling handmade sterling silver earrings for Cindy. One was a kitten, and the other was a ball of yarn.

I leaned over a counter of handmade letter openers. One of them, shaped and bejeweled like a medieval sword, seemed right for Tom.

Tom and I would give bonus checks to our employees, but I wanted to give them each something personal, besides. Olivia walked to and from work while Jocelyn rode her bike, walked, or, in weather like we'd been having, skied. Hand-knit scarves with matching hats and mittens would help keep both women warm. I chose a set in warm shades of red and auburn for Jocelyn and a set in blue and turquoise for Olivia.

Before Hooligan and Samantha were married, I gave them separate gifts. I could still do that, or I could give them something to share.

I would give Misty and Scott separate gifts, but I wasn't sure what.

I had no idea what to get for Brent, who had brought a different date every year to Christmas dinner at Tom and Cindy's when Alec was still alive. Brent had begun coming to Christmas dinner again, as one of Tom and Cindy's friends, not as my date. He no longer brought dates.

I hadn't seen the interior of Brent's new home, but I had a good idea of his taste from the old one. He liked plain and sturdy furnishings with no frills, but there were little touches of whimsy that might surprise people who didn't know him well. I'd learned to look closely at his ties.

What would he like that wasn't too personal? What would say "good friend, but not trying to be pushy" when I was actually considering becoming pushy? Staring at some mugs, I felt myself blush. Not because of the mugs. They were rather plain, in a slightly gleaming shade of pewter gray with white interiors.

Summer appeared beside me. "Look inside." She lifted them down from the shelf. The mugs were identical except for a darling three-dimensional dragon in the bottom of one of the mugs. "You fill them," she said, "and give the one with the dragon to an unsuspecting guest. They drink two-thirds of their coffee or mulled cider, and this fire-breathing dragon emerges. And your mug will just be normal."

My smile became so big it almost hurt. "They're perfect. I'll take them." I led Summer to the glass jewelry case and pointed out the earrings and letter opener that I wanted.

Summer laid them on the glass countertop.

They were exactly right. I carried them and the scarves, mittens, and hats to the cash register. Summer brought the mugs. While she rang up my purchases, I asked her, "Who made the mugs? I wouldn't put it past Cindy, my mother-in-law."

"No, it was Whitney Valcriffe, you know, the woman who organized the Ice and Lights Festival. She's an artist of many talents. I'm pleased that she joined the co-op. That woman has survived a lot and come out smiling."

Chapter 13

✂

I tilted my head in question. "What did Whitney survive?"

"Being fined and incarcerated for a crime she didn't commit and having her driver's license suspended for a couple of years."

I was surprised, but a small and probably unruly part of my brain teased me with a theory. If Whitney had committed a crime before, could she have killed Travis now? I repeated what Summer had said, but I made it into a question. "Whitney was incarcerated for a crime she didn't commit?"

"Yes."

"What crime, and how do you know that Whitney didn't commit it?"

Summer wrapped the letter opener in tissue paper. "Hit-and-run. I know she couldn't have done it because she would never have hit someone and then just kept going. My parents and her parents are friends. She's younger than I am, but I know her well. Even as a little girl, she was kind and caring. She still is. When that accident happened, she was planning to become a nurse. She would have stopped and helped."

"Who did you think was driving if it wasn't Whitney?"

Summer wrapped the earrings I'd bought for Cindy. "I'm almost certain it was the guy she was dating. Not Leo."

I fiddled with the mugs. "Travis Tarriston?"

Summer darted a quick look at me between half-closed eyelids and then focused on wrapping Jocelyn's scarf, hat, and mittens. "I'm surprised that people still remember that old scandal. Aren't you younger than Whitney?"

"I didn't remember. I guessed. Do you know our fire chief?"

"Scott?" She glanced up at her high ceilings. "He changes our smoke detector batteries. He's great, isn't he?"

"He is. He changes ours, too, even though Tom says he can do it. Scott and his crew check on all of the downtown businesses and help keep us safe. He was in Deputy Donut this morning. He told me that Travis dated Whitney for a little while."

"Only long enough to break Leo's heart and nearly break Whitney's. Plus put her in jail for a crime she didn't commit."

"How did he manage that?"

"Whitney's parents' car hit a couple of pedestrians up in Gooseleg but fled the scene. Whitney called the Gooseleg police the next day and admitted that her parents' car was the one they were looking for. She said that she'd been in the car and that Travis had been driving and refused to stop because he'd been drinking and didn't want to be caught. He denied being with Whitney that evening. His parents told the police he'd been with them."

I asked, "The Gooseleg police?"

"Yes."

"Whitney lived in Fallingbrook at the time, though, right?"

"She did. She and Leo moved to a country property about a half hour from Fallingbrook a few years ago and moved back into town last week." Remembering skiing around that property with Brent only a day ago, I smiled. Summer tilted her head in question.

"The mugs are for the person who bought the property."

Summer raised an eyebrow.

"A friend. Brent. You've met him."

Her smile became huge. "That gorgeous detective."

"We're just friends."

"Uh-huh."

It was time to direct the conversation back to my original intention. "I wondered if my father-in-law, Tom Westhill, helped investigate that hit-and-run. It would have been before he was chief."

Summer shook her head, bouncing the cute earrings against her neck. "I think the Gooseleg police handled it all. Travis's grandfather was a congressman with a reputation for corruption that no one ever proved. I don't know if he did anything to prevent Travis from being charged, but people feared him, and maybe some of the Gooseleg police were afraid of what he might do to them." Summer's mouth made a sour downturn. "Whitney's folks are good people without wealth or influence, so maybe it wasn't too surprising that Whitney was charged and convicted for something that I truly believe Travis did."

I told Summer about Travis's death that morning. She hadn't heard, but she wasn't shocked. "When Whitney was dating him, my parents were afraid he would hurt her, and maybe other people, too. He was reckless and self-centered. I'm surprised he stayed out of jail this long, if he did."

"He was driving the bus that went off the road last night with a bunch of families on board, so he must have been holding down a job, working for a tour company."

Again, Summer gave me that look between half-closed eyelids. "Was he drinking while driving the busload of families?"

"I suspect he was. His girlfriend was the tour guide on the bus. She's staying with me."

"She must be pretty broken up."

"She was, even before Brent took her to identify Travis. I haven't seen her since. Brent said she wanted to be alone."

"Did Travis have family who could have identified him?"

"Paige—that's the girlfriend—told me that Travis didn't know where his sister and brother were and that his parents were dead."

Summer folded layers of tissue paper around the whimsical mugs. "That's odd. I thought I saw Travis's mom up in Gooseleg last summer. Maybe it was someone else, but the woman I saw had this wild red hair and big, wide-open eyes like Mrs. Tarriston had. She always looked electrified. She was wiry, too, which added to the effect. Maybe she died since then."

Hadn't Paige told me that Travis's parents had died years ago? Maybe I'd heard or remembered it wrong. I asked Summer, "Did the people who were hit say that a woman was driving?"

"As far as I know, the man never remembered what had happened. His child was about eight. I don't know if it was a boy or girl, but I heard that the kid was too traumatized to say much except to scream about eyebrows."

"Would Whitney have been charged based on a traumatized child's screaming about eyebrows?"

"Probably not, but I don't know. Although the child wasn't made to testify or anything like that, Whitney's thick eyebrows might have swayed the police's and the prosecutor's opinions."

"There's nothing wrong with her eyebrows."

"No, and many women would kill for those eyelashes." Summer grimaced with something like horror. "Well, maybe not actually kill . . ."

I thought back to the crash scene. I had particularly noticed Travis's eyebrows. Maybe they had always tilted downward toward the sides of his face like that, or maybe he couldn't have helped making that amazed expression when he was about to crash a vehicle or had just crashed one, and that's why the child had obsessed about eyebrows. I described them to Summer.

She nodded. "His eyebrows were always like that. Whitney wasn't the only one who fell for him based on his looks. I think that some women get the impression that men whose eyebrows slant down toward the sides of the face are concerned about other people and are therefore more open to caring. In Travis's case, he only looked concerned and caring. He wasn't."

I asked, "Do you remember the victims' names?"

"I don't think I ever heard them. Names aren't usually published when kids are involved." Summer tucked my purchases and some folded gift boxes into an embroidered cloth shopping bag I'd bought during a previous visit to The Craft Croft. "What I do know is that even though Whitney has a legitimate reason for being angry at Travis for lying about who was driving and letting her suffer the consequences, Whitney doesn't keep grudges. I'm sure she's put it all behind her. Leo has always been very supportive of her. She was only incarcerated a couple of months, you know, to teach her a lesson and warn other people not to leave the scene of an accident. Whitney and Leo are happy together, one of those perfect couples. Look at the display they've created in the square! The ice sculptures were beautiful before Leo strung up the lights, but after he lit them, wow! That couple are community treasures."

"Do they have children?"

She handed me the bag of gifts. "No. But they're about thirty-five, so it's not too late, if they want them."

Wishing that Summer hadn't reminded me about the ticking of biological clocks, I thanked her and took my bag of gifts outside.

Beautiful big flakes were drifting down, and Christmas music played softly from speakers on lampposts decorated with swags of cedar, silver balls, and big red bows.

A bell jangled as I opened the door of Booked. I didn't see either of the store's owners, a married couple. Both former police officers, they retired from the Fallingbrook Police Department and opened their aptly named bookstore a year or so after Tom and I opened Deputy Donut.

A teenager at the checkout desk told me to let her know if I needed help and then went back to reading. I smiled. She understood people who loved browsing in bookstores.

The store smelled of pine boughs, of the honey-colored wood in the bookshelves, and of new books.

Passing comfy reading nooks and shelves of colorful paperbacks, I headed to the cookbook section. I could have spent hours there reading recipes, but I disciplined myself and looked only in the grilling and barbecuing section. Just as I'd hoped, I found a book that I knew Hooligan would like—and our friends and I would benefit from his outdoor cooking in nice weather.

The central part of the store housed children's books. Small chairs off to one side could be arranged around low tables or placed in a circle for story time.

The back of the store was dedicated to puzzles, craft kits, and games. After spending too much time lingering over fun things to do, I selected an origami kit, complete with directions and a pack of beautiful papers, for Samantha. She was the one who folded napkins into surprising shapes at the dinner table.

Near the back wall, I couldn't resist a display of jigsaw puzzles. With a mental cackle, I chose one that looked almost impossible—a photograph of pebbles under a thin layer of rippling water—for Scott. He could put it together at home or enlist other firefighters to help him in the fire station. Even better, he could invite our friends and me to his apartment to help. Maybe after Hooligan barbecued our meal.

During her breaks in Deputy Donut, Misty sometimes stopped to watch the Knitpickers work and asked them, "How do you do that?" Maybe she wouldn't thank me, but I wandered into the arts and crafts section and chose a teach-yourself-knitting book. Knowing Misty, she would follow the illustrated directions easily. If she did run into problems, she could come into Deputy Donut any weekday morning and ask the Knitpickers.

Also fascinated by knitting and knowing that I had access to experienced knitters to help me if I got myself in a tangle (or if Dep got me into one . . .) I almost bought a copy of the book for myself. I remembered just in time that I was supposed to be finding gifts for others.

The clerk put several small candy canes into another of my cloth shopping bags along with the books, the puzzle, and the origami kit.

I crossed the street to a yarn shop, On the Lamb. Inside, garlands of tiny knit mittens, sweaters, and stockings hung nearly everywhere. The clerk helped me choose needles and a ball of yarn that would be easy for a beginning knitter.

Walking up the other side of the street again, I thought about Paige and Whitney as possible murderers. I didn't know either of them well, but I'd spent more time with Whitney than with Paige. As Summer had said, Whitney seemed like a good person.

Paige's grief made her seem innocent, and I was reluctant to believe that a woman staying in my house could be a murderer.

In the library, Jocelyn and I had overheard Dustin Loyvens saying that Travis had deserved to die. Jocelyn had been about to tell me more about Dustin, but she had stopped when we heard people approaching. Maybe she knew something that might cast light on whether Dustin's anger at Travis could have led to murder.

Back at Deputy Donut, I put my bags of gifts underneath the desk, as far back as possible. Standing and stretching on the couch, Dep eyed me. "Mew?"

I kissed the top of her furry little head. "Don't unpack those bags. There are gifts inside them for some of the people in here, and we wouldn't want to spoil their surprises, would we?"

"Mew."

"I knew you'd agree, Dep. Maybe you can help me wrap the packages after we get home." She turned around three times and settled back down on the center cushion of the couch. She didn't need to worry—not that she seemed to worry about much of anything—that I might have forgotten her. I had already hidden toys for her at home. The ones containing catnip were in the freezer. She had to know a little about her Christmas surprises. Ever since I'd set the carton they'd come in on the kitchen floor, she'd been shoving it around, climbing into and out of it, and curling up inside it for catnaps. The box would probably turn out to be her favorite gift.

I shut her into the office and went into the kitchen. Tom, Olivia, and Jocelyn had made small, old-fashioned cake donuts. They had cut some of them in the traditional way—a circle with a hole in it. They had cut others in the shapes of pine trees, bells, stars, and extremely chubby gingerbread men.

On my way to the storeroom, I beckoned to Jocelyn. She followed me in. "What?"

"You started to tell me something in the library about Dustin, the man who's staying with you and your parents and who seemed enraged at Travis in the library."

Chapter 14

Jocelyn glanced around as if checking for eavesdroppers lurking in the storeroom and then lowered her voice. "I heard someone leave the house about one thirty this morning. My parents would have had to walk past my bedroom to go downstairs, so I know it wasn't them. They wouldn't go out in the middle of a blizzard, anyway. At about three, I heard the front door open and close again, and someone tiptoed upstairs. I'm pretty sure that the person went into the room where Dustin and Ashley are staying, and I'm guessing that it was Dustin. And here's the strange thing—I smelled exhaust fumes."

"Not smoke, as if he'd gone out for a cigarette?"

"Or ten! He was gone about an hour and a half. No, it was definitely exhaust fumes from a gasoline engine, one that doesn't burn cleanly, like maybe an old snowmobile. We don't have anything like that, except for a lawn mower locked in the shed."

Jocelyn's parents lived a few blocks from me. Paige and Dustin had both left the homes where they'd been staying around one thirty in the morning, and they'd both returned about three. Was it possible that they had arranged to meet each other to remove Travis from the hospital and leave him out in the cold to die? It didn't seem likely. The night before, in the bus, Dustin had been angry at Paige, and she hadn't seemed any fonder of him than he'd been of her. Had it all been an act?

Based on Paige's emotions, I preferred to go on believing that she'd had nothing to do with Travis's death other than not stopping him from drinking and driving.

"You might have solved the murder," I told Jocelyn. "But that would mean your family has a killer staying with you." I conveniently failed to point out that I might also have a killer staying with me.

"We'll be okay. Ashley seems to keep him calm. She would never let him hurt us or their kids."

I pulled my phone out of a pocket. "This could be important. I have Brent on speed dial."

"Of course."

Ignoring her smirk, I tapped Brent's number and handed her the phone. "Tell him what you just told me."

Jocelyn's eyes widened. "Okay." My phone to her ear, she became serious. "Hi, Brent. Emily said to call you."

Unashamed, I listened as I tied my apron strings and put on my hat. I wondered how Dustin had managed to take Travis out of the hospital and whether Travis had gone into the storm willingly when he was wearing only a hospital gown, robe, paper slippers, and his coat, although Brent had said the coat had been near Travis, not on him. What had become of Travis's street clothes and the duffel bag Brent had taken to the hospital to give him?

Jocelyn disconnected and handed the phone back to me. "Brent said he would come to the back door." She went into the office.

Minutes later, an unmarked cruiser slowly passed the front of the building. Peering from the kitchen through the window into the office, I saw Jocelyn open the back door and let Brent in. He removed his parka, shook Jocelyn's hand, and picked Dep up for the cuddle that she was undoubtedly demanding. He had shaved and changed into a charcoal gray suit, a white shirt, and a dark red tie with a pattern on it that I recognized from the Christmas before. His hair was neatly combed. While Jocelyn talked to him in the office, the other three of us arranged plates of donuts for the kids to decorate. The donuts were small, so we put three donuts, all different shapes, on each plate. We set out individual bowls of frosting along with blunt knives for spreading the frosting.

Olivia suggested, "Let's not give the sprinkles and other sugar decorations directly to the kids. The sprinkles could end up crammed into mouths or rolling around on the floor. How about if we help the kids place them where they want them?"

Tom and I agreed. Tom glanced toward the office where Jocelyn was talking and Brent was writing in his notebook. "We might need to enlist a few adults to help." He shot a devilish grin at me. "Brent doesn't look busy."

Brent lifted his head. Although he couldn't have heard what Tom said, he narrowed his eyes. He could probably tell from our faces that we were involving him in our plots and plans.

Families streamed into Deputy Donut. We directed the kids to the tables we'd set up for them near the kitchen and let the parents sit as far from their children as possible in our little shop, close to our Christmas trees and the windows overlooking our snowy patios and the street.

Ashley Loyvens sat by herself at a table for two. Before I could ask what she'd like, she explained, "My husband is on his way. You might as well bring us each a coffee." Huddled into her coat as if she were cold, she glanced toward the kitchen. "Where's Jocelyn? I thought she worked here."

I pointed toward the large window into the office. "She's in our office. She'll be out soon."

Ashley stared toward the office. "What's she doing talking to that man?" Her voice sounded raw, as if she had a sore throat. "Isn't he the police officer who came onto the bus last night before the rest of you got there?"

"He's a friend of everyone in here. He comes in often." That wasn't exactly true, but that day, he was already making his third visit to Deputy Donut, probably a record. I added, "Jocelyn's probably trying to get him to help the kids decorate donuts." And that was even less true. Jocelyn couldn't know that Tom, Olivia, and I had joked about involving Brent in the party.

Ashley turned down the corners of her mouth. "He's in a suit. Police officers don't usually work in suits unless they're detectives."

I saw no reason not to tell the truth. "He is a detective. His tie has Santas and reindeer all over it."

Ashley gave me a funny look as if to remind me that a Santa tie had nothing to do with whether or not Brent was a detective. She obviously didn't find Brent as adorably fun-loving as I did. She leaned toward me. "I hope someone has told that detective about the tour guide. I don't know what's become of her, if she's in the hospital or what, but yesterday morning before we started out, she was arguing with the bus driver outside the bus. They went on and on. The bus windows and door were closed, so I couldn't hear what they were shouting, but they were really going at it, waving their arms and shaking their fingers at each other. And she was crying. It was bad enough that they'd already made us late. They explained something about getting fuel for the bus. Seems to me they could have thought of that earlier and picked us up on time instead of making us stand around in the cold at a bus stop while they bought gas." She glanced down toward her hands, tightly grasping each other on the table. "You know what? Dustin's coffee might as well wait until he gets here."

I agreed. "It's best fresh and hot."

While I was pouring her coffee in the kitchen, I saw her thumbs busily texting on her phone. She put it away. I set her steaming mug on the table in front of her and pushed the creamer and sugar bowl closer to her.

I was about to go serve another parent, but Ashley went on talking about Paige as if there hadn't been a break in our conversation. "Anyway," she said, "that tour guide was really angry at the bus driver, and I wouldn't be at all surprised if she grabbed the steering wheel and aimed us into a ditch." Ashley nodded toward the office. "Someone needs to tell that detective that if the driver died of something besides his injuries, the police need to pay attention to the tour guide. They should pay attention to her even if he did die of his injuries. I'm pretty sure she caused them. On purpose."

Did Ashley suspect, as I did, that her husband had killed Travis? Did she suspect that her husband and Paige were involved together in Travis's death? I asked Ashley, "Would you like to talk to Detective Fyne? I could go get him."

"No, thanks, but I'd appreciate it if you'd pass the message along." She folded her arms across her chest and glared toward kids milling around tables near the kitchen and shouting demands for different colors of frosting and sprinkles.

"I'll tell Detective Fyne what you said." Ashley probably didn't realize that Brent would want to hear the story directly from her. I thought, *I know where you're staying. . . .*

Meanwhile, Cindy was holding the front door open to let the family she and Tom were hosting into Deputy Donut. I excused myself and went to greet the newcomers. I asked, "Cindy, would you mind helping the kids with the deco- rating?"

"Not at all." She stooped to unzip the three-year-old's snowsuit. "Tom called and told me about the party, and I said I'd help. Sorry for taking so long to get here."

"How was the driving?"

"I've seen better."

Both of the little girls' parents chimed in with sincere praise of Cindy's driving.

The girl pulled off her mitten and showed me the back of her hand. "I have a new friend. It's a Christmas elf!"

I admired the bandage on her cute little hand. The father hung up everyone's coats, and Cindy and the mother ushered the girl to where the other kids were spreading frosting on donuts, the plates, the tables, and sometimes on themselves and one another. Not on purpose. Probably.

It looked like Brent was about to leave by the back door. I went into the office. "Brent, do you have a few minutes?"

Jocelyn smiled at the chaos out in the dining area. "It looks like I'd better go help."

"Thanks, Jocelyn. It's getting a little rowdy out there, but we've recruited Cindy, so everything should settle down soon. I'll be out in a few seconds after I talk to Brent."

Jocelyn left the office. Near the front of the dining area, Ashley was talking on her phone.

Brent asked me, "What is it, Em? Want me to give you a hand with the kids?" He grinned. "Or with their parents?"

"We could use your help, and you might like to hear what some of the parents are saying. But before you go out there, Ashley Loyvens, the woman sitting near the front who I was just talking to, asked me to pass along some information to you."

One of his eyebrows raised the tiniest bit, not enough for

anyone, like Ashley, still in the dining room, to notice. "That's the woman staying with Jocelyn and her parents? The wife of the man Jocelyn was just telling me about?"

"Dustin's wife, yes. And I suspect that if you go out there, she'll leave, even though her three boys are here."

Brent pointed at the couch. "Let's sit down."

We sat on the couch. Dep trotted down a kitty-width staircase and plunked herself between us. Brent took out his notebook again.

Stroking my purring cat, I told Brent what Ashley had said about the supposed argument between Travis and Paige after the tourists boarded the bus. "I had a feeling Ashley was making up the argument to cover for her husband. Maybe she knew he'd made a threat in the library and that Jocelyn and I could have heard, or maybe she guessed that Jocelyn heard him go out during the night. Maybe Ashley also smelled the exhaust fumes when he came back. She didn't say anything about his threat in the library or his possible excursion on a snowmobile. And then she wanted me to tell you the story. She might have been afraid you'd know she was lying, if she was."

He reached over and squeezed my shoulder. "Most people aren't as willing to talk to police officers as you are."

I suggested that Paige and Dustin could have met during the night and worked together to take Travis to the village square. "But it seems unlikely, since they didn't seem to like each other last night on the bus."

"Stranger things have happened."

Gazing into Brent's eyes, I realized I was leaning toward him, and our heads and his shoulders were visible to a dining area full of guests, most of whom had been on that crashed bus the night before. Without backing away, I quickly said, "I told her you were the friend of all of us who work here."

"True." His hand stayed on my shoulder.

I still didn't move away, even though being this close to him made me want to pick up Dep, scoot to the middle of the couch, and fold both my cat and myself into Brent's arms. Remaining staunchly where I was, I said, "I also told Ashley that Jocelyn was probably enlisting you to help the kids." I explained Olivia's concern about sprinkles and frosting ending up everywhere except on the donuts.

Those gray eyes twinkled. "Then I guess I'd better lend a hand. But if you don't mind, I'll pour coffee for the grownups instead of helping with the kids. The adults' gossip could be more useful. At least it would be more likely to be admissible in court."

"That's fine."

He squeezed my shoulder and let me go. He plunked his parka on the couch where he'd been sitting and followed me into the dining room.

Cindy, who was a teacher, Jocelyn, who was studying to become one, and Olivia, who, according to Jocelyn, had experience raising a child when she was barely out of childhood herself, had turned the decorating frenzy into civilized requests for specific colors of frosting, sugar stars and spheres, snowflake sprinkles, and tiny gingerbread-flavored teddy bear sprinkles. Small boxes of milk had miraculously appeared when Cindy did. The donut decorators guzzled it.

I helped Brent put on an apron and bring the strings around the front to tie it like the rest of us did. He didn't seem to mind that we didn't have a Deputy Donut hat for him. He gamely carried a carafe of coffee to the front of the shop to refill mugs. And also, no doubt, to listen to conversations and accusations. Before he got to Ashley, however, she left her table and brought her mug of coffee to the kids' tables. She was still wearing her coat. Leaving her, along with Olivia, Tom, Cindy, and Jocelyn to wrangle the kids and their donuts, I made more coffee. When I joined the decorating party, Brent was still offering coffee and chatting to people as if he'd worked in a donut shop all his life.

Some of the kids wanted to eat their donuts on the spot, but Jocelyn must have decided that since most of them had eaten donuts in the library only a short while ago and dinnertime was looming, they should hold off. She put her index finger near her lips and said, "Sh. Don't tell your parents"— smiling at Jocelyn, Ashley covered her ears—"but the donuts you decorated can be surprise early gifts for them. I'll get bags, and you can hide the donuts in the bags." Jocelyn headed toward the storeroom.

Ashley told her kids it was time to go back to Jocelyn's.

The middle-sized boy crossed his arms and scowled. "I want my bag of donuts first."

Ashley dismissed him with a wave of her hand and then pointed at me. "This nice lady will tell Jocelyn to bring your bags home after work."

Although surprised, I nodded.

Ashley's smallest boy looked up at her. "Where's Daddy?"

Ashley pulled her phone out of her coat pocket, glanced at it, and shoved it back into her pocket. "He decided not to come. We'll see him at Jocelyn's."

"I want him to carry me." The boy started crying. "I don't want to walk to Jocelyn's! It's too far!"

Ashley asked him, "How about if we play in the snow in the square, and then go to Frisky Pomegranate? Daddy will meet us there for dinner. It's right beside the square, and we won't have to walk far. After dinner we're going to see the ice sculptures all lit up, and we'll sing Christmas songs on the way back to Jocelyn's. You'll get to stay up past your bedtime. Would you like that?"

The boy let out a huge sigh and a pathetic, "Okay." His biggest brother rolled his eyes.

Brent went into the kitchen, set down his empty carafe and

took off his apron. He passed Ashley on his way to the office. She didn't look up. "See you later," he said.

Through the window, I watched him remove Dep from where she must have made a comfy nest in his parka on the couch. He snuggled her against him and rubbed her chin. Finally, he set her down, put on the parka, waved at me through the window, and let himself out the back door.

Ashley's middle-sized boy built his complaints to a full-sized wail. "I want to put my donuts in a bag and take them with me!"

Ashley scolded, "You can't have a paper bag of donuts when you're playing in the snow."

The kid stuck out his lower lip. "I don't want to play in the snow."

The littlest boy demanded, "I want Daddy to come here first, and then I'm going to give him my donuts, and then we'll play in the snow. And I'm not giving you any of my donuts, Mommy."

"Fine." Ashley's voice shook as if she were having trouble controlling her temper.

"Me neither," the middle-sized boy said.

The oldest boy told Ashley she was welcome to his. "I don't like how I decorated them, anyway. They turned out ugly."

Ashley didn't contradict him. She conceded, "I guess we can stay here a little longer since none of you seem keen on playing in the snow." I wondered if Ashley's change in plans had anything to do with Brent's having left.

"I want to," the biggest boy said. "I'm going to build a snowman."

Jocelyn returned from the storeroom with a stack of our smallest paper bags printed with the Deputy Donut logo. "Sorry I took so long. I had to open a new box, and I found crayons. You can decorate the bags and write your parents' names on them."

Ashley looked after her own kids while Jocelyn, Cindy, Olivia, and I distributed crayons and helped the other kids decorate bags and write their parents' names on them. We held the bags open. The kids slid their donuts inside. With enthusiastic muscle that threatened to smash donuts, the kids stapled the bags shut. When they finished, there was no way that any of their donuts could escape. And none of the donuts were stapled to the bags, either, I hoped.

Shortly before four thirty, Cindy announced that everyone could walk with her to the square for a scavenger hunt before dinner at Frisky Pomegranate. "We don't have a list, and we're not actually picking up anything. I'm going to tell you what to look for, and you'll all have to raise your hands when you spot it and not say a thing until everyone has raised their hands."

Ashley's biggest boy asked, "Are there prizes?"

Cindy put on her encouraging-teacher voice. "The prize is seeing fun things!"

"Fun," the boy grumbled.

Cindy and the families went to the coatrack and put on their outdoor clothes. After everyone piled outside, I asked Jocelyn, "Are Dustin and Ashley's kids always so difficult?"

Jocelyn was diplomatic. "Dustin and Ashley seem to lack a few parenting skills, but they're under a lot of stress." I didn't point out that the same was true for other parents on the tour, parents whose kids were active but not constantly testing their parents.

But maybe Dustin and Ashley were under more stress than the other parents. Maybe they knew that Dustin had murdered Travis. Being stuck in the town where the murder had occurred could not have been comfortable, especially after Ashley saw Brent talking to Jocelyn. Ashley could have feared they were talking about Dustin, and she'd have been right.

Intending to turn the sign in the front from OPEN to CLOSED, I headed toward the door.

A woman stomped inside. Her eyes were red, and so were her cheeks. Her hair, which stuck out every which way, was also red, brilliant ruby red. Her heavy wool coat barely padded her wiry frame.

Someone had described someone like her to me. . . .

Very recently.

And then I remembered. This woman fit Summer's description of Travis Tarriston's mother, the woman that Paige had told me was dead.

Chapter 15

This woman was very much not dead. After one look at her tear-streaked face, I knew that none of us would consider telling her we were about to shut our doors for the night. She sagged into a chair near the door. As Ashley had, she kept her coat on.

I asked her, "What can I get you?" This close, I noticed that tiny broken blood vessels near the surface of her wrinkled skin gave her cheeks their rosy tone.

"Anything. Something sweet and something hot."

"How about a donut and some chai?"

She slung her heavy handbag onto the table. "What's that?"

"Spiced tea with sugar and milk."

She brushed a tear off her cheek. "I don't care. Don't you have coffee?"

"Yes. Would you like some? Our special today is Sumatran, but we also have Colombian."

"I don't care."

In the kitchen, I used a single-cup French press to make her a cup of the Sumatran. I took it to her along with a cream-filled donut covered with vanilla frosting. Olivia had turned the donut into an elegant Christmas ornament by piping thin lines of red frosting onto it and placing tiny gold and silver balls in a pattern resembling a traditional ornament.

The woman didn't comment on the pretty donut. I wasn't sure she noticed it. She waved her hand toward Olivia and Jocelyn, who were cleaning tables and taking away creamers. "I'm sorry to come in here like this. It looks like you're getting ready to close."

"It's okay. You got here in time."

"I couldn't stay on my feet one second longer. I've had the most terrible news."

I pulled out the chair and sat down beside her. "I'm sorry. Is there anything I can do?"

She dumped three teaspoonfuls of sugar into her coffee and stirred it. "Look, he wasn't the best son in the world, but he was my son, and after all these years, he was finally coming to see his old mother, and now he's gone."

I felt like icicles were forming on my spine, and all I could manage to do was repeat her last word, "Gone?" This woman had to be Travis's mother. Had Paige lied to me about Travis's mother being dead, or had Travis lied to Paige? Maybe Travis's father was alive, too. I glanced outside. Streetlights lit the dusk. No bereft man was stumbling toward our door.

The woman's words confirmed my suspicions, at least some of them. "He was hurt in a bus crash in last night's storm. He sacrificed his life to save the people on the bus. He swerved to keep from hitting a drunk driver who had strayed into his lane. No one knows who or where that guilty driver is. He or she got off scot-free." She bit off a chunk of donut and glared at me. "Travis ended up in the hospital, and then someone kidnapped him, threw him in a snowdrift, and left him to die."

I felt my eyes opening wider and wider. Where had she gotten the story about the drunk driver? It didn't match what passengers on the bus had said, and if Paige had seen a vehicle heading toward the bus, I was sure she would have mentioned it to Brent and me. I told the woman how sorry I was about her son. "Did he leave a wife? Any children?"

She stuffed the piece of donut into her mouth and licked cream filling off her fingers. "None of my children gave me grandchildren. He was alone on this earth. And he died alone." She dabbed at her eyes with her napkin. "No mother there to hold his hand." She leaned toward me and muttered, "I know who kidnapped him."

I tried not to look even more startled than I already was. "Who?" The question came out like a croak.

She blew air out through a gap where a front tooth must have once been. "He did have a girlfriend long ago, but after the way she treated him, he never could trust any woman again. And now she's gotten back at him for the way she treated him."

Trying to wrap my head around the idea of a former girlfriend getting revenge on Travis for something she did to him, not something he did to her, I asked, "How did she treat him?"

"Unfairly. She snitched on him. She told the police he was driving her car when it hit a pedestrian, but it was her car, not his, so how could he be driving it? Besides, when the policemen asked us about that accident, we told them that Travis was home with us eating dinner and watching TV. That's what we did. As a family. Ate and watched TV. But here's the thing. That old girlfriend, and she wasn't really much of a girlfriend, went to jail, but not for long enough. And then she waited. As soon as Travis showed his face in this town again, she pounced." Travis's mother made her hand into something resembling a claw and pounced on an imaginary critter on the table. Cutlery jangled. "He never should have come back, but he must have heard that I'd moved down here from where we brought him up, in Gooseleg, so he thought it would be safe to come see his old mother, but that Whitney, she just pounced." Again, the woman's clawlike hand pounced on prey I couldn't see. Coffee sloshed.

"Are you saying that she wanted him to lie for her and go to jail for her, and he didn't, so she wanted revenge?"

Travis's mother's eyes went squinty. She plunked her spoon into the spilled coffee on the glass tabletop. "Yes. That's exactly what she did. She wanted him to take her punishment for her, and he refused. Why should he have taken the blame for something she did? But she got mad, kidnapped him from the hospital although he was severely injured from saving all those other people, and she left him out in the cold to die." She gulped at her coffee and set the cup down. "Too hot." She emptied the cream pitcher into the mug. It overflowed. "I could tell the police what I know about her, but talking to them doesn't do any good now that my father-in-law, Congressman Tarriston, is gone. At least when the congressman was alive, the police knew they had to be honest, or else. But now, as far as I can tell, they're worthless."

"You said you once lived in Gooseleg. Are you talking about the Gooseleg police?"

"Yeah, but they're all alike. Worthless. They got some floozy to identify my boy before they even bothered to look me up. They just found me and flat-out told me my darling boy was dead. Dead! He was an angel even in life." She sniffed. "Perfect grades in school, captain of the Gooseleg High football team . . ." She bit off another chunk of donut. "He even won a scholarship. First Tarriston to go to college. Even his grandfather didn't do that, or his father, either." Mrs. Tarriston's description of her son was only minimally similar to what I'd heard from Scott and Summer. Neither of them had mentioned angelic qualities.

However, Paige seemed to think he'd been special.

With sympathy and more than a little curiosity, I asked Mrs. Tarriston, "Are you the one who has to break the news to Travis's father?"

She sniffed again. "He's gone, too, and luckily doesn't have to outlive a child like I have to."

"I'm sorry that you've lost both a husband and a son."

"The husband was a long time ago. I've learned to live with my sorrows."

"Do you have other children?"

"That I can't tell you. I mean, I did, but I don't know where they are, or if they're living or dead. A beautiful girl and a gentle boy, both gone off and never came back, never cared to find out what's become of their old mother. Or their old father, for that matter."

She slurped at the top of her coffee, gobbled the remainder of the once-beautiful donut, and wiped her mouth on a napkin. "I should let you folks finish cleaning up so you can close."

"No rush," I said.

But apparently there was a rush. She hurried out into the darkening evening. I hadn't been about to give her a bill, and she didn't ask for one.

I cleared her table and mopped up the spilled coffee. While Tom, Jocelyn, Olivia, and I tidied the shop, I described my talk with Mrs. Tarriston.

Tom advised, "I wouldn't believe much of what she says."

I glowered at him in a way I hoped was accusatory. "Do you remember anything about Travis Tarriston and a hit-and-run that his girlfriend at the time was convicted of?"

My glare failed to daunt him. "I might."

"The girlfriend was Whitney."

Olivia gasped, "Whitney Valcriffe? The Ice and Lights Festival organizer? She seems too nice to do that."

"That's what I thought," I said.

Jocelyn contributed, "I know who she is, but you folks made all of the arrangements with her for the festival before I came home for Christmas."

Olivia turned a chair upside down on a table. "I only met her twice, but as far as I could tell, she's a sweetie."

I asked Tom, "Do you know who the victim was? Summer said it was a man, and there was a child with him."

Tom moved another chair onto a table. "I don't remember off the top of my head. Brent will look into all of it. I'll call him tonight and tell him as much as I remember, and he can look up the rest."

I thanked him. I had to be satisfied with that answer. I couldn't believe that Whitney was a murderer, let alone a hit-and-run driver. I'd told Paige I'd do what I could to help her prove her own innocence, but I suspected that looking for evidence that Whitney was a murderer would lead exactly nowhere.

When everything in the shop was ready for the Jolly Cops Cleaning Crew, four retired policemen who would come in during the night to drain the oil from the deep fryers and do the heavy cleaning, Olivia asked, "Who's going for dinner at Frisky Pomegranate?"

Jocelyn said her parents were walking there and would meet her. "And our houseguests." She almost managed to not contort her face into an expression of trepidation. "I hope the boys won't sail any paper napkin airplanes into my soup again tonight."

"I'll walk with you," Tom told her. "I'm meeting Cindy there with our houseguests."

I explained that I wasn't going. "Paige didn't want to eat there last night, and now that she's grieving for her boyfriend, she's even less likely to want to be around the stranded passengers. I'll take Dep home and make certain that Paige gets a decent meal."

Jocelyn asked, "Who's going caroling this evening?"

We all said that we were. The other three bundled up and headed toward Frisky Pomegranate. I tucked Dep into the carrier inside my parka, grabbed the bags of gifts I'd bought that day, and started walking home in the dark. The snowflakes had become lazy, infrequent, and just plain pretty.

On my street, every house displayed bright holiday cheer. I hummed underneath my breath until Dep stretched her neck up and bopped my chin with the top of her head. I stopped humming and Dep nestled deep inside my parka again.

By the glow of the streetlights, I could see that someone had cleared the walks of the house belonging to the woman I thought might be Paige's snow angel. The woman was sweeping a dusting of snow off her porch steps.

Calling, "Merry Christmas!" I started up her walk.

She beamed. "Merry Christmas to you, too. You're burdened down. Have you been Christmas shopping?"

I grinned. "Yes, and I finished today."

"Show off! That's a lot to carry. Would you like to come in and rest your arms?" I'd been right that she'd be the type to rescue a foundering skier.

I shook my head. "I don't have far to go."

Dep wormed her head out of the top of my parka again. "Meow!"

The woman laughed. "You have that darling kitty with you! I wondered what you did with her when it's cold or snowy and she might not enjoy walking on the end of a leash. I bet she likes being carried around all cuddly like that."

"She does." I glanced at heaped-up snow beside her walk. "Did you shovel all that snow yourself?"

"I certainly did not! A crew of off-duty police officers, firefighters, and EMTs came along and cleared the snow away from the walks of every senior's home on this block. And probably a lot of others, too. They said they can use the exercise, and besides, they don't want us calling them with heart attacks. Such a sweet bunch of hardworking people! Fit, too."

I agreed. We chatted a little about the blizzard and about

other winter storms she remembered, and finally, I asked her, "Did you come out in the middle of the night and help a woman on cross-country skis?"

She tilted her head as if perplexed. "It's funny you ask. A charming police detective came by and asked the same thing. I'm afraid I can't take credit. I stayed inside all night. I didn't exactly sleep well, though, and I looked outside several times. Around two, snow was coming down so hard I couldn't see from the house to the sidewalk."

"I looked out about then, too, and I couldn't see that far, either."

"That detective asked if I saw any vehicles, and of course I didn't, so he asked me if I heard any. I heard the snowplow go by a couple of times. How about you?"

I admitted, "I must have slept through that. My bedroom's in the back. I didn't hear snowplows. Snowmobiles probably went by, too, and they can be noisy enough to hear over the wind."

"I suppose so, but that would be different from a plow, don't you think? Plows make lots of scraping and banging. Snowmobiles roar like overpowered leaf blowers."

I agreed with her.

She whacked at a snowdrift with her broom. "Why do you suppose that detective wanted to know all those things? Did something happen?"

"A man died in the square during the night."

She pressed her mittens to her cheeks. "What a dreadful night for it. But you said that a woman was out on cross-country skis. Was she okay?"

"Someone rescued her. I thought it might be you."

"Not me." Her eyes glinted with mischievous lights. "Maybe if she'd flung herself into my hedge like you did that time, I'd have come out with my pruning shears to disentangle her, but my pruning shears are oiled and put away for the winter. Do you know the woman?"

"Yes, and I wanted to thank you for rescuing her, but since you didn't, I won't." I grinned to show I was teasing. "She's staying with me, and I guess I should go home for dinner. There's Christmas caroling tonight starting at seven near Frisky Pomegranate. Are you going?"

The woman shook her head and gazed at the heaps of snow. "I'll just finish sweeping these steps, and then I think I'll heat up some beef stew and stay inside with a nice cozy fire and something warm to drink." She smiled at Dep. "If I had a cuddly cat like you, the evening would be perfect." She took off a mitten and stroked a finger across the orange stripy patch on the top of Dep's head. She switched to baby talk. "You're a sweet little kitty, aren't you?" I felt the vibrations as Dep went into full-purr mode.

Finally, I left the woman. I told myself I should ask her name. For now, she'd have to go back to being the pruning shears lady. Dep stopped purring.

I wondered if Paige had made up the story about being rescued.

Had she actually been stealing a snowmobile and using it to push an ice sculpture onto her boyfriend, maybe with the help of Dustin Loyvens?

Chapter 16

✿

The rest of the way home, I pondered whether to tell Paige that the woman I thought might be her snow angel had denied it. I wasn't sure how to break it to her. If Paige was a murderer, would I be putting myself in danger if she thought I suspected her?

I opened the front door and was greeted by one of my favorite aromas—pizza.

With her hands clutched together in front of her waist, Paige came through the dining room into the living room. "I hope you don't mind. I scrounged around and made pizza. I took it out of the oven a minute ago." Her eyes were red and puffy, and a cascade of flour trailed down the front of her long black sweater and leggings.

I was glad to set the bags of Christmas presents on the floor. They weren't terribly heavy, but holding the bulky bags away from my body had been tiring. I slipped my feet out of my boots. "Mind? It smells wonderful. It's exactly what I needed on a chilly night like this. Did you make the dough?"

"Yep. The books on your shelves look interesting, but I couldn't focus on reading. I found your cookbooks and hoped that cooking might distract me." She thinned her lips, obviously swallowing back tears. "It did, sort of."

"That's why Tom and I own a donut shop. Alec also loved

to cook, and making donuts was how Tom and I managed to cope with some of our grief."

This wasn't helping Paige. Her eyes welled with tears.

I quickly added, "Alec used to make pizza, too. Coming inside after work and smelling it brought back wonderful memories. Brent has brought take-out pizzas over, and I sometimes make or order them myself, but this is the first time in years that someone has made one to be ready when I got home."

She gave me a watery smile. "I'm glad I timed it right. I made Caesar salad, too. I figured, since you had the ingredients, you like it and were planning to make it."

"Thank you. I was." Hoping that Dep would go comfort Paige, I let my tortoiseshell tabby out of her carrying pouch. She climbed partway up the stairs, sat on the landing near the coat closet door, and stared toward the Christmas tree.

Paige had not only made a pizza and Caesar salad; she had washed the dishes and utensils and put them away. She and I set plates, cutlery, and napkins on the kitchen island. Dep roamed into the kitchen, but she didn't stay. She trotted into the sunroom, jumped onto a cushioned radiator cover, and sat looking at her—and probably our—reflection in the otherwise dark windows.

Again, I didn't offer alcohol to drink, and again, Paige didn't ask. Sitting on stools at the kitchen island, we drank sparkling water and ate Paige's excellent pizza and salad.

Finally, Paige asked the question I'd been dreading. "Did you find the woman who took me in during the night?" Paige's voice was tentative and scared.

"I talked to the woman I thought might be her, but I was wrong. She said she told a handsome detective the same thing, so Brent had already talked to her, and he also knows she didn't help you."

Paige twisted her hands in her lap. "But she did. I'm telling the truth. I never hurt Travis. I . . . I wouldn't have. You believe me, don't you?"

"Yes."

"Someone else hurt him, probably one of the people from the bus."

"I suspect you're right. People from the bus are going Christmas caroling with people from Fallingbrook at seven. I'm going. Would you like to come along? Maybe we can learn something from the passengers. We'll stay together, and we'll be careful."

Her tears welled up again. "I couldn't. Can't bear it. Being around those people, I mean, blaming Travis and me for things that weren't our fault."

"I'm sorry. Asking you was insensitive."

"No, it wasn't. It might be a good idea, I guess, and I'll have to go back to being around strangers sometime, just not yet."

"I get that."

"And thanks for asking." She glanced toward the sunroom where Dep was still staring intently at her reflection in the mirrorlike window. "Is Dep going with you?"

"She probably wouldn't like being confined inside my jacket for so long, especially if she had to listen to my singing, or what passes as singing. Do you mind if she stays with you?"

"I'd love it. Maybe I can read if she sits on my lap."

"She might do that."

"Or I could bake cookies if that's all right with you. Or both."

"It's fine. Meanwhile, for dessert, let's have more of the ones my friends and I baked."

This time, her smile seemed more confident. "I was hoping you'd offer."

While we munched cookies, I told her about the woman

who had come into Deputy Donut and claimed to be Travis's mother.

Paige shook her head as if trying to shake loose a memory or make sense of the impossible. "He definitely told me that both of his parents were dead."

"She said his father is. Also, that she doesn't know where his sister and brother are."

"He never said much about any of them. I thought he didn't want to talk about them, so I didn't ask. Do you think she really was his mother? She could have been an imposter, or maybe an aunt or something."

"I don't know, and—I'm not sure how to explain this—her grief seemed self-serving, like his tragedy was more about her than about him."

"Maybe she's trying to benefit from his death. Like raise money." She dipped her chin, and I could barely hear her next words. "Like, if she really is his mother, for his funeral."

She ran from the kitchen.

I tidied up and started the dishwasher, and then went into the living room. Paige was gazing at books on my bookshelf. Dep stalked in and positioned herself in the middle cushion of the couch as if showing Paige where she should sit after she selected a book.

Feeling guilty about leaving Paige and her grief, I put on warm layers, said goodbye, and walked as briskly as possible along mostly cleared sidewalks to Wisconsin Street. Peeking past the dark Christmas trees inside Deputy Donut, I felt reassured by the comfort of our sweet little shop. Farther up Wisconsin Street, yellow police tape surrounded an investigators' tent where our Frosty the Donut sculpture had stood—and where Travis had died. I was glad for Paige's sake that she hadn't come with me, even though she hadn't seen much of the Ice and Lights Festival the night before when I drove her past and snow had billowed around my car and the sculptures.

I walked farther before I crossed the street into the square. I started along a diagonal path leading toward Frisky Pomegranate.

"Emily!"

I turned around. Hand in hand, Samantha and Hooligan walked toward me. Corey Ides, Samantha's EMT partner from the night before, was with them. Misty and Scott were not far behind.

I waited, and then, teasing one another and laughing, we all walked farther north and joined the group across the street from Frisky Pomegranate. Olivia, Jocelyn, Tom, and Cindy were there along with the family staying with Tom and Cindy, other passengers from the bus, and Fallingbrook citizens. I greeted several Deputy Donut regulars. One of the women from the bus had left her coat mostly unbuttoned to make room for the cast on one arm. I gave her a sympathetic look. "How are you feeling?"

She glanced down at the boy by her side. "Not great, but Noah has been really helpful."

Noah smiled at me. One of his front teeth was missing. He pointed at the gap. "My tooth fell out last night, and the tooth fairy came all the way here and found me!"

Worried, I asked, "Did your tooth fall out because of the crash?"

He shook his head. "It was very wiggly before. None of us were hurt in the crash, except Mommy. I can't wait to get home and tell my friends all about being in a big crash." He flexed his muscles.

His mother and I traded smiles. "Oh, to be young," she said.

I asked, "Did you have to spend a long time in the hospital?"

She groaned. "It only felt like it. They let me out with this millstone around my neck about one. Your fire chief, Scott, took me to the house where we're staying. You folks are really kind."

"You'd have done the same for us. Where's your husband? He wasn't hurt, was he?"

"No, he's fine. He stayed back to help shovel and bring in wood for the fireplaces in the house where we're staying." She smiled. "The good news is I can't help with any of that."

Irma the librarian passed song sheets to everyone. Singing, we started through the square. With the heaps of fluffy snow, the shining ice sculptures, and the fat snowflakes landing softly on us, we were definitely walking in a winter wonderland. Naturally, Samantha and Hooligan walked hand in hand, and so did Cindy and Tom until their three-year-old guest broke their grasp and walked between them, hanging on to their hands and looking up saucily at them. Scott took Misty's hand and smiled down at her in a way that should have made her heart race.

Olivia, Jocelyn, and I walked together. Corey joined us. Olivia's pure soprano harmonized with his rich tenor. They stayed in tune, and both of them had a smooth country twang in their voices. They sounded amazing together. Jocelyn and I smiled at each other. We were already helping Olivia make friends. With an impish wink, Jocelyn held me back so that Olivia and Corey would have to walk together and we would walk behind them.

A few minutes later, Jocelyn's natural exuberance must have taken over. She handed me her song sheet, burst out of line, and ran ahead. She executed a perfect cartwheel in the snow beside the pathway.

Most of the youngest carolers dashed ahead and attempted cartwheels, also, and then Jocelyn flopped down and made a snow angel. Children surrounded her, lying in the snow, swishing their arms and legs back and forth, and hollering with glee that outshouted those of us who were singing, or in my case, trying to sing.

Jocelyn helped the kids stand and brush snow off their snowsuits. One yelled, "I can see my breath!" They all huffed and puffed like fire-breathing dragons, and I was warmed by imagining Brent's smile when he unwrapped the mugs I'd bought him.

Blowing fog in front of his little face, Noah ran to his mother and bumped into Corey. With her good arm, his mother corralled the boy. As if embarrassed by Noah's behavior, she tossed a quick apology Corey's way and then stepped aside with Noah to let us pass. And probably to remind Noah to watch where he was going. She had to be hyperaware of how being bumped could hurt.

Olivia's soprano soared into the chorus, and Corey found the right harmony to blend with her again. It sounded to me like Olivia and Corey could entertain others by singing together. I would be willing to pay to hear them.

At the south end of the square, we crossed the street and serenaded the police station. Brent was one of the police officers who stood on the building's broad stone porch and applauded. We finished our carol. I waved. Brent waved back. Our motley group walked to the other end of that short street and sang another carol in front of the fire station. The big doors rolled all the way up, showing the bright interior and the gleaming red trucks. When we finished singing, a firefighter climbed into one of the big red trucks and turned on the flashing lights and, for only a few seconds, a siren. Kids cheered and covered their ears.

After the siren became silent, Scott stood beside Irma in front of the group, raised his hand for silence, and announced, "Tomorrow, if you're all still in Fallingbrook, please join us around five for our annual kids-of-all-ages party. There will be snacks, and we'll be decorating and lighting our trees."

One of the fathers from the bus yelled teasingly, "With candles?"

Smiling, Scott shook his head.

We walked to Wisconsin Street, and turned south. We passed the Fireplug, a pub around the corner from the fire station, and Deputy Donut. We meandered, singing, through my neighborhood of older homes all dressed up for Christmas. We didn't go as far as my block.

Listening to everyone else's voices as they belted out Christmas carols, I decided that my attempts at singing were a detriment to everyone's enjoyment, including mine. I closed my mouth and listened.

At one street, most of the carolers crossed, but Jocelyn and I had to wait for traffic. A couple of women behind us held a discussion that seemed to include a lot of hissing noises.

One complained, "That tour company still isn't answering their phone. They need to send another bus right away."

The other woman agreed. "They need lessons in customer relations."

The first woman asked, "Don't you think that bus driver, Travis somebody-or-other, deserved what he got?"

The other woman was quiet for a few seconds. Then she seemed to choose her words carefully. "I'm not sure he was at fault. That tour guide, Paige, distracted him the whole trip. I hear she grabbed the steering wheel, bumped into him, covered his eyes, or something. You can bet she's to blame. There was that argument before we left."

"So unnecessary. It made us late. What were they arguing about?"

"I guess it was about his drinking. I saw her take a bottle from him and stuff it into that big black tote bag she never let out of her sight."

"Were they drinking when we were riding along?"

"Could be. I'd like to know what was in that water bottle he was sipping from while he drove. Paige kept standing between him and us like she hoped we wouldn't see. Is she here tonight?"

"I haven't seen her since we got off the bus."

The traffic cleared. Jocelyn and I started across the street. The two women stayed behind us, and I continued hearing most of their conversation. Neither Jocelyn nor I attempted to catch up with the carolers. I was certain that Jocelyn was as intent on eavesdropping as I was.

One of the women guessed, "Paige must have caught a ride into town, and sometime during the night, she went and finished what she tried to do to Travis with the bus."

The other woman spoke more quietly. "We could be in danger. If Paige guesses what we know about her, she might try to silence us."

I wasn't sure what else they said, but I picked up the word "careful."

Chapter 17

✣

Jocelyn and I traded glances and hurried to join the other carolers. I didn't look back to see if the two women followed us. Families came out onto their front porches and shouted Christmas greetings.

We sang in a semicircle in front of the hospital. If there were surveillance cameras, they were hidden by the roof over the glass entry doors. I was certain that Brent would have already commandeered any videos that might have been created in and around the hospital during the night. I wondered if he'd had time to review them yet, and if so, what he had discovered.

And when would I see him? Saturday was only two days away. Would he have to postpone his Saturday-before-Christmas cross-country skiing party?

Daydreaming, I barely paid attention as we belted out all of the verses of three carols.

By the time we finished, it was after eight. Cindy and Tom organized a carpool back to Frisky Pomegranate for host families and their guests.

Olivia set off on foot for her apartment, a few blocks southeast of the hospital. Corey and Samantha left in Corey's pickup to return to their Emergency Medical Services headquarters.

Although Jocelyn and I were close to our homes, she made me wait and let Dustin, Ashley, and their three boys get a head start. Dustin carried the smallest boy on his shoulders.

Jocelyn and I started up the street with Hooligan, Misty, and Scott, who were walking back to work at the police and fire stations. I asked Scott what goodies he'd like Deputy Donut to supply for the next night's annual tree-decorating party.

"You don't have to bring anything."

"But I'd like to."

Jocelyn agreed, "We would!"

He smiled down at us. "Surprise us, then."

When Jocelyn and I turned west, toward her house, Scott, Misty, and Hooligan continued north. Dustin, Ashley, and their boys were nowhere to be seen. Jocelyn checked behind us as if to make certain we were alone, and then she said quietly, "Those women who were behind us seemed to think that Paige killed Travis. Are you afraid of her? Should she be staying with you?"

"She's torn up about Travis's death, so I can't believe she caused it. I'm more afraid on your behalf because of Dustin and his anger. You and your parents need to be careful."

"I don't think he would do anything drastic around Ashley and their boys. We're probably in more danger from the boys racing around the house and knocking everything over."

"Maybe you should put them through a few gymnastic routines out in the nice, soft snow before their bedtime."

"Ha! Good idea. See you tomorrow!" Waving, she continued toward her house.

I turned north, and then west again. At my house, the porch light and strings of outdoor Christmas lights showed that Paige had not only kept the porch, porch steps, and sidewalks clear, she had shoveled a path to the driveway, brushed snow off my SUV, and cleared the driveway. My front window was almost dark except for my cheery Christmas tree.

I opened the front door and breathed in the fragrances of pine, cedar, ginger, and cinnamon. Candles on the mantel and coffee table helped the Christmas tree give the living room a soft holiday ambience. The candles flickered realistically but were battery operated, thanks to Scott. He'd made certain that he and his firefighters wouldn't be called to any of his friends' homes to put out fires caused by real candles. The soft lighting and holiday aromas were calming, but they also reawakened the simmering excitement of Christmas.

Paige was on the couch with a book beside her and Dep on her lap. I kicked off my boots. "It's nice and Christmasy in here."

Paige stroked Dep. "Your house is wonderful, and I love Dep. I lucked out getting to stay here."

"I'm the lucky one, having such a good guest. Thank you for clearing the snow again."

"Not a problem. It's kind of fun, and I think the storm is mostly over." She pointed toward the landing near the front door. "I moved your bags to the floor of the closet. Dep was about to unpack them."

"Thank you. I should have thought of it."

Paige looked toward the ceiling light fixture near the door. "And I hope you don't mind, but I bought some mistletoe at a Christmas bazaar when we were on our way to Fallingbrook, and I . . . I have no use for it, so I hung it up there. If you hate it, take it down. I don't think it's a fire hazard. It's on a long wire."

"Cute! I'm not sure I'll put it to good use, either." As if to prove me wrong, Dep jumped off Paige's lap and trotted to me. Laughing, I picked her up, kissed the top of her head, and told her what a good kitty she was. "Most of the time,"

I added. She wriggled. I set her on the floor and studied the mistletoe. "I love the festive look." This sprig of mistletoe had a red ribbon tied around the stem. "And I seldom turn on that light, anyway." I patted my cheeks. "There's a reason they call overhead lighting 'hag lighting.' "

Paige scoffed, "You could never look like a hag."

"You either."

She stood up and brushed cat hair off her leggings. "I feel like a hag." She gave me a lopsided attempt at a grin. "Not from Dep's hair. From crying."

I told her again how sorry I was that she'd lost her boyfriend. The mistletoe made it even more poignant. Tears pricked the corners of my eyes.

Paige asked, "How was the caroling?"

"We could have used your voice."

"Did anyone from the bus say anything that made you suspect they . . . hurt him?"

"No." I didn't tell her that the only gossip I'd heard was about her. She probably guessed that, anyway. I made a point of sniffing toward the kitchen. "What did you bake? It smells delicious."

"Gingerbread men. We can decorate them later if you like, or we can just gobble them up."

I opened the closet door. "I predict some gobbling in our future." I slid the bags of gifts out of the closet. I took my box of wrapping paper, ribbons, tape, scissors, and gift cards off the top shelf. Paige helped me carry everything to the table in the dining room. "Tea?" I asked. "To go with your cookies?"

"That would be great." She followed me into the kitchen.

We chose herbal tea flavored with orange, ginger, cinnamon, and nutmeg. While the water was heating and hot water was warming the insides of a rotund and jovial Santa teapot, I lit a fire in the dining room fireplace, set the screen in front, and started gentle piano and guitar Christmas music playing from hidden speakers that Alec and I had installed in the ceiling.

Paige carried a platter of gingerbread men in from the kitchen and set them on the dining table. "The tea's steeping in your cute Santa pot." She turned and gazed at the dining room fireplace. "You have enough stockings hung by your fireplaces for an entire extended family."

Although the homey flames in the fireplace wouldn't be as visible, I turned on the chandelier above the table so I could see to wrap packages. With its many bulbs, the chandelier didn't quite qualify as hag lighting, but I turned on wall sconces, anyway. "I guess I've been collecting Christmas stockings." I told her about The Craft Croft. "Most of them were made by local crafters. I bought some of the gifts there."

"I love wrapping packages. Could I help?" She sounded wistful.

"Sure. We'll have a wrapping and cookie-eating party." I reached into a bag and pulled out the barbecuing cookbook. "This is for Hooligan, the auburn-haired policeman who was in the bus last night. He likes to cook outside."

"Nice. Which paper should we use?" Her hand hovered over a roll of paper featuring impish elves. "He seems kind of mischievous." Her pale skin showed every flush. "In a nice way. With that name and his freckles."

"He is, and that's the perfect paper for his gift."

She unrolled just enough paper on the table and reached for the scissors.

Dep jumped up and stretched out on the paper.

I lifted her off and set her on the floor. "I'm not wrapping you up for Hooligan, Dep, as much as he might like me to."

Laughing, Paige cut the paper.

I returned to the kitchen, poured tea into Santa mugs that matched the teapot, and brought the mugs to the dining room.

Paige had wrapped Hooligan's book with the sort of neatly folded corners that I never quite achieved. She fingered rolls of ribbon. "Red?" she asked.

"Perfect." I bit into a cookie. "And so is the gingerbread man, even without decorating."

Paige tied the ribbon. "I hope I can stop imposing on you soon."

"You're not imposing." I chose paper featuring knit mittens and Christmas stockings for Misty's gift. "You're a great guest. Besides, this is the perfect season for taking in stranded travelers."

"You're right." She cut a square of paper off the roll. "I don't know how or when I can get back home."

"You're welcome to stay as long as you need to." I tied Hooligan's gift tag to the ribbon. "Passengers from the bus have been calling the tour company trying to get them to send another bus, but no one is answering."

Looking totally relaxed, Dep was again on the table, lying on the wrapping paper Paige had cut. Paige slid her aside. "Those calls would go to Travis's phone, but . . . maybe his phone landed underneath a seat when we hit that tree. Or it could have been flung out of the bus when the door opened. Maybe it's still by the side of the road, buried in snow."

"Could his phone have been on that little shelf where he kept his wallet? Brent might have made certain that it went to the hospital with him, along with his wallet." And that could explain why no one was answering Travis's phone. The police would have it now, and even if it were still charged, the police might not answer it. Maybe it was shut away in an evidence room. The police could get a search warrant for the call records, which might give them clues about who had killed Travis.

Paige bit her lip. "I don't think so. After the accident, I noticed the wallet on that shelf, but not the phone."

I pulled Samantha's origami kit out of the bag. "Is there no one else in the office?"

Concentrating on wrapping Misty's book, yarn, and knitting needles, Paige lowered her head. Her long hair concealed her face. "There isn't an office."

"Can they call the tour company's owners?"

"Travis owned the company, so, no."

"Can anyone send another bus and driver?"

Paige unrolled teal ribbon for Misty's present. "There isn't another bus or driver. There was, but Travis had to end the lease on the bus and let the driver go. He didn't want anyone to know how small the operation was. He was afraid they wouldn't sign up for tours."

For Samantha's gift, I unrolled paper featuring big-eyed kittens tangling one another in red and green yarn. "Could a bus and driver be hired to take you all home?"

Paige made a bow for Misty's package. "I don't know where to find a bus and driver, and Travis was the only one who could have known what to do."

"Are there other employees?"

"No. It was just Travis and me." She took a shaky breath. "Travis was hoping to make enough from this tour to, you know, sort of get back on his feet." She passed Misty's wrapped gift to me and made a noise like a sob. "Financially, I mean."

Wondering how much Travis must have charged each passenger if he expected one tour to make him financially solvent, I pointed out softly, "The passengers are going to want refunds."

"They . . . I think they all bought trip insurance. Most of them, anyway. They should have. Travis recommended it."

I attached Misty's gift card to her package. "Did Travis have good insurance?"

"Probably. You can't run a business like that without it, I don't think. At least the bus must have been insured."

I wondered if Travis had purposely totaled the bus for the insurance money. That would have been an iffy proposition, especially since front-end collisions tended to injure drivers. Besides, I suspected that the bus was leased, and the bus's owners would receive the insurance money. Gently, I nudged Dep's face and one paw out of the bag and pulled out Scott's jigsaw puzzle. "Paige, when I climbed onto the bus, you were standing beside Travis. Were you there when the bus went off the road?"

She finger-pressed the corners of the paper on Samantha's gift. "I think I was. I feel like a tour guide should ride standing up. I like to be able to see out the front, but also turn around to keep track of our customers to, you know, make sure they're happy and having a good time, and make announcements about what they should look out and see. But right after the crash, I ended up kind of half lying and half sitting in the seat behind Travis. I think I was thrown there when the bus swerved, which was lucky, or I might have gone through the windshield when it hit that tree. As it was, I wasn't hurt, but I wonder if I could have done anything to keep us on the road."

"Do you still think the steering failed?"

"That's the only thing I can think of. It happened so fast, you know? You try to go back and think through exactly what happened, and you just can't. Red ribbon or green? Or both?"

"Green. Maybe I should have bought yarn to go with some of these papers. Do you know if Travis had any enemies, like someone on the bus?"

Paige cut off a length of ribbon. "I don't think any of the people on that bus knew him before, and there were no fights or anything like that with the passengers, so no, he probably didn't have any enemies on the bus. But he had an enemy here in Fallingbrook."

The fire popped. We both jumped.

Chapter 18

❧

I recovered first. "Did you tell Brent?"

Paige broke the legs and arms off a gingerbread man. "I wasn't sure if I should."

"Who was it?"

She poked a gingerbread arm into her mouth. "The woman who organized the Ice and Lights Festival had a big grudge against Travis."

I suggested, "Whitney Valcriffe?"

"Yeah. Do you know her?"

"I worked with her because of the ice sculpture Deputy Donut was sponsoring."

I probably shouldn't have reminded Paige of the ice sculpture that had ended her boyfriend's life. She brushed the back of her hand against her eyes and then said, "I never met her, but I could tell that Travis thought she was really mean. They were a couple for a while. They broke up and, well, let's just say she was what they call 'a woman scorned.' So, she just hated him."

I set the mugs I'd bought at The Craft Croft on the table next to Paige. "At The Craft Croft, they told me she made these."

Paige looked down into the mugs. "Ew. There's something

inside one." She put her fingers into the mug as if trying to dislodge the little figurine inside. "Oh, I see. A monster is stuck to the bottom to scare people. You're giving this mug to someone?" She sounded scandalized.

"I'm giving both of them to Brent. He can surprise guests with the dragon one. Don't you like them?"

"I like the one without the monster, the dragon, whatever it is, though it's kind of plain, you know, gray and white like that. Some flowers on the outside would brighten it up. I'd freak out if I saw that thing in my coffee. I'd probably drop the mug and spill the coffee."

I teased, "That would never do!"

"It proves that Travis was right about Whitney being mean, if she'd make mugs that scare people." Paige was sort of joking, maybe. I unfolded one of the boxes that Summer had tucked into my bag, wrapped the two mugs in tissue paper and nestled them inside the box. Paige stared at the white box with its Craft Croft sticker, but I wasn't sure she was really seeing it. "After I found out that Travis might be coming here to see an old girlfriend who hated him, I tried to convince him to take Fallingbrook out of our schedule, but he refused. I wish he had listened to me."

Wondering if Paige's real motivation had been to prevent Travis from reconnecting with the old girlfriend, I asked, "When did they break up?" According to Scott it had been back in high school, which would mean that at least seventeen years had passed. The tattoo had remained, but emotions usually changed between people's teens and their late thirties.

"I don't think it was very long ago, but maybe she's one of these people who never give up a grudge. Or maybe she found out how much he was charging the people taking the tour to visit the Ice and Lights Festival, and it made her mad."

"Our village square isn't fenced off. No one has to pay to see the festival. The idea is that it's for everyone to enjoy, and when they come here, they'll spend money in shops and restaurants."

"I know, but he had to charge people for everything. He didn't list the costs separately. It was just part of their tour. I mean, he wasn't trying to cheat our customers or anything, but he didn't want me to tell anyone that the festival here and some of the other places we were going were free. See, he planned this entire tour based on sightseeing we could do without spending a lot, and he added a little to cover more than basic expenses. I mean he had to, right? There's the lease on the bus and fuel and maintenance and all that. Plus, he had to pay me and himself, too, though we weren't getting our cut until maybe the next tour. Only there won't be one."

"Maybe you can get a job as a guide with another company."

She sniffled. "Maybe. If I wanted to. Right now, I'm afraid to leave your house. Whitney could be after me, you know? She'll know I figured out that she killed Travis, and she'll want to shut me up."

It was almost funny that Paige's words almost echoed what the two women behind Jocelyn and me had said about Paige. I didn't mention that. I only said, "Then I guess you won't want to go to the annual tree-trimming party the firefighters are throwing tomorrow night at five. People from the bus are invited. You're welcome to join me."

"Sorry to be so unappreciative, but I'm not brave enough."

"I'll go there after we close Deputy Donut, so I probably won't be back until around seven tomorrow evening. If you get hungry before that, check the freezer. I freeze lots of single and double portions of meals for nights when I'm hungry for something and don't want to take time to make it."

"I saw those when I was making the pizza. Don't worry, I'll be fine." Despite her fears about Whitney, Paige had carefully wrapped the box containing the mugs. Without asking, she had chosen the paper with the mischievous elves for Brent, the same paper she'd thought was right for Hooligan.

"And help yourself to whatever appeals for lunch."

She thanked me. "I did that today. You might want to buy more cheese and crackers."

"I'm glad you found those. They were leftovers from my cookie-baking party, and I needed help eating them."

She said with a lightness that I suspected she wasn't feeling, "I'm always willing to help eat things."

She didn't look like someone who ever overate, and despite the shiny hair, she was thin and pale, as if she might have been hungry during parts of her life. I had pale skin, too, but I had never needed to worry about where my next meal was coming from.

I rescued a spool of ribbon from Dep. We wrapped Tom's letter opener and Cindy's earrings.

Paige asked, "What about gifts for your parents? You said they were staying in Florida for Christmas."

"They live year-round in their RV. They can't cram much more into it, so I give them gifts they can eat. My father's family passed down a recipe for steamed plum pudding, but he and my mother aren't likely to mix up a large batch and steam it in their tiny kitchen, so he's always happy to receive a homemade plum pudding from me. My mother had a traditional fruitcake recipe, and my parents and I are in the fruitcake-loving category, especially when it's soaked in rum, so I sent them one of those, too."

"I like fruitcake, too."

"I also gave them a four-month subscription to a Wisconsin wine-and-cheese-party-of-the-month. My folks seldom arrive back in Fallingbrook before July, but maybe a subscription ending in May will encourage them to return sooner for Wisconsin wines and cheeses."

Paige laughed. "I hope for your sake that it does." She didn't offer information about her family. Knowing that she didn't seem to want to talk about them, including the deceased sister, I didn't ask. We finished our tea and ate more gingerbread men than we probably should have, and I cut us each a slice of rum-soaked fruitcake.

Paige finished hers and licked her fingers. "That was delicious."

The fire had stopped crackling and had burned itself down to only a few glowing embers. Paige helped me carry the packages to the Christmas tree and arrange them artistically. By the time we finished, we were yawning, and the fire had gone out completely. We turned out lights and went upstairs.

In my bedroom, Dep curled next to me and purred while Christmas music played in my head and I thought about Whitney and her supposed hatred of Travis because, as Paige had said, he'd dumped her. Or because, as Travis's mother had said, Travis had refused to take the blame for a hit-and-run when Whitney was the driver.

I'd talked to both Whitney and Leo while we were planning Frosty the Donut. The couple's affection for each other was obvious. Whitney didn't act like someone who had carried a grudge for years after being, as Paige had put it, "a woman scorned." It was easier to believe that serving time for a crime she didn't commit, which was what I suspected had happened, could cause a long-smoldering rage, but Summer, who knew Whitney well, didn't believe Whitney could have hurt anyone. Paige probably didn't know about that hit-and-run accident. I doubted that Travis would have told Paige about a car crash that an ex-girlfriend had been in when he was supposedly home with his parents.

I reminded myself that someone who seemed too nice to be a murderer could be one. Still, I was like Summer. I couldn't imagine Whitney killing anyone.

The same went for Leo. I guessed that someone might believe that Leo could have killed Travis in revenge for what Travis had done to Whitney. Leo was muscular enough to physically overcome nearly anyone, but as I'd said to Scott, he was like a big teddy bear. Whitney and Leo seemed to enjoy their life too much to put their happiness at risk.

But, I reminded myself, criminals seldom, if ever, expected to be caught.

Eventually, I slept, so soundly that Paige could have made several trips outside and roared past the house on a dozen snowmobiles one at a time, and I wouldn't have heard her.

I did hear Dep, though, only moments before my alarm was set to go off. She'd managed to swat a plastic Christmas ball off the garland decorating the frame of my bedroom window and was rolling it around on the floor, making it clatter more loudly than seemed possible.

I got out of bed, hung the ornament on the garland, and went off for my shower.

When I arrived downstairs in the living room, Dep was sitting on the couch looking perfectly innocent. The ornament had somehow come off the garland in my bedroom and had made its way to the mat near the front door. Paige wasn't stirring. I hung the ornament on the tree, fed Dep, and made breakfast for myself.

It was Friday, trash-collection day. I took the bag out of the kitchen wastebasket, slid my feet into boots, and carried the full bag outside. I didn't bother with a coat, but my phone was in my pocket, and I made certain that the front door didn't lock behind me.

It was cold outside, and dark except for streetlights and colorful displays of Christmas lights reflecting on blankets of white snow. My trip down the porch steps and along the pathway to the garbage cans beside the house was quick, thanks to Paige's snow shoveling the day before.

I lifted the lid of one can and was about to heave the bag of kitchen garbage into it.

The streetlight glittered off something inside the can.

I leaned the lid against the brick wall of the house, set the bag beside the garbage can, and turned on my phone's flashlight.

A silvery survival blanket like the one we'd given Paige at the bus crash was crumpled on top of wadded paper towels and other garbage. I pinched a corner of the blanket and lifted it. Something wrapped in the blanket jingled like broken glass.

A large piece of clear broken glass slithered out. The label on it was intact.

Bourbon.

I pulled on the blanket. More broken glass slid out along with a cell phone, a clear plastic sandwich bag with a small white ball inside it, and a rather large stainless steel water bottle.

Chapter 19

❦

The small white ball hadn't rolled inside the plastic bag as the bag tumbled out of the blanket.

Mistletoe berries were sticky.

Paige had hung mistletoe near the front door the night before.

The plastic bag had been with a phone, a water bottle, and a broken bourbon bottle, all of them wrapped in a rescue blanket like the one I'd given Paige.

I didn't remember ever having bought or being given that brand of bourbon. Paige had reeked of alcohol even after I drove her away from the crash scene.

She had hinted that she didn't know where Travis's phone was and that it might have been flung out of the bus. She could have brought his phone, his water bottle, the bourbon, and her bag of mistletoe to my house in her shiny black tote bag.

Maybe I had discovered why she'd done a thorough job of shoveling the pathway from the porch steps to the driveway—she had made it possible to carry trash to the garbage cans without leaving footprints in the snow. Had she thrown out those things during the night while I was sleeping? Or had she done it earlier, while I was at work or Christmas caroling? And then, during our gift-wrapping and cookie-gobbling party, she'd told me plausible stories.

She'd seemed innocent. . . .

And I'd been gullible.

Frowning and shivering, I phoned Brent's personal line. I was outside, and Paige wasn't likely to hear me. However, her room was in the front of the house, and it was possible that she slept with the window open, so when Brent answered, I murmured, "I know it's not even six yet. Sorry for calling so early. I've found things in my trash cans that Travis might have owned."

He caught on. "Is Paige still staying with you?"

"As far as I know, but I haven't heard a peep from her this morning. She could have left while I was sleeping. I'm outside."

"We'll be right over. Do not confront her, and stay on the line."

"Okay."

My phone to my ear, I crept into the house and listened to partially muted sounds of Brent's voice. I couldn't tell what he was saying or who he was talking to. It was probably whoever he'd meant when he said that "we" would be right over. Had the DCI detective arrived?

There were still no signs that Paige was awake. I slipped on a coat, grabbed my keys, and tiptoed out to the driveway. If Paige followed me and seemed threatening, I'd get into my SUV and drive away. I wouldn't have to brush off the snow, either. Paige had done that the day before, and hardly any snow had fallen since. I wouldn't go to my car unless I needed to, though. If she eased behind my computer desk and leaned forward, she'd be able to see my car from her bedroom window.

In the darkness, I went around the corner of the house and tucked myself against the brick wall beside the trash cans and the bag of kitchen garbage. Over the phone, I heard car doors slam. An engine started.

I again asked myself the question I'd mulled over before,

about both Paige and Whitney. *How could such apparently decent people be murderers?*

Everyone had secrets, but if Paige had tossed out Travis's phone and pretended that she didn't know where it was, she had big secrets. And discovering them could endanger me.

Still, I argued with myself, Paige seemed to be honestly mourning Travis.

The most likely person to have killed Travis was Dustin. He had been furious at Travis for endangering everyone on that bus. He could have picked up Travis's phone, water bottle, and bourbon. We'd given one of his sons an emergency blanket to use as a superhero cape. He could have walked to my place and thrown those things into my garbage can. And he or his wife might have bought mistletoe at the Christmas bazaar where Paige had bought hers.

I'd barely warmed up the inside of my coat when a dark unmarked cruiser pulled up to the curb. The headlights went off. Brent got out of the driver's seat.

DCI Agent Kimberly Gartborg unfolded herself from the passenger seat. *Oh, great,* I thought. The glamorous and intelligent woman seemed like a good detective, such a good one that she had undoubtedly detected that Brent was single, attractive, available, and would make a great role model for her twins. I had never met the boys, but Misty had, and she'd told me that they were mature for their age and they excelled in sports and academics. To add to Detective Gartborg's sterling qualities, she and the boys owned a big, floppy, shaggy dog who, when I'd met him in August, had been only about half grown and adorably puppylike. The Gartborgs could live happily ever after with Brent in his chalet on his new property. *Stop it, Emily,* I told myself.

Staying out of sight of Paige's window, I took a step away from the brick wall and waved my phone's light at the two detectives. Brent and Gartborg closed their car doors quietly and came to me. Brent reintroduced me to Gartborg.

Shaking her hand and welcoming her back to Falling-brook, I again apologized for calling so early.

"It's okay," Brent said. "You're not the only one who gets up early and finds things before others do."

I shuddered. "I wish I hadn't had the bright idea of brushing snow off our ice sculpture yesterday morning. I would have been perfectly happy not to have made that discovery."

Brent became grim. "Someone was going to find him, and sooner was better than later. Sorry it was you, but at least we taped off the area before families and kids came along." He cocked his head toward Gartborg. "Kim arrived even earlier than your call. I was briefing her when you phoned."

Gartborg's mouth twisted in a rueful smile. "You called before anyone at the police station made coffee." She heaved a sigh. "Other than some vile brew that must have been sitting on a hot plate since yesterday."

I couldn't help a grimace of horror. "I'll make up for that."

Her smile became happier. "Your coffee is the best, Emily. When does your shop open?"

"Seven."

She pulled back the sleeve of her black leather coat and checked a watch on her feminine wrist. "That's an hour away. I guess I'll last."

I grinned. "We might let you in sooner. Meanwhile, I'll be happy to make you some here."

She straightened her coat sleeve over her watch. "You might have just saved my life, or at least my livelihood." She pointed at the garbage cans. Her gloves matched her coat. "So, what did you find?"

I shined my light into the trash can and explained the significance of the survival blanket, the broken bourbon bottle, the phone, the bag that had once held mistletoe, and the oversized stainless steel water bottle.

Gartborg responded in a voice as quiet as mine, but sterner. "Did you touch any of it?"

"Only a pinch of the blanket. When I pulled at it, the other things fell out." I gestured to the garbage can lid propped against the wall of the house. In the darkness, the yellow bricks could have passed as gray. "And I touched the lid."

"We'll need the entire bag," she told me.

Not surprised, I nodded.

Brent bunched the top of the plastic bag in one fist and pulled it out of the can.

"We should take all of the garbage," Gartborg said, "if the woman is staying here."

I wrinkled my nose. "Ew. But be my guest."

Brent pulled the bag out of the other can and picked up the bag I'd brought outside. "We'll take you up on the guest part. Kim's not the only one who could use a cup of real coffee."

"Perfect," I said. "I need some, too." Ordinarily, I drank my first cup of the day at Deputy Donut, but I suspected that I was not going to make it to work before I really started craving that warming first sip.

Brent carried the bags toward the cruiser.

Gartborg gave me a half smile. "And if your houseguest just happens to wake up when we're having our coffee, we might have a little chat with her. But do you need to get to work, Emily?"

Brent shut the bags of garbage into the trunk.

I thanked Gartborg for considering my responsibilities at Deputy Donut and added, "The others can open without me. I'll warn them I'll be late." I led her toward the porch. Brent met us there.

I opened the door carefully. As I'd suspected, Dep was on the other side of it. She started toward the stairs, and then twisted her head back and mewed up at Brent. The living room was still dark. I kicked off my boots, threw my parka over the carved newel post, and turned on the Christmas tree lights and a lamp.

Taking off their boots, Brent and Gartborg were both underneath the mistletoe. I hadn't told them where Paige had hung it, but Brent glanced up as if he'd guessed where it was. Then he looked at me. One of his eyebrows raised slightly, but he didn't say anything, and I couldn't read his expression. In his stocking feet, he walked farther into the living room and away from the mistletoe.

Heading toward the kitchen, I offered, "Have a seat. The coffee won't take long." I made no attempt to be quiet. I wanted Paige to wake up and come downstairs without my having to knock on her door and tell her that a couple of detectives wanted to talk to her.

Gartborg called toward me, "Need help?"

I turned around. "No, thanks." Gartborg and Brent were taking off their coats. Brent was wearing a black suit and a red tie with Christmas trees on it. Gartborg's black wool slacks and red tunic-length sweater looked like they were at least partly cashmere. Brent reached for her coat, grabbed mine off the newel post, and headed toward the closet.

Gartborg scooped Dep off the floor and cradled her in her arms like a baby. Dep appeared to go almost boneless. "Then I'll entertain your cat. Her name's Dep, right?" Dep wasn't boneless, after all. She reached a cautious paw toward Gartborg's necklace, a rope of holly leaves and berries all made of silver that matched the detective's premature silver bob.

Crossing the dining room, I called back, "Good memory."

Gartborg laughed. "She's a memorable cat, aren't you, Dep? And that was a memorable evening." From the kitchen, I was too far away to be positive, but I was almost certain that Dep was purring.

I hoped that neither Brent nor Gartborg would have a good look at the presents underneath the tree. Brent and I had exchanged gifts ever since he had started eating Christmas dinner with Tom, Cindy, and me. Brent wouldn't be surprised to see a present for him among the others underneath my tree, but in some ways, I didn't want Gartborg to know how close he and I were, maybe because I feared she was competitive enough to try to steal him from me only to see if she could, the way Travis had supposedly stolen Whitney from Leo when they were all teenagers.

Grinding coffee beans, I sighed. Gartborg couldn't take something from me that wasn't mine, no matter how determined I was to change that. And maybe she would notice that I still wore my wedding ring, and she wouldn't feel the need to compete.

I started the coffee brewing, called Deputy Donut, and told Tom I'd be late.

He demanded, "Is everything okay?"

"Sure. Brent brought the DCI detective over for coffee."

"And to talk to your guest?"

"How did you know?"

"I remember how these things work. Take as much time as you need. Stick around while they're talking to her. You don't need to be in the same room, just be there so she might be more comfortable and more candid."

"You're terrible."

"Once a cop . . ."

I laughed. We both knew how that sentence ended. "See you in a while."

I got out a platter and put three mugs, three dessert plates, a sugar bowl, and a creamer on it. They all featured widely smiling snowmen with sticks for arms. I added matching paper napkins. The spoons and forks were plain stainless.

I opened a large, almost flat bakery box from Cookies and Bakies and removed a kringle, a popular Wisconsin delicacy that had originated in Denmark and was basically an over-sized Danish pastry that was usually, like this one, twisted into a pretzel shape, again larger than life. Although the name sounded Christmasy, kringles were eaten year-round in Wisconsin. Almonds and dried, sweetened cranberries and cherries filled the light, flaky pastry of this one. A liberal amount of vanilla glaze topped it.

By the time I cut off a slice for each of us and put them on the dessert plates, the coffee was ready. I poured it into the mugs and carefully carried the loaded platter through the dining room and into the living room.

Gartborg was sitting on the end of the couch nearest the fireplace, while Brent was facing her on the armchair between the Christmas tree and the fireplace. I guessed they'd chosen those spots so they could watch the stairs for Paige.

Dep had apparently abandoned Gartborg and was now stretched out on one of Brent's thighs with her eyes closed in bliss and front paws dangling over his bent knee. I hoped she wasn't about to curl her toes and stab through his pantlegs with her claws.

Gartborg leaped up and helped me set the platter on the coffee table. I appreciated the gesture, even though I had years of experience carrying trays of food and mugs of hot liquids. I thanked her. Luckily, Brent was able to reach the coffee table without disturbing Dep much. I sat in the wing chair, on the other side of the tree from Brent and facing the empty end of the couch.

After Gartborg's first sip of coffee, she closed her eyes in contentment almost like Dep's and took a deep breath. "Thanks, Emily. I needed that."

"Brent said you just got here. How did you make it to Fallingbrook at such an hour?"

"I drove. I left home insanely early."

Remembering my latest drive through a fierce snowstorm, I made a face. "How were the roads?"

"Mostly clear."

I reached for a plate of kringle. "Did you bring your boys and the dog?"

"I left them behind to look after one another. The boys want to attend a party tonight. They'll drive up tomorrow, with the dog, for the rest of the weekend. We all enjoyed our mini-vacation up here in August."

"Drive." I couldn't help sounding surprised. Although I hadn't encountered her twins face to face in August when Dep and I became acquainted—to put it mildly—with their dog, I remembered hearing that the boys were sixteen then.

She looked up at the ceiling. "They got their licenses in September. They're good and responsible." Of course they were. She added, "But I can't help worrying."

Upstairs, a floor creaked and a door closed softly. Brent looked at me and raised an eyebrow again. I remembered Summer's comment about women falling for men whose eyebrows slanted down toward the sides of their faces because the men looked concerned and caring. Brent's eyebrows were almost straight, with a slight arch to them, like most people's. Maybe what we fell for was believing we were the recipients of silent communication meant solely for us.

I nodded to show Brent that I'd heard it, too, and it meant that Paige was still in my house, and she was awake. Almost afraid of Gartborg's answer, I asked her, "Where are you staying?"

"Out at Lake Cares Away again, but in the lodge this time. The cabins are closed for the winter, but that's okay. They allow pets in the lodge, too. The boys wouldn't dream of leaving Ivan behind in a kennel."

Remembering the goofy dog, I couldn't help smiling. Maybe my smile was partly due to relief that Gartborg and her family weren't staying with Brent. I supposed that could change.

Upstairs, water ran. Alec and I had attempted to soundproof the bathroom, but with only limited success in a house built more than a century before.

The floor in the upstairs hall creaked, and a door closed softly again. It sounded like the guest room door.

Brent, Gartborg, and I drank coffee, ate kringle, and waited for Paige to come downstairs.

She didn't, and I heard no more creaking floors or closing doors.

Chapter 20

✤

After a few more minutes of silence from upstairs, I asked Brent and Detective Gartborg, "Would you like me to go invite her to talk to you?" I gave my mouth an ironic twist at the word "invite."

Gartborg asked, "Is there another way she could have left the house?"

I turned my head and glanced out past the Christmas tree to the front porch and the street beyond. It was becoming light outside. "She could climb out her window, slide down the porch roof, and leap into a snowdrift. But we probably would have noticed."

"Back stairs?"

"No."

"What about other windows upstairs?"

"I think she returned to the front bedroom. That's the door I thought I heard close."

Gartborg set her mug on the coffee table. "Would you mind getting her? Before she goes back to sleep?"

"Of course not." But I did mind. Paige had probably been awake a lot during the past two nights, and forcing her out of bed earlier than she wanted was unkind. Besides, the whole thing was awkward. Who wanted to tell a guest that the police had come to speak to her, especially right after the police had probably raised the guest to the number-one spot on their suspect list?

Mentally rehearsing how to say it, I headed for the stairs. Dep jumped off Brent's lap and raced up past me. I found her sitting in front of Paige's closed door.

"Meow."

Smiling down at the helpful kitty, I tapped fingernails against the old, solid wood door. "Paige?"

From inside came a tentative, "Hi?"

"Can you come downstairs?"

"But . . . don't you have company? I thought I heard voices."

"Yes, and there's coffee and kringle for breakfast. For you, too."

There was a pause, and then a breathless, almost squeaked-out question. "Are they people from the bus?"

"No, it's Brent and one of his colleagues. They'd like to talk to you, informally, but you don't have to answer their questions without a lawyer present."

There was another pause, and then she opened the door a crack and peeked out. Long strands of hair hung in front of her face. "I can't . . . I don't need . . . want a lawyer. I don't have anything to hide, and I'd like to help them figure out who did this to Travis so they can be arrested and never hurt anyone else again." She spoke quietly. Like me, she probably thought the listeners downstairs were straining to hear everything we said. They'd been quiet since I left them. Sniffling, Paige turned her head away and whispered, "I'll be down in a few minutes." She sounded resigned. She closed the door. A heavy-duty zipper like the one on her duffel bag zipped or unzipped.

About as thrilled as she seemed to be about Brent and Gartborg questioning her, I walked slowly down the stairs. Paige had said she didn't have anything to hide, but I suspected that wasn't true. Throwing out a used survival blanket, a dirty plastic bag, and a broken bourbon bottle was understandable. Throwing away a possibly expensive water bottle and an even more expensive phone might require some explaining.

I'd hoped that Dep might stay upstairs to cheer Paige, but she rushed past me down the stairs. By the time I got to the living room, Dep was standing on her hind legs and sniffing warily at my empty kringle plate.

I told Brent and Gartborg, "Paige is coming. More coffee and kringle?"

Gartborg wanted more coffee but nothing else to eat. Brent wanted more kringle but said he'd had coffee at the station before Gartborg arrived.

Gartborg wrinkled her nose. "If you call that coffee."

Brent winked at me. "I prefer Emily's."

Gartborg came with me to the kitchen and asked quietly, "Can you stick around? Maybe you can find something to do in your dining room, so Paige won't feel quite so outnumbered and alone?"

"Sure. Tom, my partner at Deputy Donut, is also our former police chief. He suggested the same thing when I told him I'd be late." I confessed, "I reminded her about needing a lawyer, but she didn't want one. I suspect she can't afford one and doesn't know how to go about finding one."

"That can be looked after, but she's not a suspect. We only need information. Don't worry. We'll read her rights to her, and she doesn't have to answer our questions." Gartborg returned to the living room.

By the time I ground more coffee, Paige was dressed in her usual black leggings and tunic and was perched on the edge of the seat of the wing chair. Her red socks with green Christmas wreaths knit into them were made more noticeable by the way she sat with one foot curling around the other ankle. I handed her a fork and a snowman plate with a big chunk of kringle on it. The fork rattled as she set the plate on her lap. "Thank you," she whispered. The Christmas tree bulbs gave her shiny brown hair multicolored highlights. Now neatly combed and parted in the middle, it hung like curtains beside her face.

I gave Brent his slice of kringle and put Paige's and Gartborg's mugs on the coffee table. "I need to write Christmas cards," I told them all. "I'll be in the dining room. Let me know if you need anything."

Brent and Gartborg said they would. Paige sent me a pleading glance before lowering her head as if to study the kringle on her plate. Her hair fell in front of her face.

Wishing she didn't have to endure more painful questioning, but now having doubts about her, I went into the sunroom and retrieved my cards, envelopes, stamps, Christmas stickers, and pens. I took them to the dining room and sat at the table. Dep jumped onto my lap, stomped in a circle, curled up, and purred. From where I was sitting, I could see Gartborg's head from the back and Brent's head and shoulders from the front, but I couldn't quite see Paige and she wouldn't be able to see me. Ordinarily, I would play Christmas music while I wrote and addressed cards, but I didn't want to miss one word of the interview.

Brent gently questioned Paige about the tour, the trip from Green Bay, and the crash. Paige told them, "Because of the weather on Wednesday, I tried to get Travis to remove Fallingbrook from the tour so we could be in Duluth before the storm. Travis said our guests were expecting the Ice and Lights Festival, and they wouldn't like to miss one of the tour's highlights." She'd told me that she'd tried to convince Travis to stay away from Fallingbrook so he could avoid Whitney. Why had she changed the story, especially considering that Whitney's previous connection to Travis could cause the two detectives to suspect Whitney? Paige burst out, "I wish he'd listened to me! Everything would be fine."

After I addressed each envelope, I wrote a personal note to the recipient. As always, the notes turned out longer than I expected, and I kept slowing down and stopping when the conversation in the next room distracted me.

Paige finally mentioned Whitney when Gartborg asked about enemies Travis might have had, and then Paige didn't hold back. She portrayed Whitney as a vindictive old girl-friend. Paige said she didn't know about other people in the area or back home in Green Bay who might have wanted to harm Travis, and then she raised her voice as if casting suspicion on Whitney had given her confidence. "Detective Fyne, you heard some of those people on the bus after the crash, didn't you? Some of them were really mad at Travis as if he purposely crashed the bus. He didn't. It was totally an accident. Did investigators check the steering?"

"They did," Brent answered. "They found nothing wrong with it."

Gartborg had been watching Paige, but now she turned her face toward Brent. "Detective Fyne, you told me you noticed a strong smell of alcohol when you first boarded the crashed bus."

"I did," Brent said. "Others reported it, too."

Gartborg asked, "Paige, had Mr. Tarriston been drinking?"

"No."

Gartborg pressed her. "You're sure?"

I quietly pulled another envelope off the pile and started copying the next address from my list.

Paige finally answered, "Pretty sure." She didn't sound it.

Brent took over. "Passengers said that Mr. Tarriston—Travis—was sipping from a large stainless steel water bottle, possibly an insulated one, during the trip. Do you know what was in his water bottle?"

"I assumed it was water."

Gartborg asked, "Did you smell alcohol when you were on the bus, Paige?"

"Maybe a little. I don't know what the passengers were eating and drinking. Travis didn't want to make any rules about it, you know? He wanted them to have a good time. It was a family tour, so we didn't expect drinking, and if there were smokers, they could smoke outside the bus during stops. Because of having kids along, we scheduled lots of stops, even though there's a john on the bus."

Brent asked her, "Do you know where Travis's water bottle is now?"

"Probably still on the bus."

I looked up from inserting a card into its envelope. Brent's attention seemed to be on his notebook, which was probably on his lap.

Gartborg asked, "May we have your phone number, Paige?"

Paige dictated a number. "But my phone's not working."

Brent continued staring toward his notebook. I guessed he was writing down the number.

Gartborg looked down for a few seconds and then focused her attention on the stairway as if she were listening or watching for something upstairs. I guessed she'd tried phoning the number Paige had given them. I didn't hear a ringtone anywhere in the house, but a professional male voice, the kind of voice that comes with messaging services, came from near Gartborg: "You have reached—" Gartborg ended the call and asked Paige, "What's wrong with your phone?"

"I don't know. It must have been banged around in the crash."

Pressing a Santa's elf sticker on the back of an envelope, I thought of the many times I'd dropped my phone and it had continued working. One of my phones hadn't appreciated the thorough soaking it had received in the Fallingbrook River, however. Had Paige's phone gotten wet? If the bottle of bourbon had broken while it was in her enormous black vinyl tote, could that tote have contained enough liquid long enough to soak and ruin Paige's phone? Had she thrown out her own phone, not Travis's?

Brent asked the question I was thinking. "Do you know

where Travis's phone is? It wasn't with him when he arrived at the hospital and it wasn't in the duffel bag that I took him later."

Paige told him what she'd explained to me, that his phone was probably still on the bus or underneath snow at the crash site.

Brent was still leaning forward, peering around the ends of decorated pine branches toward Paige. "When I talked to you outside the bus after the convoy of Fallingbrook locals drove the passengers away, the smell of alcohol was still lingering near you. Do you have any idea why that would be?"

I could barely hear Paige's answer. "No."

Brent persisted. "Passengers said you argued with Travis outside the bus on Wednesday before you started out. What was that about?"

"We were talking about routes, nothing major. He didn't bring maps. I wanted him to stop at his place on the way so he could get them, but he said we were already late, and I could navigate using my phone. I said I would, but we might go out of reach of satellites and cell phone towers. And that's what happened. My phone did lose the satellite connection, and we did get lost, which was why we were so late coming to Fallingbrook."

Brent tilted his head. "Did Travis give you anything during that argument? Or did you take something from him?"

Again, Paige paused, and I quickly signed a card featuring a cardinal on a snowy holly bush with red berries peeking through the snow. Finally, Paige answered, "I don't remember."

Brent prodded, "Could it have been a bottle?"

"I . . . oh, yes, now I remember. He was carrying a bottle of bourbon that we were going to share evenings during the tour. I told him it would look bad if he carried it onto the bus in front of all of the passengers, so I put it into my tote bag."

Gartborg asked, "Did that make him angry?"

"Not really, but maybe that's how it looked to the tourists. They were already in their seats on the bus and might have been spying on us through the bus windows, I don't know."

Gartborg fired another question at her. "Where is that bottle of bourbon now?"

"I don't know. I think that it must have broken and fallen out of my bag during the crash. Maybe that's why you smelled alcohol, Detective Fyne. Everything happened so quickly, I couldn't keep track of it all. Now that you mention it, I remember smelling something like bourbon after I was flung into the seat behind Travis, but by the time you got there, I must have been used to the smell, and I stopped noticing it. And then, with so much going on, I forgot. I guess I was in a sort of shock."

Brent gave her a gentle smile. "You were, understandably, but you did a good job of preventing Travis from falling off his seat and becoming more injured."

"Thank you." She sniffled. "I loved him."

Brent looked down. I heard the flipping of notebook pages. He turned his head toward Paige again. His face showed empathy. And regret. "We measured Travis's blood alcohol level at the hospital about an hour and a half after the crash. He had high levels of alcohol in his blood, enough to force us to suspend a normal license. Travis had a commercial license. He wasn't allowed any alcohol in his blood. None. Or he'd lose his license."

"I . . ." Paige's voice trailed off. She cleared her throat and went on more loudly. "I don't know how that could be. He wasn't drinking out of that bottle of bourbon."

Brent asked softly, "Do you think that if we found his water bottle, we would find alcohol in it, not water?"

Paige got up and walked to the coffee table. Now I could see her from the side, although her hair hid her face. She set her mug down and then hacked at the air with stiff, splayed fingers. "How could he do that to me? I told him he couldn't drink and drive. He knew he could lose his license, and his company. We'd lose everything we were just beginning to have!" She covered her face with her hands and backed out of my sight, toward her chair.

Gartborg called to me, "Emily, do you have any tissues?"

Chapter 21

"Sure." I ran into the sunroom, grabbed the box of tissues I kept near the love seat for when I watched tear-jerking movies or read emotional books, and took it to the living room.

With her head down and her hands covering her face, Paige was still sitting on my wing chair.

I set the box of tissues gently on her lap. "Here you go, Paige."

She mumbled, "Thanks."

Having inserted myself into the conversation, I considered myself to be part of it. I stayed next to Paige's chair and said softly, "I'm sorry, Paige, but I have some advice. You should have a lawyer, and you definitely need to tell the detectives the truth." I threw Brent an apologetic glance and confessed to the crying woman, "And I need to tell you the truth, too, Paige. When I took out the trash this morning, I saw some things in my garbage can that I hadn't put there—a survival blanket wrapped around a broken bourbon bottle, a phone, a plastic bag with a mistletoe berry inside it, and a reusable water bottle. If you're the one who threw them out, you need to admit it." I was a little surprised that neither Brent nor Gartborg interrupted me. I was also surprised that Dep hadn't joined me in the living room.

Paige plucked a tissue from the box and wiped her eyes. "My phone's upstairs." She jumped out of her chair, whirled, and ran up to her room. Seconds later, while I was still standing awkwardly near her chair, she returned and thrust her phone at Gartborg. "It's been plugged in to charge the battery ever since I got to Emily's, but I can't get it to turn on."

Gartborg pointed at the coffee table. "Put it there, please. We'll have an expert check to see if it really is your number."

Paige eased toward her chair and said with quiet dignity, "It is."

"Then," Gartborg suggested, "could the phone that Emily found in her garbage be Travis's?"

Paige fell into her chair. "I suppose."

I moved closer to the dining room but stayed in the living room. I wasn't snooping. I was merely being available in case one of the others needed me for anything, like another slice of kringle or a coffee refill. Or a clumsy but well-meant pat on a shoulder.

Pen in hand, Brent gazed down toward his open notebook. "Do you have any idea who put a phone into Emily's garbage can, Paige?"

"If it's Travis's phone, anyone who was on that bus, including Emily, you, other police officers, EMTs, and firemen could have picked up Travis's phone. And his insulated bottle, too." Her mouth a thin line, she glanced up at me. I thought I saw the hurt of betrayal on her face, but when she spoke, I heard anger. "Who would be surprised to find a broken bourbon bottle in someone's trash? Anyone could have come along and thrown out an empty bottle. It probably happens all the time. And I wasn't the only one on the bus who was given one of those survival blankets. And I wasn't the only one who bought mistletoe at that Christmas bazaar. A woman named Ashley bought a bag of it, too. She was right in front of me in line."

Gartborg counted on her fingers. "A phone. A broken

bourbon bottle. A large stainless steel insulated bottle. It's quite a coincidence that three things that seem to have gone missing from the bus ended up in Emily's trash can at the house where you're staying, along with a blanket like the one that you and a few others were given at the site, Paige. And a bag with a mistletoe berry in it." She glanced up toward the light fixture near the door.

As if hurt feelings and anger strengthened her, Paige sat up straighter. "Maybe not. People from the bus were mad at Travis and me. They thought we'd caused that crash. They could have collected those things. Maybe they picked them up to give to Travis later, but when they heard he died, they knew he had no use for them. Or maybe they weren't being kind. Maybe they planned to keep or sell the phone, but if it was banged around like mine was and didn't work, they just gave up and threw it out. But if they caused Travis's death"— her voice trembled—"they had to be afraid of being caught with those things. Some of them must know I'm staying here. When I first got here, I was wearing my jacket right side out, and it plainly says TOUR GUIDE on the back in big white letters. Someone could have seen me. They could have come over here on purpose in the middle of the night and thrown those things out. They probably didn't think anyone would find them, but if someone did, then I would be suspected of harming Travis." She flicked a glance at me. "Or Emily would be." She pulled her lips into her mouth as if to bite off specific accusations.

Gartborg asked, "Emily, did you tell anyone that Paige was staying with you?"

I thought back. "I didn't keep it a secret. The people I work with know, and one of our assistants, Jocelyn, has a family from the bus staying with her—Dustin and Ashley Loyvens and their three little boys." I gave Brent an intense stare, hoping he'd remember that Dustin was the man I believed had stolen a snowmobile early Thursday morning.

Brent didn't say anything, and I realized too late that if Paige was a murderer, I probably shouldn't have mentioned anyone by name.

Paige spat out, "Dustin Loyvens! That's the man who was angriest at me on the bus, the one who claimed that Travis had been drinking. And his kids had one of those blankets. And Ashley bought mistletoe." She gave Gartborg a pleading look. "You . . . you should get those things out of the garbage and check for fingerprints. You'll find mine on my phone, there." She nodded at the phone on the coffee table. "Or I'm happy to let someone make copies of my prints from my actual fingers, however you do it. You can compare them to prints on the other phone, whoever's it is." She leaned back and folded her arms. It was like a challenge, a well thought out challenge, as if she'd prepared her speech even before Brent and Gartborg showed up at my house. Had she thought of Dustin as a possible culprit before, or had she added him to her story after I mentioned him and Ashley?

Gartborg told her, "Emily's trash is already locked in the cruiser's trunk. We will check for fingerprints." She gazed sternly at Paige. "I suspect that fingerprints have been wiped off, probably with the paper towels that were nearby in the trash."

Paige only shrugged, and I had to give Gartborg credit. I had dismissed those paper towels as legitimate household trash.

Gartborg stood and placed the phone that Paige had said was hers into an evidence envelope. "That's all we need from you right now, Paige, but we'll probably have to talk to you again, especially if we find your prints—or no one's—on those objects."

She turned to Brent. "We have Ms. Usinor's address in Green Bay, don't we?"

His answer was curt. "Yes."

Gartborg said firmly to Paige, "Let us know when you arrive home so we can return your phone and anything else of yours that we might have, but it might be a while."

Brent added gently, "And call us if you think of something we should know or if you feel threatened, anything that could help us find out who killed your boyfriend or who might be a danger to you."

Paige stared at him for a second, then brushed her hair away from her cheeks and grabbed the box of tissues. "Okay." Her voice was almost too quiet to hear. She ran up the stairs. "I'll be in my room, Emily." She sounded about to cry again.

Brent went to the closet and pulled Gartborg's black leather coat out. Standing underneath the mistletoe, she put on her boots. Brent handed her the coat along with a key fob. "Do you mind driving the evidence back to headquarters, Kim? I need a walk."

She accepted the fob from him. "I don't mind at all." Her icy voice reminded me of why I wanted to protect Brent from her. "See you back at the office." She slipped on her coat and left.

I heard her walk down the wooden porch steps. A car door slammed.

All this time, Brent had stood still as if also listening to her departure. He hadn't made a move to get his own coat. He locked the door and then came farther into the living room, away from that mistletoe. "Are you going to work, Em? I'll walk with you."

I glanced up toward the second floor and said softly, "Maybe I should stay in case Paige needs me. Or my phone."

Thinning his lips, he shook his head. I studied those gray eyes for a moment and guessed what he was thinking. He didn't want me staying alone with her. He strode to the coffee table, picked up the mugs and plates, stacked them on the platter, and carried the loaded platter to the kitchen.

Following him, I discovered why Dep had stayed in the

dining room. With her paws tucked in and her tail curled around her, Dep was on the table, neatly covering my address list. Only the tips of her fur strayed off the piece of paper. "Funny girl," I cooed. "Why do you like to lie on pieces of paper?"

She merely opened her eyes halfway as if to remind me that boxes, paper bags, blankets, laundry, and sheets of paper were automatically donated to cats for their use as beds. Or for whatever they wanted.

In the kitchen, Brent washed the dishes. I dried and put them away, and then I went into the dining room and gathered my cards so I could drop them into a mailbox on the way to work. Brent took our coats out of the closet. Apparently, Dep noticed our preparations and did not want to be left behind. She stepped off my address list and positioned herself near my feet until I picked her up and tucked her into her carrying pouch.

Ever since Paige had run upstairs and shut herself into the guest room, I hadn't heard the slightest noise from her, not even one floorboard creaking.

Chapter 22

Brent helped me slip on my coat. I appreciated it even though I could have done it myself. Standing behind me, he let his hands linger on my shoulders for a few seconds, and then he slid his hands down to my upper arms, squeezed, and let go. Uncomfortably aware that I was underneath the mistletoe and that he was on duty, I avoided turning toward him. I zipped my parka to Dep's chin and put on my boots. Brent and I clomped outside. I locked the door.

It was fully light, but cloudy. With its Victorian homes decorated for Christmas and covered in white snow, my neighborhood resembled an old-fashioned Christmas card. It only lacked horses wearing jingle bells and pulling sleighs filled with laughing people and wrapped packages.

Out of earshot of my house, and still without turning to look up into Brent's face, I patted Dep through the front of my parka. "I'm sorry for letting the cat out of the bag about finding those things in the garbage. I thought if Paige knew I found them, she might confess, which would be better for her than lying to you. And might help your investigation." The top of Dep's furry head warmed my chin.

"It's okay, Em. Kim and I didn't want to endanger you by revealing that you'd been the one who called us, but Paige probably figured it out. We were about to warn her that lying wouldn't help her case. Hearing that advice from you could make her think it over and contact us."

Relieved that he didn't seem annoyed, I risked a glance up at his face. "But maybe she wasn't lying. Someone, Dustin Loyvens, for instance, could have taken the blanket from his kids, the mistletoe bag from his wife, and the bottle and phone from the bus and put them in my garbage can to make Paige look guilty."

"Maybe." He frowned down at me. "But she's the one who reeked of alcohol at the crash site, and she's the one who's staying at your place. If she threw them out, we have to ask ourselves why, and if she's not telling the truth about it, we have to ask ourselves why about that, too. Yesterday, I told her to give me anything she had of Travis's that might have a bearing on his death and to let me know everything she could think of that might shed light on why anyone would have wanted to harm him. She should have handed over his phone and water bottle then, if she had them, and she should have told us about the bourbon that she conveniently admitted, only this morning, to having taken from him on Wednesday before they left Green Bay. She seemed a little smug when she told us to check for fingerprints."

"That could be because she knew she hadn't handled those things since before the crash, if at all. And now that she admitted taking the bourbon bottle from him, no one could be surprised if her prints are on some of the glass fragments."

"True." The cleared section of sidewalk narrowed. Brent slowed to let me walk ahead of him. "It's possible that she made an earlier attempt on Travis's life. She might have engineered the bus crash to try to kill him."

I turned my head back to look at him. "Wouldn't that have been risky? It could have killed her, too."

"She could have aimed the bus toward the ditch and then flung herself into that seat behind Travis so she wouldn't go through the windshield. Passengers have told us that she stood near Travis almost the entire trip, talking to him, distracting him, standing where the passengers might not notice him drinking from his water bottle. Right before the crash, Paige moved closer to him. Passengers said she took his water bottle from him and stashed it in her tote bag. Some people said they thought she then grabbed the wheel and turned it sharply, sending the bus off the road."

"But you tested him. You know he'd been drinking. Maybe he drunkenly veered toward the snowbanks beside the road, and the passengers saw her grab the wheel, but she was trying to straighten it and keep the bus on the road."

Near the home of the woman I'd mistakenly believed could have been the snow angel, the sidewalks had been shoveled enough for Brent to walk beside me again. "That's possible, but don't you think she'd have volunteered that information?"

"Maybe shock made her forget."

"That happens. She guessed almost immediately that the steering failed, as if she'd planned to cause a crash and blame the steering."

With one mittened hand, I scooped snow off a hedge. "If I came up with a theory like that, you'd say it was a stretch." I packed the snow into a ball, threw it down onto the ground beside the hedge, and flattened it with the heel of my boot.

Laughing, Brent wrapped an arm around my shoulders and pulled me close to his side. "Maybe, but detectives can make these guesses. We'll say we're carefully examining every possibility." He let me go. I regained my balance, or most of it, and he went on with his explanation. "Other passengers thought she hit him over the head with her tote bag. If her bag contained both the bourbon and the stainless steel water bottle, clobbering Travis with it could have done a lot of damage to his head, and the heavy insulated bottle could have broken the bottle of bourbon. I'm guessing that Travis's and Paige's phones were also in that bag, and that both phones were soaked when the bottle broke and spilled the bourbon. What a waste, though it's not a particularly good brand of bourbon."

"Snob. Could her tote bag have accidentally hit him over the head in the tumult, and the passengers mistakenly believed she did it on purpose?"

He cast a sideways glance down at me. "It's possible. You really don't want to believe she could have murdered her boyfriend, do you?"

"She seems kind of naïve and shy, and maybe not completely honest, but she doesn't seem dangerous. She's afraid of the people from the bus, and also afraid of police officers."

He grinned down at me. "Am I scary?"

"Very."

His bare hand landed for a second on the back of my neck. "I'm going to find somewhere else for her to stay."

I tried to ignore the fleeting sensation of warmth that his hand had given me. "That's disappointing. I've enjoyed her company, and Dep likes her." I bent my head and kissed the tip of a fuzzy little ear. The back of my neck felt cold. I pulled my scarf higher to cover it.

Brent's voice became earnest, almost stern. "We don't know where she was between when she left your place and returned early Wednesday morning, which also spans the time when a snowmobile, which could have been used both to transport Travis and to topple Frosty the Donut onto him, went missing from this neighborhood and was later found."

I insisted on remaining stubborn. "Maybe Dustin Loyvens kidnapped Travis with the snowmobile, took him to the village square, and rammed Frosty the Donut until it fell on top of Travis."

"During a blizzard, would a hospital patient wearing only a hospital gown, bathrobe, coat, and paper slippers be more likely to accept a ride on a snowmobile from his girlfriend or from a man who was angry at him?"

I sighed. "His girlfriend. But maybe Travis was confused due to his head injury and wandered out of the hospital. Dustin might have been joyriding on that snowmobile, but when he saw Travis outside, he thought of a way of getting revenge on Travis for endangering Dustin and his family. And everyone else on that bus." Remembering how many children had been on that bus, I shuddered. "Did anyone see Travis leave the hospital? I mean, hospitals aren't exactly un-staffed, even at night."

"A nurse in the lobby did. Travis told her he was going for a smoke. She told him not to stay out long, but he seemed in his right mind, so she let him leave. She went to check on an-other patient. About ten minutes after he left, she wondered if he was still outside. She looked out at the spot where peo-ple usually smoke. He wasn't there, so she figured he went back to his room."

"Didn't she check?"

"She didn't know his name or room number."

I admitted, "I guess that makes sense."

"Closed-circuit cameras in the lobby corroborated the nurse's story but didn't show Travis crossing the lobby again. But we already knew that he must not have come back in-side."

"Last night when we were caroling at the hospital, I couldn't tell if there were surveillance cameras at the front entrance."

"There are, but Travis was heading toward the back. There's an exit there that leads to an alley. And no cameras near that entrance, unfortunately."

"Wouldn't that alley be even farther from the village square than the front entrance?"

"Yes. Whether he went out the back or the front of the hospital, he probably wouldn't have been able to walk all the way to the square in paper slippers. He would have needed a ride."

"Riding a snowmobile would have been colder than walking. Isn't it possible that he could have made it to the square on his own, and then, you know, don't people sometimes just lie down in the snow when they have severe hypothermia?"

"It's a possibility." I heard doubt in his voice. "The slippers would have ended up tattered, though, and they were only a little scuffed."

"When I first realized that Frosty the Donut had been knocked over, I thought a vehicle had slid off the road and hit it."

"Again, it's a possibility, but a deliberate attempt is more likely than a simple skid off the road. To get through the snow that was in the road and then through plowed-up snowbanks and over the curb, and then after that, through deep snow between the road and your sculpture, the vehicle would have to be powerful and speeding. A snowmobile could have ridden over the top of the plowed snowbank. Whatever vehicle did it, plows came along later and piled more snow on any tracks over or through the snowbank."

We turned onto Wisconsin Street. I shoved my Christmas cards into a mailbox and then continued up the street beside Brent. I asked him, "Did the nurse hear vehicles around the time that Dustin left the hospital?"

"She was closer to the front of the hospital, but she said she heard snowmobiles off and on during the night. I heard a few, too, from the police station."

I reminded him, "Snowplows were out, too. How well do you know that snowplow operator who came onto the bus briefly? He knew Travis, and from the way he said Travis's name, I got the impression that he didn't like Travis."

"Ronald seems okay, but we haven't ruled anyone out. Including you."

I gave him a playful jab with an elbow. "You never ruled me in. Did the nurse see anyone in the hospital around the time that Travis went out? Maybe someone resembling Dustin?"

"Several people came in, including a short woman in what appeared to be cross-country ski boots and a red parka with something white like fake fur around the hood. The short woman managed not to get picked up by any of the cameras, and the nurse didn't get a good look at her face. Her hood was up, and a scarf covered her nose, mouth, and chin."

"Are you sure about the fake fur on the hood? Paige might have borrowed the red parka she wore yesterday when she went with you to identify Travis's body, but it doesn't have any sort of fur around the face."

"Memories aren't as clear as people think. The nurse admitted that she didn't feel the need to pay close attention to the woman."

"Did the nurse see any skis and poles outside, like leaning on the building?"

"She said people often leave them near the front entrance, and she didn't notice any near the back when she checked there for Travis. She said they could have been there, but she wasn't looking for skis and didn't see any. Even if she had, they'd probably have been snow-covered, and she wouldn't have known if they were red like yours or some other color."

We were at the driveway leading to the lot behind Deputy Donut. I stomped a foot onto the slightly snowy sidewalk. "You think of everything."

He gazed down at me with warmth in his eyes. "It's kind of my job. And I should let you get to yours."

He gave the top of Dep's head, still sticking out of my parka beneath my chin, a knuckle rub. "Take care, you two. I'll see what I can do about finding Paige somewhere else to stay."

"You don't need to. I don't think she harmed her boy-friend."

He gave me a skeptical frown.

"Dep likes her, and I trust her judgment."

He bent and spoke into Dep's face. "You like me, too, don't you, Dep?" His hair smelled like clean, cold, fresh air.

"Meow."

He straightened. "See? She said yes."

"That might have been no."

He laughed and headed toward the police department.

Chapter 23

✿

I left Dep and my coat, boots, and backpack in our office and went into the dining area. Now that the roads were clear, our shop was full of customers. Greeting regulars, newcomers, and tourists from the wrecked bus, I headed toward the kitchen.

Tom stood beside a deep fryer where donuts turned golden and spun lazily. "Is everything okay?" he asked.

I said it was, but after I went into the storeroom for my hat and apron and rejoined him in the kitchen, I described my morning.

He looked up from the hot oil and narrowed his eyes. "I'm glad Brent's going to find somewhere else for this tour guide to stay."

I rolled donut dough on the marble counter. "She's been fine, so far."

"Until you called the cops on her."

I teased, "There's no arguing with you, is there?"

"Not when your safety is at stake."

I pressed a round donut cutter into the rolled-out dough and twisted the cutter to make certain it cut completely through the dough. "You're as bad as Alec was."

"Worse." He spread cooked donuts on a rack to cool.

Decorating donuts, Jocelyn beckoned to me. "I told you Olivia's coming out of her shell. She's chatting with customers. That's the good news. The bad news is they're almost old enough to be her grandmothers, and she needs more friends closer to her own age besides you and me."

Olivia was not only chatting with the Knitpickers, she was examining Cheryl's knitting. Olivia pointed at something in the whatever-it-was that Cheryl was making.

I smiled back at Jocelyn. "Olivia seemed to get along with that EMT last night. They're singing together was awesome."

"It was."

"Maybe Samantha and I can throw them together."

Jocelyn placed a white snowflake sprinkle on a raised donut with frosting tinted to match the lavender-blue tones of a winter sky at dusk. "Has he ever come to Deputy Donut?"

"Not as far as I know." The Emergency Medical Services station was too far away for the EMTs to walk to Deputy Donut to take their breaks like police officers and firefighters did. "Maybe I can convince Samantha to stop by on their way back from a call. Or Samantha could try sending him for the coffee beans she buys for the Emergency Medical Services staff."

With a coy grin, Jocelyn suggested, "Maybe Samantha can figure out a way to bring him to Brent's cross-country skiing party."

"I like that!" Brent's party was in only slightly over twenty-four hours. Samantha would have to quickly come up with a ploy.

Looking forward to Brent's party, I took another carafe of coffee to the Knitpickers' table.

"Why are you grinning ear to ear?" Cheryl asked.

I topped up her coffee. "Because I'm looking at you in your gorgeous silver Christmas sweater."

"Flattery will get you nowhere."

Virginia turned in her chair to look at me. She flapped her own knitting toward Cheryl and Olivia. "Emily, do you know who this is?"

"Cheryl?" I asked, a little confused. The Knitpickers had been spending nearly every weekday morning in Deputy Donut since we opened.

"No, her!" She pointed a knitting needle at Olivia. "Your new employee. She's okay!"

I smiled at Olivia. "She's more than okay. She's wonderful."

Virginia gave me a look that was both amazed and pitying at the same time. "She's OK. The initials. OK Kritters. That's critters with a K."

I was still lost. I looked to Olivia for help.

"Virginia's under the impression that I'm famous," she explained.

Virginia asserted, "You are. Among crafters." Her look of pity deepened. "Emily crafts perfect donuts, but . . ." She shook her head.

Cheryl must have decided to help me out. "Olivia does felting, you know, taking rovings and poking it with needles until she comes up with the cutest little creatures."

Her explanation didn't really help. More confused than ever, I asked, "Rovings?"

Virginia explained. "Unspun lambswool, big balls of soft stuff. It's cleaned and carded, but not spun into yarn."

Cheryl pulled a keychain out of her knitting bag. A tiny masked raccoon was holding his little hands up. "Like this. I bought this a couple of years ago. Isn't it darling? She made it. She sells them online. She knits, too, and sews. She's a wonder at all of it."

I threw Olivia an apologetic glance. "Sorry, I didn't know. Wait. During your job interview, you told us you liked crafting. Is that what you meant?"

Blushing, Olivia nodded.

Virginia tried folding her arms without putting down her knitting, but it didn't seem to work, and she gave up. " 'Likes crafting.' Now that's an understatement if I ever heard one."

I asked Olivia, "Do you belong to The Craft Croft?"

"I never joined."

I was relieved, sort of, to discover that she probably hadn't knit the scarf and hat I'd bought for her. If she had a wardrobe of her own creations, I hadn't seen any of it.

As if reading my mind, Cheryl piped up. "OK, I mean Olivia, hardly ever makes anything for herself. She was just telling us that she sells her creations as soon as they're finished."

I asked Olivia, "How long have you been doing that?"

"I've been making them since I was about twelve, but I turned it into a business after I graduated from high school." That was around the time that she and her sister were orphaned and Olivia became a full-time mom to Hannah.

Maybe Cheryl was having similar sad thoughts. She picked up her mug and changed the subject. "It's almost Christmas! Are you two ready?"

Olivia smiled with anticipation. "I will be as soon as my sister gets home from college. Then we'll celebrate."

I tried to look crestfallen. "Is it ever possible to be ready for Christmas? I've done my shopping and cards, but there's always more baking that I can do."

Cheryl laughed. "I'm that way, too. I always say I'll stop, but I always end up having to take another cake or batch of cookies out of the oven at the last minute." She called across the table, "Priscilla! Are you ready for Christmas?"

"I have to be. I'm leaving tonight for my daughter's. My son's family is coming, too. Four grandkids! I can't wait to see them."

Virginia said that her entire clan was coming to her. "I would never trust anyone else to roast and stuff the turkey right. They can make some of the sides if they insist."

Kathleen and Barb, both widowed for many years, were planning a holiday together in a resort. "We're not cooking anything," Kathleen said. Without slowing the pace of their knitting or dropping a stitch, they each managed to turn two thumbs up.

Leaving the Knitpickers to discuss whether anyone could call it "stuffing" if it wasn't stuffed into anything, Olivia checked on a family farther back in the café, and I moved to the retired men's table. None of them were concerned about what they might eat on Christmas Day. They merely wanted more donuts. Now. "That's easy," I said.

After the Knitpickers and retired men left at noon, we weren't busy. Tom suggested that each of us could take more than an hour off if we needed to. He and Jocelyn wanted to shop. Olivia had a hair appointment. "I don't deserve a lunch hour," I told them, "after coming in late. I'm not happy about taking parts of yesterday and this morning off."

Tom's eyes twinkled. "Don't make it a habit. Why don't you wait and see how busy we are after Olivia and I come back?"

While they were gone, Jocelyn and I made deep-fried bacon-wrapped scallops and spicy sweet-potato fries for lunch for ourselves and for customers in the midst of their Christmas shopping. One mother and her three preteens sang along with the Christmas songs we were broadcasting through our sound system.

After Jocelyn and I finished our lunches, she looked up

from the puffy raised donuts she was turning into green wreaths trimmed in frosting bows and sugar ornaments. "Scott said to surprise him with something tonight at the fire station. Do we have a donut cutter that looks like a fire truck? We could frost them in red." She gestured toward her tray of donuts. "And we could put green wreaths on the fire trucks."

"We have a generic truck cookie cutter, but after the donuts puff up, it would be hard to tell that they're trucks and not squarish red blobby things."

She glanced toward the storeroom. "We have ingredients to make sugar cookies. That would really surprise Scott."

"Let's! We can have the cookie dough ready when Olivia and Tom get back. Then you can go do your shopping, Olivia can bake and decorate the fire truck cookies, Tom can make donuts, and I can wait tables."

When Olivia and Tom returned, Jocelyn and I were taking the first batch of cookies out of the oven.

"You can take a break, Emily," Tom said. "We have enough donuts for the rest of the day. I'll happily wander around talking to everyone."

Olivia shooed us out. "Baking and decorating fire truck cookies will be fun. Thanks for thinking of it."

Jocelyn and I went into the office, paid our respects to my demanding cat, and then put on our coats and boots and walked down Wisconsin Street. I stopped at the library. Jocelyn headed toward shops farther south.

Irma looked a little surprised when I asked her where to find Gooseleg High yearbooks. She informed me nicely, "You can't take yearbooks out of the library." She pointed toward tall bookshelves near the middle of the main room. "They're in the reference section over there."

Scott had said that Travis Tarriston graduated from Gooseleg High the same year that Scott graduated from Falling-brook High. Scott had been three years ahead of Samantha, Misty, and me, so finding Travis's senior year among the Gooseleg yearbooks was easy.

I carried the book to a table near a window and sat down.

It didn't seem that Travis had won academic prizes or starred in musicals or joined the chess club or science club, but he had definitely been a football star. And he'd had those devil-may-care good looks, complete with those eyebrows that I'd noticed and that Summer had commented on. Back in high school, when his face was slimmer and he hadn't ac-cidentally met forcefully with the windshield of a bus, his eyebrows made him appear both surprised and interested in whatever anyone had to say.

Gazing at his senior picture and trying to remember if I'd ever noticed Travis at football games, I heard a noise that seemed totally out of place in a library—paper tearing and being crumpled. Then I remembered that kids had been mak-ing ornaments out of construction paper.

But the children's voices inside the library at the moment were farther away than the noises had been. And construc-tion paper would have made a softer sound. I was certain that the paper I'd heard being ripped and crumpled was heavier and glossier than construction paper.

Maybe a child had decided to work by himself where the others wouldn't bother him or see what he was making. He must have finished the tearing part of the project. I didn't hear the noise again. I bent my head over the yearbook and turned pages. I wasn't sure what I was looking for.

Someone clumped past on the carpeting between me and the front desk. The footsteps stopped. I looked up.

No one was at the front desk, but a large man in a bulky khaki coat, heavy canvas work pants, and thick rubber boots was staring at me. His face red, he turned and walked toward the door. He pulled a glove out of a coat pocket. Something fell out of the pocket and landed silently. He picked it up, shoved it back into the pocket, and strode out of the library. Between homemade construction paper ornaments and cards plastered over the front windows, I caught glimpses of him heading south on the sidewalk, and I realized who he was.

The last time I'd seen him had been in semidarkness, inside a wrecked bus. He was the snowplow operator who had spoken Travis's name with derision. Brent had called the man Ronald.

Plows usually ran almost constantly during snowstorms, and their drivers worked long hours. Maybe Ronald had seen Travis smoking outside the hospital when he was plowing the lane behind the hospital. Maybe he'd offered Travis a ride—for more cigarettes? And Travis had accepted. But Ronald had taken him to the village square and had used the snowplow to topple Frosty the Donut onto him.

The thing that had fallen from Ronald's coat pocket could have been crumpled wrapping paper or a Christmas shopping list. Maybe because I'd heard paper tearing only moments before, I'd believed that the strangely shaped object resembled a scrunched-up page torn from a book or magazine.

I put the Gooseleg yearbook on the re-shelving cart. Trying to appear casual, I strolled around high shelves to approximately the spot where I'd heard paper tear.

On a bottom shelf, a tall, thin maroon book turned out to be a Fallingbrook High yearbook from Scott's junior year. It was out of chronological order. It should have been to the right, not to the left, of the ivory one. I pulled it out and took it to the desk where I'd sat moments earlier.

I turned the heavy, glossy pages slowly, one by one. I smiled at Scott's junior picture. There was Whitney, too, and

Leo. They all looked incredibly young. Scott was serious, Whitney was dewy-eyed, and Leo scowled.

I came to a section labeled FOOTBALL.

And there it was, a ragged edge near the center of the book, between pages sixty-one and sixty-four. The page that would have been numbered sixty-two on one side and sixty-three on the other had been sloppily torn out.

Chapter 24

Had Ronald removed the page from the yearbook just now? I considered asking Irma if she knew how or when the book was damaged.

However, Brent wouldn't want me showing anyone possible evidence before he examined it. The front desk was hidden from me at the moment, beyond more bookshelves. If Ronald had been standing where I was and had torn a page out of the book, no one at the front desk would have seen him do it.

I bent, quickly pushed the previous year's Fallingbrook High yearbook to one side, and slid the damaged book into its correct position on the shelf, to the right of the ivory one. How often did people look at old yearbooks? According to Irma, no one would be allowed to remove this one from the library. Still, I felt like everybody in the community might suddenly take a notion to come into the library and inspect that particular yearbook, and that I should tell Brent about it before it disappeared.

If Ronald was trying to keep anyone from seeing those pages because they showed he had a motive for killing Travis, maybe Brent and Detective Gartborg would focus on Ronald instead of on Paige.

Irma wasn't at the main desk, so I didn't have to worry about my undoubtedly guilty expression about keeping the book's damage a secret. I could tell her later, after Brent had a chance to see the book.

Walking back to Deputy Donut, though, I had second thoughts about calling Brent about the torn-out page. I didn't know who had removed it, or when. I was jumping to conclusions based on Ronald's tone of voice on the wrecked bus when he'd recognized Travis, and on the sound of paper tearing in Ronald's vicinity in the library. And because I wanted to believe that Paige wasn't a killer? Even if Ronald had torn that page out of the yearbook when I was behind other bookshelves, I couldn't prove that it had anything to do with Travis's death.

I'd barely gotten into our office at Deputy Donut and removed my boots and coat when Brent phoned me. "Misty and I are going to move Paige to Misty's, but we're not sure when we can make it to your place. It won't be until later this evening." Although Dep had been dozing in one of her little beds near the ceiling, she must have recognized Brent's voice over the phone. She trotted down from her catwalks, sat on the desk in front of me, stretched up, and bumped the phone with her lips.

I told Brent, "That's fine."

"Can you wait until I call you to go home? We can meet you outside and go in with you, and you can help keep Paige from worrying that she's being arrested. Can you find things to do after Deputy Donut closes this evening?"

"Sure. Tonight's the annual kids' tree-decorating party at the fire hall." Gripping my phone tightly to keep Dep from nudging it out of my hand, I added, "I guess you're not coming to that."

"No, sorry. I would if I could. Do you think Paige will attend?"

"She said she wasn't."

"Okay. I'll call you tonight. It probably won't be until after the party ends."

We disconnected. I picked Dep up, hugged her, and muttered, "If he thinks Paige is so dangerous, why is he willing to let her be alone inside our house for so many more hours?"

"Mew."

"I guess I agree with you, Dep. Paige wouldn't damage anything in the house she thinks she's staying in."

"Mew." *Purr, purr.*

"Besides, Brent's mainly concerned about keeping you and me safe."

Purr, purr, purr, purr.

"Unfortunately, I have to set you down and get back to work."

Silence. Dep turned her back to me, sat on the desk again, and bathed a front paw. Beyond the window into the kitchen, Tom gave us both a big smile. I waved and went through the dining room and into the storeroom. I washed my hands, put on my hat and a clean apron, and returned to work.

Tom was taking a tray of fire truck–shaped sugar cookies out of the oven. Olivia had spread red frosting on cooled cookies. She was adding green frosting wreaths and decorating them with tiny red and silver sugar balls. The cookies were adorable.

Jocelyn and I waited tables and served customers, many of whom were singing along with the Christmas music quietly playing in the background.

After the last customer left at four thirty, we packaged the fire truck cookies. We finished our usual evening cleanup and trooped into the office. Dep wound around our ankles, making putting on boots difficult. I cuddled her while the others got ready, and then Jocelyn held her while I slipped on my boots. It took all four of us to encourage Dep to stay inside the office while we edged out onto the back porch and locked the back door.

Olivia and Tom each carried a bakery box of red fire truck cookies. I brought two platters.

Jocelyn asked me, "Want me to carry those?"

I held on to the platters. "What if you feel a sudden urge to turn a few cartwheels?"

"Would I do that?"

Laughing, I handed her a platter. Mingling with other groups of excited holiday partygoers, we walked up Wisconsin Street toward the square and the fire station. Snowflakes drifted down, adding to the picturesque white fluff covering everything like vanilla icing.

With its ladder extended upward, a fire truck was parked on the far side of the apron in front of one of the fire hall's oversized open doors. Other fire trucks were parked along the street between the fire station and the police department. The brightly lit firehall was full of people instead of trucks. We went inside and wended our way through the laughing, chattering crowd. Only about half of the guests were adults.

Toward the back of the huge garage section of the station, strings of white lights festooned a realistic-looking pine. Firefighters were lifting tots and helping them place ornaments on high boughs.

Scott greeted us with a big smile. "We recruit height-loving firefighters at early ages here in Fallingbrook." He glanced toward a table on the other side of the fire hall. "Our buffet table is almost full, and every surface in the kitchen is covered, too, so if you want to put anything in my office, go ahead."

It looked like we might be able to squeeze one of the platters we'd brought onto the buffet table. Carrying our bakery boxes and platters, Olivia, Tom, Jocelyn, and I went into Scott's office. Tom set his box on Scott's otherwise clear metal desk. Smiling in anticipation, Tom left to wait outside near the street for Cindy and the family staying with them.

Olivia watched him go, and then said, "He's really enjoying being a temporary granddad figure." Flushing, she turned to me. "Oh, sorry, Emily. That was insensitive."

"It's okay. I'm enjoying seeing him having a great time with the parents and the little girl. Cindy, too." And I suddenly pictured Brent and me with a couple of toddlers in Christmas-patterned sleepers, all of us singing around a Christmas tree with Tom and Cindy. If I ever did have children, no matter who the father was, we would treat Tom and Cindy as another set of grandparents. I shook myself out of the daydream.

Jocelyn and Olivia were arranging the cookies prettily on the platter. Hiding my undoubtedly blushing face, I looked away from them.

I'd been in Scott's office before, but its neatness always impressed me. Except for this one night of the year when the fire station's kitchen might be messy, Scott probably automatically avoided clutter that could add to a fire or be in the way of fighting one. Cabinets were closed. None of the books on his bookshelf leaned. He had technical manuals and other reference books, but he was also fond of fun. There were shelves of novels and jigsaw puzzles for the time between calls and between restoring vintage and antique toys to donate to kids. The lower right side of his bookshelf caught my eye. Four tall, thin books stood there together, a green one, an ivory one, a maroon one, and a blue one.

I had lined up four identical books in that same order in the library.

Scott had a yearbook for each year he had spent at Fallingbrook High. The maroon one would be from his junior year. I itched to pull it out and open it to pages sixty-two and sixty-three.

Jocelyn picked up the beautifully arranged platter of whimsical cookies. "Coming, Emily?"

"Sure." I followed Olivia and Jocelyn out of Scott's office and closed the door.

Jocelyn placed the platter on the table with the other food. Kids descended. "Fire truck cookies!"

Other kids near the gaping doorways shouted, "Popcorn!"

A big man in a bulky khaki coat wheeled in a festive red and white popcorn cart with added decorations of red, silver, and green tinsel garlands.

Scott called out, "Over here, Ronald!"

Ronald smiled and pushed his popcorn cart toward Scott. The two men positioned the cart close to an electrical outlet, and before long the inimitable and mouthwatering smell of hot, buttered popcorn wafted through the fire hall.

Most of us in that building with one side open to the elements were wearing coats. Ronald took his off and tossed it on the chair behind him. His muscles bulged underneath the short sleeves of his bright red T-shirt. At first I thought the picture on the front of his T-shirt was Santa in his sleigh pulled by reindeer.

And it was, in a way, but Santa's face was a skull, and the reindeer were skeletons.

The little bags he was filling with popcorn featured the word POPCORN inside hearts formed by the tops of crossed candy canes.

I asked him, "Where did you find those bags?"

"We order them from the place that supplies the popping corn and stuff." He eyed me. "Were you at the library earlier?"

My face heated. "Today? Yes. I sometimes spend my lunch hours there, reading." It was true, although I didn't do it often.

"Sorry for not saying hello. I was trying to place you, but

now I think I know where I saw you before. On Wednesday night. On that wrecked bus."

"Yes. I'm Emily Westhill." I considered telling him I'd also gone to Fallingbrook High but decided I shouldn't mention high school—or football. And certainly not yearbooks.

"I'm Ronald Eamberton. I work for Fallingbrook. Plowing snow, mowing roadsides, patching potholes, you name it."

"Making popcorn at events?"

"Nah. I do this for the Fallingbrook Falcons." He pushed a tinsel garland aside and showed me the Fallingbrook Falcons emblem stenciled on the cart. He added, "Proceeds go to charity."

Never having heard of the organization, I pointed toward Tom, who was lifting the little girl staying with him and Cindy. She hung a fuzzy teddy bear high in the tree. "My father-in-law and I run Deputy Donut."

"I've always intended to stop in there."

"Do!" I hadn't meant to sound quite so enthused.

"I will." His eyes were dark and his lips thin. I couldn't read his mood. Was he chatting because he wanted to find out if I'd heard him tear that page out of the yearbook or if I had seen him drop it and then pick it up? I couldn't think of a way of searching his coat pocket for the scrunched-up piece of paper other than somehow turning off all the power in the fire station and rushing to feel inside the pockets of the coat in the dark. It was a ridiculous and unworkable idea. Emergency lights would undoubtedly come on immediately, and even if they took a few seconds, streetlights and the glow from the Ice and Lights Festival across the street would prevent the firehall from becoming completely dark inside. Besides, by now Ronald had probably emptied his pocket and discarded that page.

He was still looking at me. Imagining the expressions that must have been flitting across my face, I offered a sickly smile and shoved my red, green, and white striped stocking cap farther back. It had been squashing curls onto my forehead and threatening to push them into my eyes.

Behind me, a woman said loudly, "And where has that tour guide been all this time? Betcha she murdered her boss and skipped town."

My hand stopped mid-gesture, giving Ronald the chance to see my wedding ring. It was not totally an accident.

Another woman said, "I'm sure you're right. Lots of families have already had people come pick them up. She probably went with one of them. She was obviously mad at her boss the entire trip."

The first woman said, "I think it was a lovers' quarrel. You know what they say about your nearest and dearest. They're the ones you love to kill."

The second woman lowered her voice. "I heard that she dragged him out into a snowdrift and left him to freeze."

The first woman had a different theory. "I heard that she stole a truck and ran over him with it."

Still scratching my forehead, I looked down toward my feet.

The other woman added to the story. "And then left him to freeze. And then she probably fled in the truck."

I couldn't help checking Ronald's reaction. His face had turned bright red.

I made a show of sniffing appreciatively toward the popped corn mounding up in the cart.

Not wanting to be obvious, either to Ronald or to the two women, I waited several heartbeats before casually turning around. Two women, both in black nylon parkas similar to about a dozen others in the fire station, had their backs to us and were walking away. Their hoods were up, and I didn't have a clue about who they were. I wasn't sure if they'd been the ones talking, but I didn't see another likely pair of women nearby.

Taking the last bite of a tiny cream cheese and chive sandwich, Olivia came up to us. Dustin and Ashley Loyvens's smallest boy pushed in front of her and gazed up at Ronald. "Can I have some popcorn?"

Ronald's flush receded. "Sure."

Noticing him juggling the scoop and the bags, Olivia took the bag from him and bent toward the boy. "Here." Squealing and spilling popcorn on the cement floor, the boy dashed away. Jocelyn put out her arms and stopped him before he could knock over the Christmas tree that his older brothers were helping decorate.

The boy's vocal advertising caused a stampede of little people, including his brothers. During the popcorn frenzy, I managed to introduce Ronald to Olivia. "She works with us at Deputy Donut."

"I'm definitely stopping by there." Filling another bag of popcorn and handing it to Olivia, he blushed again.

Watching them chat with each other as they worked together to give people bags of popcorn, I eased away. I counted seven women in black parkas, but no two of them were together, and most of them weren't wearing their hoods. I tried to remember which women on the bus had worn black parkas, but I hadn't paid much attention to the colors of people's clothing, and in the dimly lit bus, all of the dark clothing had looked black or close to it.

Across the firehall, Tom and Cindy were still helping children choose and hang ornaments on the tree.

Closer to me, Jocelyn had accompanied the three Loyvens boys to the buffet table and was delivering a lesson in nutrition. They hesitated near the raw veggies but bypassed them in favor of cookies, pretzels, and potato chips. Jocelyn looked up, grinned at me, shrugged, and mouthed, "It's Christmas!"

The fire truck cookies were almost gone. Leaving the quickly emptying platter on the table within reach of Jocelyn and her charges, I inched sideways through the crowd to Scott's office. I went inside and closed the door.

The maroon yearbook was still where I'd seen it. I bent over, slid it out of the bookcase, and flipped to page sixty-two. It featured a collage of pictures from football games.

Two pictures filled page sixty-three. The top one was captioned, FALLINGBROOK-GOOSELEG RIVALRY HEATS UP.

In front of a set of wooden bleachers, Gooseleg and Fallingbrook football players appeared to be facing off in a scuffle.

The Gooseleg players were in blue jerseys while the Fallingbrook team wore red. Helmets lay scattered on the ground, as ignored as the football lying near them.

The name TARRINGTON was emblazoned across the back of one Gooseleg player's jersey. His elbow back, the player appeared to be aiming a fist at the enraged face of a Fallingbrook player. The Fallingbrook boy had a wispy goatee, but I recognized him.

He was Ronald Eamberton at about age sixteen.

Someone fiddled with the knob on the door of Scott's office.

Chapter 25

❧

I slammed the yearbook shut and shoved it into its place on the shelf.

The doorknob turned.

I pivoted toward Scott's desk.

The door opened slowly.

Trying to appear intent on the bakery box, I bent over it.

Ronald Eamberton walked into the office and seemed to take up most of the space. His gaze darted around the room. "Salt?" he asked.

Watching him, I ran my fingers over the bakery box. One of my fingers touched glossy tape. Picking at the tape and probably looking as confused by his question as I felt, I repeated in a voice made clumsy by nerves, "Salt?"

"Scott said to look for salt in here. I didn't bring enough. Me! King of the road salt!" His smile didn't quite reach his eyes.

Still with one hand on the box of cookies, I edged toward the door. "I'll ask Scott." I left the cookies behind and barreled past the partly open door and almost into Scott. "Ronald wants salt," I said. Scott gave me a peculiar look. I realized that my explanation had come out almost breathlessly. I cleared my throat, pointed beyond the door, and added, "He's looking for it in there."

Scott pushed his office door open farther. Ronald was peering down at the approximate place on the bookshelf where I'd hastily stuck the yearbook. Scott spoke with the laid-back patience of someone needing to give directions more than once. "Ronald, the salt's in the kitchen."

Ronald turned toward us. His face was flushed. He pointed at the bakery box and platter on the smooth metal top of Scott's desk. "Oh, sorry, I thought this was the kitchen."

Scott pointed. "Next door over. I'll go with you."

Ronald joined us outside the office.

I muttered, "I'll finish putting the cookies on the platter."

No one pointed out that I hadn't started.

I shut myself into the office again and looked at the bookshelf. I put my fist over my mouth to stifle a gasp.

In my hurry to hide that I'd been looking at the maroon yearbook, I hadn't slid it back as far as it would go. Its spine stuck out at least an inch beyond the other three yearbooks.

And Ronald had been looking down at that exact spot.

I stooped and pushed at the book until it was even with the others. Heart racing, I stood, peeled the tape off the box of cookies, and lifted the lid.

I set the cookies on the platter. Their cuteness barely registered. *Had Ronald noticed how neat everything else was in Scott's office? Did he figure out that I had pulled the book off the shelf, found the picture of Travis Tarriston about to hit Ronald, and had shoved the book onto the shelf in such a hurry that I hadn't put it back the way Scott would have? Even when we were in the library, Ronald could have believed that I knew for certain that he'd torn a page out of the yearbook in the library. He might guess I suspected he could have murdered Travis. . . .*

If so, what might he do to prevent me from telling anyone?

A man shouted, "Thanks, Chief." I thought the voice was Ronald's.

Someone brushed against the other side of the door. Looking as innocent as possible while mentally rehearsing running screaming from the room, I continued arranging cookies on the platter.

The door opened. Frowning, Scott came in and closed the door. "Are you okay, Emily?"

"Sure."

"What did Ronald really want?" Scott's voice was low and intense.

"Salt. Didn't he ask you for some?"

"Yes, but the kitchen door is clearly labeled and has a glass window. It didn't make sense for him to come in here." Scott's lips thinned in obvious concern. He asked quietly, "Was he following you? Or harassing you?"

I took a deep breath. "He could have been following me, but I don't think it was to harass me, exactly." I tilted my head up to look at Scott. "Can you lock your office door?"

Without asking or debating, he did. One of the many things I loved about my friends was how much we all trusted one another.

I went over to his bookshelf. "Look at this." I pulled his senior yearbook off the bottom shelf, turned to page sixty-three, and pointed at the picture showing someone named Tarriston about to punch the younger version of Ronald. I explained about hearing paper tear and seeing Ronald leave the library. "I can't say for certain, but I think he could have torn this page out of the yearbook in the library and taken it with him. Before he left the library, he saw me near where that tearing paper sound had come from, and a few minutes ago, he asked if I'd been in the library earlier today. He might have followed me into your office to find out how much I knew. I'd barely glanced at these pages in your yearbook when I heard someone coming. I put the book on the shelf but unfortunately, I failed to push it back as far as it would go. When you opened your office door, he was staring down at that shelf of books. I'm afraid he guessed by the way I'd left it sticking out that I'd been looking at it. And why."

With a whistle underneath his breath, Scott folded his arms across his chest. "As far as I know, Ronald is a good Fallingbrook employee, but stay away from him if you can, and maybe you should tell Brent what you just told me."

"I will. He and Misty are coming to my place tonight to take Paige, the tour guide, to stay with Misty. I found things in my trash that made Brent and Detective Gartborg suspect Paige of killing Travis."

"I heard about that. Not about the things in the trash, but about the tour guide being moved to Misty's because Misty is a police officer and you aren't." He stood up straight again, away from the door. "Misty's going to have to put me up, too, as long as that woman is staying with her. Or put up with me. Misty can look after herself, but I'm not taking chances."

I smiled at him. "Good. Paige seems harmless. I suspect that the actual murderer dumped those things to try to frame her. My top suspect was a passenger on the bus. That man might have stolen a snowmobile and used it to push our ice sculpture over onto Travis. But now I'm wondering about Ronald. He was driving a snowplow that night. It would have been better at knocking down ice sculptures than a snowmobile. He came onto the bus right after the crash, and the way he said Travis's name, he sounded almost murderous. And it seems as if he might have destroyed pictures from the library's copy of the yearbook that show Travis about to punch him."

Scott frowned. "Ronald was in my year in school, but I didn't know him well then, and I still don't."

"Were you here any of Wednesday night?"

"Yes."

"Did you notice any vehicles going past here or near the

corner of the square where our Frosty the Donut ice sculpture was?"

"We were called to other crashes that night in addition to the bus crash. I couldn't see outside the entire time I was here, but snowmobiles roared past, and I heard the plow at least once. It was snowing so hard that, when I did look out, I could barely see this side of the street. I couldn't see into the square at all, and I certainly couldn't have seen the corner where your sculpture was, though that corner is usually visible." Scott walked to his desk and picked up a fire truck cookie. "Ronald was our star football player, and Travis Tarriston was Gooseleg's. That brawl heated up after that picture was taken, and there were injuries. Because of that fight, almost all the members of Fallingbrook High's team were suspended from school, and our winning season turned into a losing one."

"I remember hearing about some of that, but I guess the rumors about the brawl didn't sift down to the next year's freshman class."

"The school administration tried to keep the reason for the suspension quiet, but word got around, at least in my class. To make the whole thing more difficult for us at Fallingbrook, Gooseleg High didn't suspend anyone, and their team went on to win most of their games that season. Ronald's jaw was broken in that fight. I don't know if Tarriston or someone else broke it, but from that picture, it could have been Tarriston. In any case, Ronald's high school sports career and his hopes for a career in professional football ended with that fight, the broken jaw, and the losing season. The next fall, when the college scouts came around to watch the games, Ronald's jaw hadn't healed well and was being reset. He wasn't on the squad. Tarriston was offered a football scholarship. I think he dropped out during his first year of college, though, so the scholarship was wasted, and he never became a professional football player, either. Maybe neither of them would have made it, but Ronald didn't get the chance to try. I never talked to him about it, but I guess I would understand if he still held a grudge." He bit the cookie in half. "Mmm."

I asked, "Would a grudge like that make someone want to commit murder in revenge years later?"

"Personally, I could never understand that, but you know how people can act in the heat of the moment when they get an unexpected chance."

I contorted my mouth into a regretful expression. "Unfortunately. One more thing—have the Fallingbrook Falcons, the organization supplying the popcorn, been around for a long time? This is the first I've heard of it."

"A few years. They're legitimate, a service club that donates time and money to the community."

"Are you a member?"

"No. I think it's mostly an older group. They're lucky to have Ronald as their muscle."

I grinned. "I see why you haven't joined." Scott merely smiled. He gave back to the community in many other ways. I said seriously, "Thanks for all you do."

He shook his head in dismissal.

I added, "And for rescuing me from Ronald."

He smiled down at me. "You probably didn't need it."

I twisted my wedding ring on my finger. "Probably, but . . ." I let my voice trail off, then picked up the platter of cookies. "I'd better take these out there before everyone goes home."

Those light blue eyes twinkled. "Don't rush. Firefighters can cope with leftovers." He unlocked the door, opened it, and followed me out into the fire hall's main room.

Jocelyn had gathered children around her. Still wearing their snowsuits, they were sitting in a circle on the floor and playing a Christmas counting game involving reindeer, three small ships, and, as far as I could tell, ten lords a-leaping. Tom and Cindy were among the people standing watching.

The three-year-old who was staying with them raised her hand and shouted, "Five golden rings!"

I didn't see anyone in hooded black nylon parkas. Many people had already left the party.

I put the cookies on the table next to the popcorn cart. Olivia and Ronald were laughing together while they handed out the last of the popcorn, mostly to adults. I loved matchmaking and hoped that Olivia could enjoy a social life now that she no longer had to act like a mom most of the time, but watching Olivia and Ronald tease each other, I hoped that Olivia wasn't falling for a murderer.

Seconds later, she brought me a bag of popcorn. Although small, the bag was only half full. "Try it. We used up the fire department's salt and didn't have quite enough for the last batch of popcorn, but it's still delicious." She leaned closer and muttered, "What's the worried face about?"

"Do I look worried?"

"Yes, Madam Poker Face."

I tried a bright and perky expression. "Is this better?"

"No. People are going to wonder what's in that popcorn."

"And want more?"

"Too late. Ronald's packing up."

Like all popcorn, Ronald's was impossible to stop eating until it was gone. Meanwhile, he unplugged the popcorn cart, put on his coat, waved a general goodbye, and wheeled the cart outside.

The firefighters weren't going to end up with many leftovers. The buffet table was nearly bare at six thirty when Scott rang an old-fashioned and very loud brass fire bell mounted on the wall beside his office. Everyone in the firehouse became quiet. He announced, "It's time! Join us outside for the lighting of our outdoor tree."

Firefighters directed us around the gleaming red hook and ladder truck parked in front of the fire station. We reassembled on the sidewalk near a huge spruce tree. It was surprisingly mild outside for this time of night in December. It was still below freezing, but not much. In northern Wisconsin, we knew how to dress for the weather.

I ended up standing beside Scott. Ronald was nowhere in sight. Holding hands with the littlest Loyvens boy and another small child, Jocelyn was in the front of the crowd. I turned around. Along with the family staying with them, Tom and Cindy were near the back of the crowd. The little girl was perched on her father's shoulders. Laughing, he moved her mittened hands down to cover his cheeks instead of his eyes. Near them, Olivia waved at me.

"Hey, Emily!"

In her EMT uniform, Samantha sidled up to stand on the other side of me from Scott.

I told her, "You almost missed the tree-lighting."

"I came from a call. The ambulance is around the corner."

"What did you do, turn on the strobes and sirens?"

"No, but confess. You're jealous of those of us who have them on our work vehicles."

"I've always admitted I'm jealous of that. But our Deputy Donut car has a giant donut with flashing lights, and we can broadcast a siren through the speakers if we want to, so I'm not very jealous."

"Isn't that 1950 Ford put away for the winter?"

"Yes, so I'm more jealous now than during nice weather." I looked past her. "Did Corey come with you?"

"I dropped him off at the station."

I lowered my voice so that people around me wouldn't hear my matchmaking in case it didn't work. "He and Olivia sang well together last night. Do you think you could bring or send him to Deputy Donut sometime when you pick up coffee beans? Or you could bring him in for a coffee break, and he and Olivia could get to know each other."

"I could. Also, Brent was in our station last week and mentioned the party in Corey's presence, and he invited Corey, too."

"Perfect."

Samantha had an impish side. She demanded, "Does having good singing voices mean that a couple will live happily ever after?"

"It's a start."

She grinned and pointed at the hook and ladder truck.

To applause and cheering, a fireman climbed the truck's big extension ladder and, with a dramatic flourish, fastened an unlit star to the top of the tree.

Although having watched this tree-lighting ceremony every Christmas of my life except for a couple of winter vacations and the December when I was six and my mother's leg was broken, I couldn't help joining the oohs and aahs of appreciation when the star became gold and all of the lights below it on the tree also started shining.

The fire station's big garage doors rolled down, shutting us and stray breezes out. Multicolored lights reflected on Scott's cheerful face.

I jostled him with an elbow. "You sure know how to get people to leave when the party's over."

He put on a look of fake pain. "I was afraid we'd have no leftovers. I'll bring your platters back to Deputy Donut."

"No rush."

He patted his stomach, which was always flat. "Yes, there will be. I'll have been lacking donuts for much too long."

"You were at Deputy Donut yesterday!"

He grinned down at me. "See? Too long."

I told him goodbye and found Tom and Cindy. "See you tomorrow at work," Tom said.

Cindy was holding the three-year-old's hand. "See you tomorrow at Brent's," she added.

Holding Jocelyn's hand, the youngest Loyvens boy pulled her along the sidewalk. His parents followed with their two older boys.

Olivia and I walked to Wisconsin Street. Although the investigators' tent was nearly as white as the snow, it was a blot on the landscape where Frosty the Donut should have been standing. And where Travis Tarriston should not have died. I wondered again why Travis had left the hospital. He could have stayed safe and warm inside.

We crossed Wisconsin Street and started south, toward Deputy Donut.

A white van was on the other side of the street in front of the Fireplug Pub. Its headlights were off. I might not have noticed it if its engine hadn't been running.

A Fallingbrook Falcons logo was on the driver's door of the van.

Chapter 26

The man in the driver's seat of the white van opened his window and called across the street, "Good night!"

Ronald.

Olivia and I waved and returned the greeting.

Ronald pulled out, headed north, and turned toward the fire station.

I said, "I'm glad he didn't try to hide his identity from us."

"Why would he?"

"He could be stalking me." I knew it sounded ridiculous, but by the time I finished explaining, we were in front of Deputy Donut, and Olivia was also worried.

She grabbed my arm and pointed north. Headlights were coming toward us from near that end of the square. "Is that him? Did he turn around, and now he's coming this way?"

"I don't know."

She pulled me around the corner, out of sight of the vehicle heading down Wisconsin Street toward us. We hurried up the driveway.

Dep met us inside the office with her own unique welcome. We locked the door. Dim lights were on in the dining area. Since we were in the rear of the shop and those Christmas trees were in our front windows, we wouldn't be easily visible from the street. I flicked the desk lamp on. Olivia reminded me that Ronald knew we worked at Deputy Donut and, like everyone else in Fallingbrook, he knew where Deputy Donut was. She suggested, "Maybe we should take Dep and walk home."

"And Ronald could follow at least one of us." I didn't want to stay in Deputy Donut, either. I swooped down on Dep, picked her up, and gave her a hug. "I can't go home now, anyway." I explained why Brent wanted me to wait until he and Misty could meet me at my place.

Olivia burst out laughing. "There's good news—you might be avoiding Paige and Ronald, but it's unlikely that both of them murdered Travis."

"Good point. I feel better already." I was sure that Olivia could tell I was teasing.

She bit her lip. "I hope Ronald isn't a murderer. We've met before and remembered each other. He has a son Hannah's age. Ronald and I attended PTA meetings when Hannah was in grade school. I hadn't seen him in almost ten years. This evening he told me why. His wife left him and took the kid with her, and he hasn't seen the boy in years. Can you imagine?"

"No. Maybe. What was his ex like?"

"I didn't know her, or either of them, well, but she seemed okay."

I said dryly and not entirely seriously, "Maybe she left him because she was afraid he might one day kill someone."

"I hope he's not a killer." She stared out toward the street and drummed her fingers on the desk. Guessing that she was deciding how to word something, I remained quiet. Finally, she spoke. "I have a confession. Brent said I could bring someone to his party. Ronald was kind of hinting that he and I should go out for coffee sometime, and I thought—why not? I know it's about time for me to have a life of my own now that Hannah's in college, and he seemed to want to talk to someone with a kid his son's age. Not that Hannah's my kid, exactly, but she's my sister and I've been a mom to her. Anyway . . ." She made a fake cringing motion, ducking her head between her shoulders and opening her eyes wide in something like apologetic terror. "I invited Ronald to Brent's party. Hannah's not due home until Monday, so I won't be neglecting her."

"She managed the fall term on her own."

Olivia scratched behind Dep's ears. "She probably managed better than I did without her. There's nothing like an eighteen-year-old to keep your feet on the ground and your head out of the clouds."

"Did you tell Ronald that the party was at Brent's place?"

"Yes."

"Did that seem to worry him?"

"Not at all."

"He knows Brent's a detective, so he must not be afraid of Brent's investigations." *But*, I thought, *Ronald could be pretending not to worry.* . . .

"And Misty and Hooligan will be there, too, and Tom's coming later, in case the other three need help subduing Ronald." She lifted her hand from Dep's neck and seemed to study the air above the cat. "He seems harmless."

"You don't sound positive."

"I'm not, especially after what you told me. I don't know why I invited him. We had fun talking and making popcorn, but . . ." She glanced past me toward the street. "Don't look now, but I think that's the Fallingbrook Falcons van passing. Slowly."

Naturally, I looked, but I couldn't tell if the Fallingbrook Falcons logo was on the van. I said in a dry voice, "The way he's driving slowly as if he's looking for someone or something isn't reassuring." I took off my coat and strapped Dep's carrying pouch on. "Did you give Ronald your address?"

"No, and not my phone number, either. I'm still going to

ride to and from the party with Jocelyn and Parker. I'll meet Ronald there. Unless he gets cold feet."

I joked, "He won't if he skis fast enough." More seriously, I suggested, "Maybe you shouldn't walk home right now. He might follow you, and you won't be surrounded by half of Fallingbrook's finest like on Saturday. While I wait for Brent's call, I'm going to take Dep for a tour of the ice festival."

Olivia teased, "Just what she always wanted!"

"Want to come with us?"

Olivia pretended to pull a felting needle into and out of a ball of rovings. "I can't. I need to finish some critters for people to pick up in time for Christmas. I saved the Fallingbrook orders for last." She glanced out the back window. "The parking lot's been cleared nearly as well as the sidewalks out front. I can go partway home through the lots behind the stores. By then, Ronald and his van should be somewhere else."

I tucked Dep into the carrier. "Thanks for the idea. I'll walk north through the parking lots and then cut over to the square and kill time on pathways there. If Ronald is trying to find out what I know about him, he won't see me among the ice sculptures, trees, and people." I shuddered. At best, Ronald was merely enthusiastic about getting to know Olivia better. At worst, he wanted to find and silence me. And Olivia, also, if he thought she knew as much as he feared I knew or guessed. I hoped that knowing me wasn't dangerous to her.

We turned out the desk lamp, went out onto the porch, locked the door, and stood still, listening and watching. Very few vehicles were parked in nearby lots, and I couldn't hear anyone driving through them, either. Olivia headed south. Smiling at the jaunty wreath decorating the door of the garage where our antique Deputy Donut delivery car was settled in for its long winter's nap, I started north. Dep cuddled down into her pouch. Feeling the vibrations of her purring, I patted the front of my parka.

Between the snow and the Christmas lights shining from the backs of buildings, the parking lots were bright, and I could see where I was going as easily as I would have on the sidewalks in front of the stores. The wintry air was refreshing and not very cold. Christmas lights on the rear of Deputy Donut made the loading dock and the door leading into our storage room cheery, and other shops had also decorated their rear entrances. On the other side of the strip of parking lots, festive lights decorated the backs of homes.

I pulled my hood up over my striped stocking cap and dark curls. Ronald probably didn't know that I often carried a cat underneath my parka. He might not recognize me with Dep's added bulge in front.

At the street bordering the north end of the square, I turned toward Wisconsin Street. I walked a half block, and then I needed to cross Wisconsin Street. I stared straight ahead instead of turning my face toward either direction of traffic, but my caution was unnecessary. The Fallingbrook Falcons van didn't go past. I waited until all sounds of traffic were far away, and then I did a quick visual check and crossed the street.

The square was crowded with people admiring the cheerfully lit ice sculptures. I hoped Dep wouldn't poke her head up out of her warm nest and notice that some of the people were walking dogs. I also hoped that the dogs wouldn't sniff the air and realize there was a cat hiding nearby. Their casually held leashes might not restrain them. I inched my parka's zipper higher.

"Emily!"

Beyond a pair of crossed candy canes carved from ice and trimmed with red and white lights forming the traditional stripes, Whitney and Leo Valcriffe stood as arm-in-arm as possible for a gigantic man and a petite woman. They waved their free hands at me. I pushed my hood back and walked through deep snow to them.

Whitney pointed at the top of the sculpture. "Isn't it cute? The crossed canes form a heart in the top."

I'd seen a motif like that only minutes before.

Leo said it aloud. "Fallingbrook Falcons. It's their sculpture."

Whitney brushed long blond hair out of her face. "One of the Fallingbrook Falcons just called us to report that their sculpture was leaning. After staring at it, we can't tell. Do you think it's leaning?"

I squinted at it. "It's hard to be sure since the candy canes were carved at a slant."

Leo suggested, "Let's walk around it."

Looking upward, we tramped a circle in the snow around the sculpture. We all agreed that the sculpture had not tilted from its original position.

Whitney frowned up at its top. "A few minutes before Ronald called, he drove past here. Maybe if he'd been walking, he would have seen these candy canes differently. Besides, he was on the other side of the street. He could have turned around and driven along this side for a closer look, but I don't think he did." Her lovely face became sad. "Maybe after that accident with your sculpture, Emily, people worry about their own sculptures falling down."

"Or being pushed." Leo's voice was gruff.

I tilted my head back to look up at his face. "Do you think that's what happened?"

His ball cap had slipped back. He straightened it. "Hard to tell, but we were out here about the time it must have fallen, and we heard something like a crash and then, maybe, a kind of thump down there near where your sculpture was. It could have been a snowplow, though, just plowing the street. Those blades make a racket. And you know how you can never be sure, but I thought the ground shook. Which, again, could have been because of a snowplow."

Whitney said, "I heard the noise but didn't notice the ground shaking. I'd just arrived. Leo was still putting the finishing touches on the lighting on this sculpture at two in the morning." She reached up and gave Leo's cheek a fond pat. "Knowing him, I figured he'd work all night until he got it exactly the way he wanted it, no matter how cold he got, so I hopped into my truck and brought him some hot soup." She turned to me. "Leo was working by the headlights of his pickup truck, so he was easy to find. Not that he can ever exactly hide anywhere. He's bigger than most of the ice sculptures, not to mention the trees around here."

He slapped a hand against the chest pocket of his coat. "Only my heart, babe, only my heart."

Planted in Fallingbrook's early days, the trees were about a hundred feet tall. And although Leo resembled a mountain, most of the sculptures were taller than he was.

Smiling at the couple's affectionate teasing, I asked, "Did you see any snowplows around the time you heard the crashing noise, or any other vehicles?"

Leo prodded at snow with his boot. "A pickup truck stopped beside me for a second, but when Whitney arrived, he drove on and parked near Frisky Pomegranate. I couldn't see well, but I think he got out of his truck and went in there. Two other pickup trucks were also parked near Frisky Pomegranate, though it's closed at that time of night. I can't say that I noticed any other vehicles right about then. Did you, Whitney?"

She shook her head. "Only those three trucks. Plus, I didn't stay long. I told the police that the bang we heard was about two fifteen. I went home shortly afterward."

Leo's gaze down at me was direct and seemingly innocent. "Snowplows went around the square several times while I was out here that night, and there were other trucks out, but not many cars. And snowmobiles were zipping everywhere. I was afraid some of them would roar through here and not see a sculpture or even a tree. I didn't notice any of them driving through the square, though, not up here." He pointed south. "But they could have been going through that end of the square. Such a pity that your sculpture was ruined."

Whitney reminded him, "And that a man died."

He lifted a shoulder. "That goes without saying. It's too bad he decided to come back here after all these years." Leo didn't sound very broken up about it.

Biting her lip, Whitney looked off toward the south end of the square and didn't reply.

Dep stuck her head up and meowed.

Whitney jumped and laughed. "You brought your cat! How cute. She startled me, though."

I rubbed the top of Dep's head with the thumb of one mitten. "I think she's reminding me that it's her dinnertime. She had dry kibble available all day at Deputy Donut." I wrinkled my nose. "She likes something fishy and more pungent at this time of night." I told Leo and Whitney goodbye and sauntered farther east along the north end of the square. Dep wriggled her head down into the carrier again. The sociable cat would probably pop her head up again if I stopped to talk to anyone else.

Instead of admiring the sculptures I was passing on the right, I was thinking about Whitney and Leo. Like Scott, Leo had noticed snowplows and snowmobiles near the square in the wee hours Thursday morning. Whitney and Leo had also heard a crashing noise and also maybe a thump that could have shaken the ground. I still thought that Dustin Loyvens, on a stolen snowmobile, was the most likely one to have pushed Frosty the Donut onto Travis, but if Ronald had torn that page out of the yearbook, he and his snowplow were right up there near the top of my suspect list.

Whitney and Leo were at the bottom. Paige was right above them.

I reminded myself that Whitney and Leo could have lied to give each other alibis. One or both of them could have killed Travis. I couldn't picture them being so evil, though.

Frisky Pomegranate was on my left. The last I knew, the Jolly Cops Cleaning Crew cleaned Frisky Pomegranate late at night or early in the morning after they finished at Deputy Donut.

Maybe the pickup trucks that Leo and Whitney saw belonged to the Jolly Cops.

Chapter 27

✖

I turned away from Frisky Pomegranate and followed a cleared path through the middle of the square. Colorfully lit ice sculptures loomed over me. I stopped beside a huge Santa on a throne. Shouting names of toys and games, snow-suited kids climbed ice steps and sat on Santa's lap. I checked my phone in case I'd missed Brent's call. I hadn't.

I phoned the Jolly Cops Cleaning Crew. Expecting to leave a message, I was surprised when a person answered.

"Jolly Cops," he sang out. "Hi, Emily!" Of course he had call recognition. I was at a disadvantage, though, because I didn't know which man he was. We were never in Deputy Donut at the same time, and I'd never talked to them on the phone enough to know their voices. I must have waited too long to speak. Sounding a little less cheerful, this one asked, "Is anything wrong?"

"No, not at all. I was wondering if any of you were around Frisky Pomegranate early Thursday morning, and if you saw anyone in the square at that time."

"Your ice sculpture is—or I should say was—at the other end of the square." Trust a retired policeman to know every detail that was public, and probably a few others, besides.

"Yes, but the vandal might have come from the north or

driven north after he rammed the sculpture." I didn't sound particularly sure of myself.

He chuckled. "Why do I get the impression that you're looking into a murder more than into an act of vandalism?"

"Because of my history?" I suggested. "But, you know, the killing might not have been deliberate. However, unless someone inadvertently slid off the road, the vandalism probably was deliberate." I knew it wasn't a good answer. The Jolly Cops were friends of Tom's. In a second, this one, whoever he was, would tell me to leave the investigating to the police. . . .

He didn't. Turning serious, he described what he'd seen that night. "I was driving from your place to Frisky Pomegranate a little after two. The snow was so heavy, I could barely see a thing, but there were bright lights near the northwest corner of the square. Being an ex-cop, I had to stop and see what was going on. The man doing the electricity for the Ice and Lights Festival was working by the light of his headlights. Then another pickup truck arrived, and a woman—I think it was his wife—handed him something like one of those insulated stainless steel water bottles. I went on to Frisky Pomegranate."

"Did you hear anything, like maybe someone crashing into Deputy Donut's ice sculpture?"

"No, but I might have been inside my truck with the engine running, or maybe I was already inside Frisky Pomegranate when that happened. Besides, my hearing isn't as good as it once was." He volunteered, "I went out on the patio around three thirty. Snow was really coming down, but I still saw the blur of headlights about where I'd seen those two pickups. When I left Frisky Pomegranate around four, the electrician was gone, and so were the trucks that had been near where he'd been working."

"Do you remember how many pickups you guys had at the site?"

"Three. Two of the guys usually carpool. Truck pool."

I thanked him for his help and immediately received the warning I'd been expecting all along. "Stay out of trouble, Emily. Leave the investigation to the experts."

"Right." It wasn't exactly a promise. We disconnected, and I checked again. Brent hadn't called.

Wondering if the stainless steel insulated bottle that Whitney gave Leo that night ended up in my garbage, I walked down one of the square's diagonal paths and up the other. Deciding it was more likely that Paige had discarded Travis's water bottle, I took side paths and admired every sculpture. I stayed away from the yellow police tape and investigators' tent on the corner where Frosty the Donut had been.

Close to the police station, I considered going in and asking for Brent or Misty, but I knew they would call me when they were ready. I crossed the street to avoid the investigators' tent. None of the fire trucks were parked outside the fire station, and the huge spruce glowed with its strings of lights and its big gold star. Windows near the tops of the rolled-down garage doors showed the tops of trucks. I caught a glimpse of the feathery angel at the top of the tree inside.

Around the corner, singing and laughter spilled from the Fireplug Pub. Maybe if Dep hadn't been with me, I would have joined the crowd in the pub while I waited for Brent to tell me it was safe to go home. Instead, I crossed Wisconsin Street. Deputy Donut was still only dimly lit inside. I walked up the driveway and tried the back door. It was locked.

Dep poked her head up. "Mew?"

I agreed. "We could wait in here, but let's keep going toward home. We can tour the neighborhood, looking at Christmas decorations, until Brent calls."

I returned to the parking lot. Dep scrunched herself into her cozy nest inside my coat.

As Olivia had said she would, I walked south through the parking lots instead of along the street. Not because I was afraid that Ronald might return, I told Dep, but for something different to do.

She didn't answer.

The backs of the stores to the south of Deputy Donut were also cheerful with lights, evergreens, wreaths, and garlands. The parking lots ended. I turned west, and then south again at the next street. I took my time, enjoying the season—the snow, the lights, the decorated trees and shrubs, the inflated Santas clinging to chimneys, the tang of woodsmoke. I thought I could also detect the aroma of freshly baked cookies. In one house where drapes had not been drawn, little kids sang along to a piano being played by a teenager. At my street, I turned west again. I was only a few blocks from home, and I still hadn't heard from Brent or Misty.

I found a way to delay. The woman who had turned out not to be Paige's snow angel, the woman I again thought of as the pruning shears lady, was brushing snow off her walks with a broom. I stopped and said hello. Dep wiggled her head out of her carrier and also greeted the woman.

She rested her broom against her hedge, took off a glove, and rubbed Dep's chin. Looking from Dep's upturned face to mine, she said, "I might know who could have taken in your houseguest during the worst of that blizzard. The man across the street knows just about everything that goes on around here. He didn't look outside early Thursday morning during the blizzard, but he reminded me that there's a spindly— that's what he said, 'a spindly'—white-haired woman in the next block, closer to your house. Some people get us confused." Grinning, she shook her head. "Not him, he's too observant. 'Spindly!' I hadn't thought of her when I talked to that handsome detective and to you, but I know which house is hers. I walked up there to find her address." She pulled a slip of paper from her coat pocket. "I wrote it down for you. Here."

Thanking her, I glanced at the number and shoved the

paper into my own pocket. "Have you been out here waiting for me?"

She shook her head. "No, but I was keeping an eye out in case you came along. I went on to your place and rang the doorbell, but no one answered, so I came back here to sweep the snow and watch for you."

"When were you at my house?" I hadn't meant my question to sound sharp.

"About a half hour ago, give or take."

"Maybe my houseguest doesn't like to answer the door." That was probably it. Paige wouldn't be thrilled about talking to someone she didn't know, and she might not have mistaken the pruning shears lady for the real snow angel, if the real snow angel existed. Also, Paige definitely didn't want to talk to people who had been on the tour with her and Travis. Or maybe she'd been sleeping.

The pruning shears lady had a different guess. "Maybe she went to the tree-decorating and lighting party at the fire station. I used to go to that. But after all those years, I can imagine it and don't have to walk all that way. I could drive, I suppose, but you can't count on that in this weather, and besides, I always used to walk. Seems like I should continue to, if I wanted to go at all, that is."

"Have you been to the Ice and Lights Festival?"

"No, and I hope to before they take it down or it melts. It's supposed to stay about this temperature until after Christmas. Which could mean more snow."

I wondered if she would think I was too pushy if I offered to drive her to the festival, but before I could say anything, my phone rang. Brent.

Still thinking that taking her to the festival might be a good idea and fun besides, I told her goodbye and started up the street.

"I'll be at your place in five minutes," Brent said.

"Perfect. I'm on foot about five minutes away." Actually, I

was closer, but I was including a couple of minutes to talk to the woman I hoped would turn out to be the snow angel.

It took less time than that. The house was dark inside, and no one came to the door. There was, I noticed, a wreath on the dark blue door.

I dawdled along the last block and arrived at my front walk as Brent's personal SUV pulled up beside it. No one was in the passenger seat.

Brent got out, came around the car, pulled me close in a quick hug, and told me, "Misty can't make it, but I have her key, so if you wouldn't mind, you can help me settle Paige in at Misty's."

"Sure." I led the way up onto the porch. Unlike the night before, Paige hadn't turned on the porch light or the Christmas tree lights. The house was completely dark.

I turned the key in the lock. It opened too easily. I turned toward Brent. "The dead bolt wasn't locked." He looked as troubled as I felt. I opened the door and called out, "Paige?"

No one answered.

Chapter 28

✣

I called more loudly, "Paige?"

Still no answer.

Brent touched my arm. "Stay outside. I'll check around before you come in."

I turned my face up toward him. I probably looked scared. He squeezed my wrist, parka sleeve and all. "Want to wait in my car?"

"I'm okay."

Dep stuck her head out. "Mew?" Her feet scrambled inside my coat.

I gave Brent a shaky grin. "Maybe I'd better keep moving so Dep won't think it's time for her to get out and run around. I'll be nearby."

"I'll come get you." He went into the house and turned on the light. The mistletoe's shadow danced. Brent closed the door.

My skis, poles, and both snow shovels were on the porch. I eased down the front steps and walked along the pathway that Paige had shoveled to the driveway. I peered into my SUV. No one was inside, but being close to the car made Dep squirm again. I murmured, "It's okay, Dep, we're not getting in."

My outdoor lights in back went on. Brent had made it to the sunroom.

I turned and stared at the trash cans beside the house. They looked like they had early that morning after Brent had removed the bags and I'd replaced the lids. I turned on my phone's flashlight, lifted one lid, and shined the light around inside the can.

Empty.

I closed that lid and opened the other one. Nothing was inside it, either. A light went on in the small basement window beyond the trash cans.

Biting my lip, I gazed around my side yard, driveway, and front yard. No one could have crawled underneath the porch. The crisscrossed lattice underneath it was intact.

Hugging Dep inside my coat, I backtracked to Brent's car and leaned on it. The lights on the first floor were on. Peeking between the branches of the dark Christmas tree in my front window, I could see through the living room, dining room, and kitchen to a smidgen of the sunroom. Upstairs, a light came on in the guest room. A minute later, light shined down from the bathroom window at the side of the house above the trash cans.

Breathing shallowly as if I needed to be silent, I approached my front steps.

The porch light blazed, and the front door opened. Brent was still wearing his coat. "She's not here," he said. He held the door open for me and closed it after Dep and I were inside.

I kicked off my boots and automatically switched on the tree lights. The living room glowed with holiday hues. I realized that my rush to turn on the tree lights might have looked like desperation to get out from underneath the mistletoe. Not that either of us had probably been thinking about mistletoe. I asked, "Do you have any idea where she is?"

"She left a note. It's on the bed in your guest room."

I unzipped my parka and let Dep out. She streaked toward the back of the house. I ran upstairs.

The survival blanket was, not surprisingly, gone from the guest room bed, and a note was squared neatly on my grandmother's quilt. My house key was on the note, but I didn't have to move the key or touch the note to read it. *Thank you for everything. Someone's picking me up. Paige.*

Brent had come upstairs, also. I twisted around to look over my shoulder at him. "'Someone,'" I repeated. "She doesn't give us a clue about who, does she? Or where she was going. Detective Gartborg told her to let you folks know when she got home."

"Maybe Paige sent us a message, too, or she will after she arrives. Last I knew, we hadn't received one."

"Could someone have kidnapped her?"

His lips thinned to a grim line. "Let's hope not."

I heard the *thumpety, thump, thump* of kitty feet pounding up the stairs. Dep stood in the doorway. "Meow!"

"Oops," I said. "It's past her dinnertime." I trotted downstairs to the landing and opened the closet door. Dep and Brent followed me. Dep went on toward the kitchen. I reached into my pocket and pulled out the address that the pruning shears lady had given me. Explaining, I handed it to Brent.

"I'll go talk to her."

"No one answered her door a few minutes ago. Have you eaten? I ate only a teensy bag of popcorn at the tree-decorating party."

"I had a sandwich at lunchtime."

"Then you might as well have dinner here while you wait for the woman to return home."

"Glad to." He hung up both of our coats, and I put Dep's carrying pouch on its hook.

In the kitchen, I fed Dep while Brent phoned Misty and told her she didn't need to prepare for a houseguest. He pocketed his phone. "Misty's still on duty, so it works out."

I pulled a package out of the freezer. "Carrot and ginger

soup to start? And then . . . here are some chicken wings, already seasoned and baked. We just have to heat them and then broil them in sauce. And we can have ice cream and cookies for dessert."

"Sounds great. Want me to start heating the soup?"

"Sure. And Brent, some strange things happened today. I wasn't going to tell you about the first one, but then there was a string of them, and they might go together."

He knew where the saucepans were and got one out. "Tell me."

I turned on the oven. While I told him everything that Ronald Eamberton had done that made me wonder if he'd had a hand in Travis's death, we started heating the soup and the wings. Brent opened a beer for each of us and peeled carrots and cut celery and carrot sticks. I crumbled blue cheese into yogurt for a dip, and then I mixed butter, vinegar, garlic, salt, Worcestershire sauce, smoked paprika, and my home-made hot paste for the sauce for the wings. Setting two places on the granite-topped kitchen counter, I ended the tale with, "And now that Olivia has become reacquainted with Ronald, she invited him to your party. They seemed to hit it off, but I have a feeling he's more interested than she is. She told me his wife left him and took their son."

Stirring the soup, Brent was silent for a few seconds. "I don't know him well, but he does seem emotionally vulnerable. I hope she won't hurt him."

"And I hope he won't hurt her! Physically."

"At the party, the rest of us might have more control over physical than emotional harm. Despite the way Ronald spoke Travis's name when he saw him on the bus Wednesday night, we haven't seriously considered him as a suspect. I'll check into what he was doing that night and whether the snowplow he was driving could have made those dents in your ice sculpture's base. And we'll keep Olivia safe at my party, one way or another."

"Thank you, and thank you for including her. I don't think she has many friends."

"I got that impression. Besides, I couldn't have invited everyone who works at Deputy Donut except her."

"Is Frosty the Donut's base, that block of ice with the dents, in a freezer somewhere?"

"Investigators took photos, measured, and made prints of the dents."

I put the hot sauce on to heat and stood beside Brent at the stove, both of us stirring. "I know you want to suspect Paige, Brent, especially now that she seems to have fled, but don't forget Dustin Loyvens. I still think it's more believable that he stole the snowmobile than that Paige did."

"He did steal it," Brent said in a genial voice. "He admitted it."

I lifted my whisk for a second. "He . . . what? And you haven't arrested him?"

Brent ladled soup into bowls. "He's been charged with the theft, but not with murder."

I sputtered more than my simmering sauce was about to. "Why not?" I removed the pan from the heat.

"Can you think of a good solid reason why I would say that?"

I had to be stubborn. "No." Then I thought about it. "Wait. Someone gave him an alibi."

"Haven't I always said you'd make a good detective?"

"You gave me a decent clue with the word 'solid.' It often goes with 'alibi.' "

He laughed.

I demanded, "Who gave him the alibi? His wife? Are we supposed to believe she was riding around behind him on a snowmobile in the middle of the night while her three boys were sleeping in a house belonging to people that the Loyvens didn't really know?" I eased onto a stool and patted the one beside me. "Have a seat."

He sat. "We're not supposed to believe that at all."

I should have moved the stools farther apart. Spooning up my soup without bumping his elbow wasn't easy. I again demanded, "Who gave him an alibi?"

"I'm not at liberty to say."

"But you're sure the person is trustworthy."

"I am. We are."

"I'm not sure it makes sense."

"The soup's delicious."

"You're changing the subject." I got up, took the wings out of the oven, and turned on the broiler. While I coated the wings in the sauce and put them back on the wire rack on the baking tray, I thought about what Brent had said. Finally, sliding the tray of wings back into the oven, I remembered Dustin Loyvens's anger when he was on the bus, and the way the entire bus had reeked of what I now suspected was bourbon. I went back to my stool, toed it farther from Brent's, and suggested, "Could Dustin have needed to go to an AA meeting or talk to another member of AA?"

Brent repeated, "I can't tell you, but leave it, okay? And don't tell anyone else what I've told you or your guesses about it. He's entitled to privacy. And he didn't murder Travis or anyone else."

"Okay. But of the people I know about, that leaves Ronald Eamberton and Whitney and Leo Valcriffe."

Brent put our soup bowls into the dishwasher. "And Paige."

I turned the wings over and put them underneath the broiler again. I conceded, "And she's missing." I told him about my discussion with Whitney and Leo. "One of the Jolly Cops saw them at the north end of the square around the time they claimed to hear a thump. They're a sweet couple, but I suppose they could be lying for each other."

Brent closed the dishwasher, leaned back against it, and

folded his arms. "Have you, by any chance, been asking too many questions?"

"I didn't ask Ronald any. I only heard paper tear and saw him drop and then pick up something that could have been a page out of a yearbook. And he saw me in the library, which must have been enough to make him want to follow me into Scott's office, where, unfortunately, I was snooping through one of Scott's yearbooks. And I didn't ask Whitney and Leo questions that would have made them think I suspect them, which I don't, even though they were seen with an insulated stainless steel bottle. I'm not afraid of asking any of the Jolly Cops questions." I pulled the pan of steaming and mouth-watering wings from the oven. "Unless they tell Tom I've been snooping around."

I held the serving bowl while Brent piled the wings into it. "Are you more afraid of Tom than you are of me?" I didn't have to look up at him to know he was smiling.

I put the bowl of wings on the counter in front of our plates and marched to my seat. "I'm not afraid of either one of you."

Brent muttered something like, "You should be."

I didn't ask him to repeat it.

The wings, beer, celery, and carrots kept us from talking for a while.

After we ate more ice cream and cookies than either of us felt was absolutely necessary, Brent asked if I minded checking the house to see if Paige had left anything behind or had perhaps taken something with her.

Dep woke up from her after-dinner nap and made the tour with us. The only things that Paige had left behind were the note and my key. She seemed to have taken her own garbage, if she'd had any.

At first, I couldn't find the cute little brown pottery pitcher and matching tumbler that I'd given her to keep on the night table beside the pull-out couch. It turned out that she had put it away, and her guess about where it belonged had been off by one cabinet.

Brent asked, "How did she contact someone to pick her up if her phone was broken? You don't have a landline. Could she have gone out and bought a new phone?"

"Perhaps, or maybe the woman whose address I gave you really did help her, and she went back to the woman and asked to use her phone."

"Or the woman is the 'someone' who picked her up? Maybe she's driving her home."

"Maybe they're both inside the woman's house with the lights out, and they're not answering the door."

Brent's expression darkened. "Let's hope not. I don't want to . . ." He didn't finish the sentence, but he didn't have to.

I pointed toward the ceiling. "I gave Paige access to my computer. Maybe she emailed someone."

"May I have a look?"

"Sure."

In the guest room, I logged on as a guest to my computer the way I'd shown Paige.

If she'd used the computer, she'd erased the history.

Brent put the note she'd written into an evidence envelope. He checked his watch. "I should go. If the snow angel doesn't answer, I'll look up her name and number and give her a call, maybe tomorrow, since it's getting late. And we'll check to see if Paige made it to the address she gave us. Meanwhile, in case Ronald Eamberton is stalking you, or Paige comes back, please stay inside until you have to go out in the morning, okay? And don't open the door without checking first. And don't let Paige in, even if she's cold. Call me or 911."

Promising that I would do everything he asked, I took his coat out of the closet and handed it to him.

Dep beat us to the front door. I picked her up, and Brent

put his arms around both of us in a bear hug. "Stay safe, both of you."

"You, too," I said into his coat.

"Call if you need us."

"Okay." My voice was still muffled in the warm wool of his coat. Too aware of that mistletoe dangling above our heads, I didn't look up.

He let me go. "See you tomorrow at my place." He opened the door and went out.

With Dep still in my arms, I locked the door.

Later, upstairs in my bedroom, I stared down at my wedding ring. Maybe it was time to take it off and put it away. My memories of Alec would always be special whether I was wearing the ring or not.

Then I remembered how I'd hoped that Ronald Eamberton would notice my ring and lose interest in possibly flirting with me. That was obviously not his intention now, if it ever had been. Still, I had depended on that ring for years to shield me from unwanted attention, and I would feel vulnerable without it. I curled my fingers into my palm. That ring would stay on, at least a little while longer.

Chapter 29

✻

The next morning, ducking his head as if the doorway were too low for him, Ronald Eamberton came into Deputy Donut.

Maybe he'd hoped to talk to Olivia, but she was putting the finishing touches on raised donuts filled with orange cream, frosted with fudge, and topped with tiny gold sugar stars and curling slivers of candied orange peel.

Ronald chose a small table beside the shop's outer wall and sat facing our decorated windows. I walked around other tables to him. "Merry Christmas, Ronald! What can I get you?"

He looked up at me. His eyes were wary. "I promised I'd come try your donuts." He blushed.

I couldn't help contrasting my earlier impressions of him with the way he was acting in Deputy Donut. He'd seemed decisive when he came into the bus and asked if he could do anything to help, and he hadn't been afraid to challenge Travis about returning to Fallingbrook. If he had been the one to tear the page out of the yearbook in the library, he'd been determined then, too. When he'd arrived with the popcorn cart in the fire hall, he'd seemed entirely capable. It was after that, after he'd confirmed seeing me in the library, that his personality seemed to change. He'd begun acting tentative and unsure. He claimed he'd mistaken Scott's office for the kitchen. Was he really that unobservant? And now, he was blushing and fumbling for words like a lovesick teenager. Was he putting on an act in order to appear incapable of murder?

Maybe I had to give him the benefit of the doubt. The night before, Olivia had invited him to Brent's party. He had braved coming to Deputy Donut, but he could have been hit with a bout of shyness at the thought of encountering her.

I rattled off a list of donuts and coffees. He chose the final ones I'd mentioned—old-fashioned donuts with bits of candy cane in and on them, and a mug of the day's special coffee, a Central American blend flavored with chocolate and hazelnuts.

I was about to turn around and head for the kitchen when he asked, "Do you work here full time?" He ran his words together.

"Yes."

"So, what'd you do yesterday, go to the library on your lunch break?"

"Yes."

"Do you do that often?"

"No, but sometimes it's noisy in here. The library is usually quiet. *Except for the sound of tearing paper . . .* "Do you go there often?" I tried to sound like someone merely making small talk.

"Yeah." He looked out toward the street he had probably plowed hundreds of times. "For the same reason. It's quieter than driving noisy trucks. What do you usually do when you go to the library?"

His questions were becoming pointed, but I needed to look like I didn't suspect him of anything other than maybe being interested in Olivia.

But how?

If he'd heard me ask Irma where the yearbooks were, he already had a clue about why I'd gone to the library.

The longer I paused before answering his question, the worse I would look. I darted a glance toward the office.

From the back of the couch, Dep stared through the window at me, and it was like she was silently dictating a plausible story. I tried my spur-of-the-moment fabrication on Ronald. "Whenever I think of something I would like to learn more about, I write it on a slip of paper and put it in a jar back there in our office. Before I go to the library, I pull out a slip of paper, and that's how I decide what to look for in the library. You?"

"Wow." I couldn't tell if he was amazed because he believed my story or because he didn't. He shook his massive head. "I'm not that organized. I just go in and look around until I find something I want to look at or read. Are you going there today?"

"No. I'm taking the afternoon off to go to Brent's party. I hear you're going, too."

"I haven't skied in years, but yeah."

"Brent groomed his trails for the classic kind of cross-country skiing, not skate-skiing, but if you prefer skate-skiing, the trails are probably wide enough."

He looked relieved. "I learned the old-fashioned way."

Olivia came to the table. "Hey, Ronald!" She gave him a shy smile, a mug of coffee, and one of the fudge-covered orange-cream–filled donuts she'd been decorating. She must have noticed the surprise on my face. She explained, "Ronald told me last night he was going to come in and he'd want coffee, but he'd never be able to make up his mind about a donut, so I should choose for him." She asked him, "What do you think?"

Blushing, he bit into it. "Best one I ever had."

I gave him a big smile and checked on other diners.

Olivia stayed at Ronald's table, chatting and laughing with him until he finished his coffee and donut and lumbered outside, and then she returned to decorating donuts.

I asked her, "Did you see Ronald's van again while you were walking home last night?"

"No, and I was watching and listening for it. Did you?"

"I'm sure he didn't follow me home."

Olivia looked past the half wall toward the front door and went still for a second. "Uh-oh. Is that who I think it is?"

I followed her gaze. "It's Travis Tarriston's mother. I'll go."

Travis's mother's eyes and hair were, if anything, redder and wilder than they'd been the first time she'd visited Deputy Donut.

She perched on the edge of the seat that Ronald had vacated only minutes earlier. Before I had a chance to ask what she would like, she rasped out in a hoarse stage whisper, "Call the cops! I just saw my son's murderer."

I pulled my phone out of my pocket. "Who was it?"

"I forget his name."

A man? The last time she'd been in Deputy Donut, she had said that Whitney Valcriffe had killed her son.

I tapped Brent's personal number. "Where did you see him?"

She pointed south. "Out there. On the street."

Brent answered, but instead of greeting him, I asked Mrs. Tarriston, "How do you know he killed your son?"

Brent's voice was quiet. "Em, are you in Deputy Donut?"

"Yes. A woman here wants to talk to you."

Travis's mother started out of her seat. "I have to go."

"I'll be right there," Brent said.

I quickly pocketed my phone. "Wait, Mrs. Tarriston. How do you know that the man you just saw out on the street killed your son?"

"I recognized him from when Travis was in high school.

He beat Travis up but didn't kill him that time. He beat Travis so badly that Travis didn't play as well, even the next year, and almost didn't get his football scholarship. That other kid, Don or Ron or something, I don't know, wanted the scholarship for himself. But my boy won it, fair and square. And now he's gone. I'm going to sue."

"The last time we talked, you thought Travis's old girlfriend had killed him."

Travis's mother thrust the handles of a bright yellow purse over her arm. "Well, now we know better, don't we? Maybe they worked together, I don't know. But they're not going to get away with this. They're going to owe me, big time."

"Tell the police about them. Do you know where the police station is?"

She eyed me with something like fear, but her answer was scornful. "Why would I know a thing like that?" She ran out to the sidewalk and headed south, away from the police station.

I didn't take time to get my coat. I followed her outside. Mrs. Tarriston was already a half block away.

In the other direction, near the investigators' tent, an unmarked police cruiser turned toward me. Wrapping my arms around myself, I waited. Brent pulled up beside me and opened the passenger window. I bent to speak to him. "She's about two blocks south on Wisconsin Street. She's wearing a blue coat. She has a yellow purse and ruby-red hair that's sticking up in all directions."

He thanked me and pulled away from the curb.

I looked south again. Mrs. Tarriston had disappeared, either into a store, around a corner, or into a car.

Shivering, I went inside. I hoped that chasing Mrs. Tarriston or any murder suspects she sent him after wouldn't force Brent to cancel his party.

About a half hour later, Tom was frying donuts, Jocelyn

was teasing customers, and Olivia and I were decorating old-fashioned cinnamon-scented donuts containing sweetened, dried cranberries and mini white chocolate chips. I spread white chocolate frosting on the donuts, and Olivia placed dried cranberries on the frosting.

Brent came in through the front door. He caught my eye and glanced toward the office.

"I'll be back," I told Tom and Olivia.

Chapter 30

✻

I let Brent into the office. Dep trotted down from her cat-walks and meowed up at him until he picked her up. "I didn't find Mrs. Tarriston," he told me over Dep's head. "What did she have to say?"

"She'd seen a man outside. From what she said about him and a football scholarship, I'm pretty sure it was Ronald Eamberton. He had just left." I gestured vaguely toward the table where they'd both sat, though at different times. "Seeing him brought back these football-related memories along with the certainty that Ronald had killed Travis. She threatened to sue Ronald." I told Brent everything that Mrs. Tarriston had said, including that Ronald might have worked with Leo and Whitney to kill Travis.

"Has Ronald been in here other times, before this morning?"

"I've never seen him in here, and yesterday he said he'd been meaning to come in, so I think this was his first visit to Deputy Donut. I'm sure he mostly wanted to see Olivia, but he asked me questions about the library. I guessed he was trying to find out how much I might know about his vandalizing the yearbook. If he did it."

"He could have. Thanks to you, we searched for that page in trash deposited in receptacles near the library and located the torn-out page late last night. I'll talk to him before my party this afternoon. Meanwhile, I have other news for you. I went to the home of the potential snow angel who wasn't home last evening. The woman corroborated Paige's story. The snow angel gets up at one thirty every morning to take a pill. Without fail." He imitated a stern, proud face and then winked at me and added, "She even showed me how she'd set the alarm on her phone. That morning after she swallowed the pill and drank a full glass of water, she saw a heap of something in the snow out on the sidewalk. Realizing it was a person, she threw on a pair of boots, ran outside, and helped Paige into her home. She described Paige perfectly and remembered Paige's first name. She gave Paige a cup of hot chocolate and talked to her until she felt that Paige was warm enough to ski—in the street—to your place. The snow angel is very precise. She checked the time. It was six minutes until three. She said that Paige seemed traumatized by a bus crash and was worried about her boyfriend. The woman urged her to go back where she was staying and wait until daylight before trying to visit someone in the hospital who would probably be asleep." Brent's face saddened with empathy similar to what I was feeling. When Paige left the snow angel's house, Travis was probably already dead.

I repeated what I'd told Brent Thursday morning. "I heard Paige leave about one thirty and return around three. So, based on what the snow angel said, Paige did not have time to ski to the square, push that ice sculpture over, and ski back, before or after she visited the woman."

"She certainly didn't."

"Is there a possibility that Paige went knocking on doors later, like Thursday or yesterday before she left, until she found someone who fit the description she'd given us, and then told the woman what to say?"

"It would be very slight. Remember Paige telling us about the yellow kitchen with daisies on the wallpaper?"

"Yes. Was that—"

"It was. I doubt that, after Paige described that kitchen to us, she went knocking on doors of houses that matched the way she'd described the outside of the house until she found a tall white-haired lady and then went inside hunting for a yellow kitchen with a yellow ceiling and daisies on the wallpaper."

"That would be hard to believe. So, my judgment of Paige's character wasn't too far off."

He said, straight-faced, "They might have been sunflowers, not daisies."

I batted at his arm. "Yes, Detective. Now you've eliminated every suspect I know about, except Ronald, Whitney, and Leo. And they're coming to your party."

"There could be others." He rolled his shoulders as if to work out kinks. "But I'm going to follow up on Ronald, trade in the cruiser for my own car, and go home. I have some cross-country ski trails to groom before the rest of you get there."

"The party's still on?"

"Definitely. Kim's boys made it safely to the Cares Away Resort last night, so they're all coming."

"With the dog? Ivan?"

He grinned. In August, both of us had fallen rather hard for that half-grown puppy. "With Ivan."

"Good." I added in a phonily warning tone, "He'll be bigger."

"I understand that he's still, um, energetic."

"Good," I said again.

Brent set Dep on the couch. "See you there." He checked his watch. "In about three hours."

I reminded myself that I shouldn't read too much into Brent's having invited the glamorous detective and her sons and dog to his party. They were spending the weekend nearby. Besides, Brent had invited Whitney and Leo although

he barely knew them. It was only natural for him to have invited the Gartborgs. If they'd brought skis, they would probably love Brent's property. I hadn't met the twins, but I
looked forward to becoming reacquainted with the delight-
fully bumptious Ivan.

Shortly after noon, customers picked up the last orders of
party-sized Christmas trees we'd created from stacked
donuts. Christmas was only a week away, and Tom was certain he wouldn't need help beginning the next day's orders
and waiting on customers by himself the rest of the afternoon. "You three should go to Brent's now so you can ski
before dark," he urged. "Cindy and I will be along later.
Bringing donuts."

Olivia, Jocelyn, and I bundled up, and I tucked Dep into
her carrier inside my coat. In a holiday mood and nearly
dancing in our exuberance, we headed down Wisconsin
Street. At my street, Jocelyn told Olivia, "Parker and I will
pick you and your skis up in about twenty minutes."

Olivia continued south, and Jocelyn and I walked west until
Jocelyn dashed down the street that connected with her street.
At home, I made certain that Dep had everything she needed
until I returned. "It might be quite late," I informed her.

She continued nibbling at her fishy lunch.

I changed out of my work clothes and into a pair of slinky,
midnight-blue stretch velvet leggings and a matching lace-
trimmed tank top that I would wear, along with a pair of ballet flats, for the après-ski party. I layered a big cotton shirt
and comfy sweater over the tank top and pulled on a pair of
wool socks. My lightweight ski pants and jacket went over it
all, and I packed leather-palmed gloves, my stocking cap
with its Christmasy stripes, a red scarf, and a warm parka
into the car along with my skis, ski boots, and poles. It was
sunny, so I put my goggles in the front seat to wear as sun-
glasses on the drive.

At the last minute, I went back inside.

Dep met me at the door. "Mew?"

"I have one more thing I need to do."

She accompanied me upstairs. I appreciated her company as I slowly removed my wedding ring, kissed it, nestled it into my jewelry box, and shut the lid.

Chapter 31

My finger felt naked, and looked it, too, with the slight indentation where that ring had been.

With a sigh, I turned around and left the bedroom.

Running down the stairs behind Dep, I told her, "Don't worry about Detective Gartborg. If things work out the way I plan, you might see more of Brent in the future."

She stopped at the landing, sat down, and blinked at me. "Meow." Approval? Probably not, considering that I was obviously going somewhere without her.

Since I was alone, I sang Christmas songs as I drove along roads that were now almost bare but heaped with snow on both sides. I didn't understand how my parents and other people could spend Christmas in warm climates. The snowier, the better, I thought, singing off-key about white Christmases and blue Christmases and winter wonderlands.

I parked behind the last car in the lineup along the right side of Brent's driveway, got out, and was greeted by a flurry of barking and a whirlwind with big black splotches on his mostly white body and an adorable black head with a lopsided white streak up the middle.

"Ivan!" A pair of teenage boys ran toward us from near Brent's house.

Now huge, Ivan had gained a few manners since I'd met him in August. He didn't jump on me, but he danced, twirled in circles, and wagged his magnificent white plume of a tail. I sank down to my knees and let him give me a proper and very slobbery greeting, which necessitated the removal of my goggles so I wouldn't have to clean them before skiing. "You remember me!" I said. "Either that, or you love everyone."

"Both," one of the boys said above me. "He likes people, but he doesn't greet everyone like that. He's probably hoping for another adventure like the one we heard he had with you."

I rubbed the furry black ears. "Sorry, Ivan, I didn't bring my cat today."

Still wiggling, he gazed lovingly at me with eyes the color of melting chocolate.

I looked up toward the boys. They were backlit against the bright sky. I stood and shook their hands. "How was the drive north?" Tall and slim, brown eyed, with black, curly hair, they would be hard, if not impossible, to tell apart if one of them hadn't been wearing glasses. They both had engaging grins and a direct way of returning my gaze.

"Fine," the one wearing glasses said. "Mom worries too much. You're Ms. Westhill, right?"

"Right. But call me Emily, please, or I'll feel ancient."

The boy with glasses said, "Okay. I'm Zander, and he's Rylan. We're supposed to tell everyone to go to the house for a pre-skiing drink. Keep walking down the driveway, and you'll come to the house. Some people are taking their skis to the house, but the trail runs along beside the driveway, too." He pointed. I could barely see the trail now. It was beyond mounds of snow that had fallen since Wednesday. Zander suggested, "You can leave your skis in your car if you want, and ski from here when some of the other people start from the house."

Picturing all of Brent's guests sorting out skis and poles on his front porch at the same time, I decided to leave mine where they were, along with my goggles, ski boots, gloves, scarf, and my cheerful stocking cap.

Wearing snow boots and my wind-resistant jacket and pants, I started down Brent's long driveway. Although it had been plowed, it was covered with hard snow. I'd be able to ski down it later, if I wanted to.

Ivan accompanied me until one of the boys whistled. The big dog turned around and galloped back to them. I couldn't help smiling.

I'd almost reached Brent's porch when a siren blooped once and became silent. I turned around. Zander and Rylan were directing an ambulance to park behind my car. In her EMT uniform, Samantha hopped out of the driver's seat. The passenger door opened. A lanky man, also wearing an EMT uniform, jumped out.

Uh-oh. When I'd suggested pairing Olivia and Corey, Samantha hadn't been enthusiastic, but maybe she'd changed her mind. However, this might not have been a perfect time to try my matchmaking experiment. As far as I knew, Olivia was meeting Ronald at this party. . . .

With his tail wagging full speed and his enormous paws churning powdery snow into clouds that billowed in the sunshine, Ivan bounced from one EMT to the other and back to his boys.

I ran up onto Brent's porch. As before, the railing was decorated with cedar garlands and red bows. Now, a colorful conglomeration of skis and poles leaned haphazardly against it. Voices and laughter came from inside the large timber chalet. I was admiring the honey-toned wood door and the cedar wreath nearly covering the multi-pane window near the top when the door opened.

In jeans and turtleneck, Hooligan stepped out onto the porch and hugged me. "Have you seen Samantha? She has to transport a patient from a nursing home to his daughter's place for the holidays, and she's coming here after that."

I pointed down the driveway. "That must be what she did. She just arrived in an ambulance. With Corey."

He beamed a happy smile at me. "Thanks, Emily!" Without a coat, he bounded off the porch and tore down the driveway.

Smiling, watching the happy groom rushing to greet his bride of several months, I stepped over the threshold and practically ran into Brent.

He crushed me in a bear hug.

I almost didn't notice the hug.

I was gazing around the two-story great room. I was a little disappointed to see Ronald. I was afraid he was a murderer and might harm Olivia, who was standing near, but not too near, him and smiling. Also, his being here complicated, perhaps, my hope that Olivia and Corey might one day discover that they harmonized in more than singing. Scott, Misty, Jocelyn, and Parker, a compact but broad-shouldered young man I'd met only briefly before, were talking and laughing with Ronald and Olivia.

Beyond them, in the open-concept kitchen, Detective Gartborg slid a baking sheet out of the higher of the two wall-mounted ovens. Unlike other guests, who wore comfy jeans, yoga pants, T-shirts, and sweaters, Detective Gartborg was already dressed for the après-ski party in a sophisticated black velvet tunic and matching pants.

Mostly, I was paying attention to the great room. Like the outside of the house, the interior was amber-toned logs and acres of glass. The floor was a lighter color of wood, rock maple, I thought. I recognized some of Brent's area rugs and furniture. They all went perfectly with the chalet's timber-frame architecture and luxury cottage style. A stairway led upward past windows to a loft. Ropes of cedar decorated the railing beside the stairs and along the loft. Twigs of holly, with red berries and pointy, shiny green leaves, were entwined with the cedar, and I thought I saw a sprig of mistletoe tucked into the garland near the center of the loft railing. I smelled cedar, bacon, and Brent's wool sweater. "Wow!" I breathed.

Laughing, Brent let me go. "Wow, what?"

"The inside is as gorgeous as the outside, and as your wooded hillside."

"Disappointing."

"What? How much have you had to drink?"

"I was hoping the 'wow' was for the hug."

"You *have* had too much to drink."

"Have not. And I'm at home and not on call, so it wouldn't matter, anyway."

I slipped off my snow boots and added them to the others on mats beside the door. "Yes, it would. It's not like you." I was sounding much too prim. "Where should I put my jacket?" Not only prim, but pragmatic.

"I'll show you."

In my thick socks, I padded behind him down a white-painted hallway. He stopped at an open door. "Sorry you didn't get a tour last time you were here. This is a guest room."

The most noticeable feature of the bedroom was the glass door leading to the room's own little deck, surrounded by snow-covered trees. "Wow," I said again. I added my jacket to the ones already on a quilt covering a peeled-log bed. After seeing how the others, except Detective Gartborg, were dressed, I decided to stay casual for now. I left on my wind resistant pants, my oversized shirt, my sweater, and those heavy, long socks. My slinky stretch velvet could emerge later.

Two guitar cases stood together in one corner. I asked, "Whose guitars?"

"Zander's and Rylan's. They brought their guitars in out

of the cold before I sent them outside to direct traffic." He pointed at a door standing ajar near one corner of the room. "The bathroom's in there."

I ran my fingers through my curls. Combing them wouldn't have done much good. "I'm okay," I said.

"More than okay." He captured my left hand and stared down at it for a second. "Did you lose your ring?"

Like a child, I pulled my hand away and hid it behind my back. "I took it off." I was afraid to look at him.

He said with urgency in his voice, "Listen, Em, before we go back to the others, I have something to tell you."

Chapter 32

I hoped Brent's news wasn't that Detective Gartborg and her family were moving in with him. "What?" I tried not to sound apprehensive. I was still afraid to meet his gaze.

"You don't have to worry about Olivia being with Ronald. He was nowhere near the village square when Travis was killed. Fallingbrook has tracking on its vehicles. Ronald's truck was plowing the miles of roads south of downtown."

I looked up at him then. "Are you sure Ronald was in the truck?"

"How did I know you'd ask that?"

"Because I always think of everything?"

"You've been known to miss a few clues now and then."

For some reason, maybe because of the warmth in those gray eyes, the only response I could come up with at first was heat rushing into my neck and face, but I finally managed to ask again, "Was he?"

"He wasn't in it the entire time. He was in a coffee shop. The proprietor and surveillance video confirmed that he was eating a substantial breakfast between two and two forty-five. He left downtown Fallingbrook about midnight and didn't plow near the village square again until four thirty. The medical examiner said that Travis probably died around two. Witnesses saw your Frosty the Donut sculpture still standing and illuminated shortly after one."

"So, Ronald is totally in the clear?"

Brent kept his voice low. "Except for the library's Fallingbrook High yearbook."

"Did he tell you why he tore that page out?"

"You guessed right. He was afraid people would see it, remember the fight, and believe he killed Travis."

"I guess I should find some way of telling Olivia that her date today is not a danger to her."

"I already let her know."

I thanked him. Half listening to the cheerful sound of people greeting each other out in the great room, I added, "There's still a problem."

"What?"

I heaved a dramatic sigh. "Olivia met Ronald here for a date, and Samantha brought her EMT partner, Corey Ides. Olivia and Corey encountered each other while we were caroling, and their voices blended beautifully. Olivia sort of has two dates to your party, except the one with Corey wasn't planned, and neither she nor Corey probably knows about it, so it isn't a real date between those two. I hope."

Smiling down at me, he squeezed my upper arms. "You had something to do with this matchmaking, didn't you?"

"Yes. I should have realized something like this could happen."

"I'd better let you go out there and smooth things over. But first . . ." He smothered me in another hug.

I pulled my face away from the wool sweater and the muscular chest underneath it. "Wow," I said.

"Wow, what?"

I started out of the room. "I'd say it was your guest room, but you might not believe me."

"I might." He followed me into the passageway leading to the great room.

"I like it a lot."

"The guest room?"

"Yes. And the rest of the house. And everything."

Behind me, he murmured in satisfied tones as if talking to an invisible third person, "She's getting better at catching on to clues."

My heart sped its pace, and I nearly turned around to face him, but Hooligan, Samantha, and Corey were coming down the passageway toward us. As always when Hooligan was around Samantha, he was beaming. "I'll show them where to put their coats," he told Brent.

My nylon ski pants made annoying swishy noises as I walked to the great room and joined the others. Detective Gartborg was carrying a tray of appetizers and offering them to the guests as if she felt totally at home helping Brent host his party. I knew I should appreciate her kindness and support, but I couldn't help feeling irritated. And, I had to admit, jealous. She had the privilege of working with Brent as part of her career. I didn't. And now she was acting like she was one of his best friends, too.

I had to admit to myself that I'd spent a lot of time with Brent during the past few days, and I might even have helped him with the case, but I hadn't been working with him like Detective Gartborg had. To be fair, she'd been in Fallingbrook, in charge of the case, for only parts of two days. And just now, Brent had been flirting with me. Maybe more than flirting.

Beyond Detective Gartborg, two enormous pots and one medium-sized one sat on the stove. The delicate aroma of hot chocolate was almost overwhelmed by Brent's famous chili. He always put his super-spicy chili in the red pot and one that he called "not so hot" in a green one, even when Christmas was nowhere near.

I joined the group surrounding Gartborg. Misty and Scott stood side by side, close together with their arms around each other's backs. With his free hand, Scott chose a spicy shrimp on a toothpick from the platter and held it to Misty's mouth. Without removing her arm from his back and smiling adoringly up at him, she pulled the shrimp off the toothpick with her teeth.

Jocelyn reintroduced Parker to me. We shook hands. The muscular young man was careful not to squeeze my hand too tightly. His gaze was direct and kind, and his smile was as wide as Jocelyn's. It was easy to tell that the two of them loved being together.

Brent opened the front door. Calling cheerful Christmas greetings, Whitney and Leo Valcriffe came in. Watching them walk toward the guest room, it struck me that Dustin Loyvens, Paige, and Ronald had all been cleared of Travis's murder. Whitney and Leo, however, had been in the vicinity at approximately the right time, and Leo and Whitney had given each other their only alibis. I didn't know where either of them had been before or after the Jolly Cop had seen them together. I felt like I should watch them carefully. Brent probably would, too, and he might have warned Misty, Hooligan, and Detective Gartborg to be careful around them. I reminded myself that even if Leo and Whitney had harmed Travis, they wouldn't call attention to themselves by doing anything dangerous to anyone else, maybe ever again. We were probably all safe around them.

Samantha, Hooligan, and Corey came out of the bedroom wing and joined the party. Samantha had changed into jeans and a sweater. Corey was still wearing his EMT uniform. Detective Gartborg and Brent brought out bacon mini-quiches and offered them to us.

Zander and Rylan came inside. I asked them, "Where's Ivan?"

Zander smiled. "In the car."

Rylan explained, "He has a double coat and very thick fur on his feet and ears. He'll be fine in the car in the sunshine for a few minutes. We have a thermometer in there. It's about sixty, warmer than he likes, but it won't go up beyond that or get too cold even though a couple of windows are open a little. It's not dangerous for him or about to be. We would never let anything hurt him."

Zander added, "He loves being in a car even when it's not moving. He thinks it's a den we can all share. It's better than letting him come in here and shed all over Brent's house."

Brent said cheerfully, "I wouldn't mind."

Whitney and Leo came out of the hallway and joined the party. Removing their coats, the Gartborg boys traipsed toward the bedroom wing.

Whitney looked around and told Brent, "The place looks great!" Leo put his arm around his tiny wife and nodded.

Brent smiled at them. "The house has great bones."

I asked Whitney and Leo, "Did you two design it?"

Standing as tall as she could beside her big teddy bear of a husband, Whitney gave the interior a proud glance. "With help from an architect. And Leo did the electrical work."

His eyes twinkling, Leo flexed his biceps. "We both worked on the interior finishes. Whitney's the artistic one." I couldn't help liking the couple.

Jocelyn and Parker took over passing the appetizers. Olivia kept smiling and didn't seem uneasy about being at a party with two men who might be interested in her.

In the kitchen section of the room, Brent stirred the chili with long-handled spoons.

Detective Gartborg joined the rest of us. Although she seemed supremely confident when she was working, she barely said a word in this social situation. Maybe, being a detective, she couldn't help staying in the background and observing, but she didn't know some of the people at the party, and I was afraid she might feel awkward. Parker and Jocelyn had been talking to her before they took over serving appetizers. Gartborg knew Misty and Hooligan from the police department. Samantha had met her before and made certain that she knew who Corey was, and she seemed to recognize Whitney and Leo. I introduced her to Olivia and commented that Olivia had recent experience raising a teen. Maybe Gartborg had helped question Ronald about the library's copy of the yearbook, but I introduced her to him in case she hadn't. I didn't mention her job to him, but I told her, "He's the one who keeps our roads clear of ice and snow."

If anyone was feeling shy, it was Ronald. He shrank a little, a difficult feat for a man his size, and said in self-deprecating tones, "I'm not the only one."

A smile flickered across Gartborg's otherwise cool expression, but she didn't say anything.

I wondered if Ronald had guessed that I was the one who alerted the police to his having damaged the yearbook.

Gartborg turned her head and watched her sons return from the guest room without their coats and with their guitars. The two boys tuned the instruments and quietly strummed them. As they launched into "Frosty the Snowman," people started singing along.

Not wanting to spoil the music, I kept my mouth clamped shut.

I noticed Whitney staring at Corey, looking away, and then examining his face again like people did when they couldn't quite place someone. Corey might have noticed, but he didn't look toward her.

The singers sent Frosty hurrying away, the boys stopped playing the guitars, and Whitney asked Corey, "Have we met?"

He looked down at his uniform. "Maybe I responded to an emergency call you made."

Studying Whitney's face, Samantha clarified. "A medical emergency."

Whitney shook her head. "No."

I suggested, "Maybe you saw him when we caroled through the festival on Thursday evening."

"That must be it." Whitney didn't sound convinced.

Samantha raised her hand and spoke loudly enough for all of us to hear. "Hooligan brought my skis, but Corey doesn't have his here. Does anyone have a spare pair?"

"That's okay," Corey said. "I can just walk around."

Leo wore a huge smile. "Brent has several extra pairs. Poles and boots, too, and I bet he has at least one set that might not be perfect for Corey but will work."

Brent's eyebrows went up. "I do?"

Whitney grinned and Leo nodded. "Remember, we told you about the closet of sports equipment we were leaving for you because you might have a use for them, and we don't? Bet you haven't looked in there yet."

Brent made a rueful expression. "I haven't." I knew why he hadn't explored thoroughly. He'd barely spent any time in his new place.

Leo gestured to Corey. "Come on. That is, if you don't mind, Brent."

Would Corey be safe alone with Leo?

It must not have worried Brent. He answered, "Of course not. I hope you find some. I'm not sure how many days we'll get that are this perfect for skiing."

Whitney was still smiling. "Lots, probably. You're going to love it here, Brent."

"I already do." He opened a kitchen cabinet full of mugs. "Who wants hot chocolate before we ski?"

We followed him to the kitchen, and he ladled hot chocolate into mugs and cups. I didn't notice any resembling the ones I'd bought him. I hoped Whitney hadn't spoiled my surprise by giving him mugs with creatures lurking in their depths.

Brent directed us to a counter where he'd set out liqueurs we could add to our hot chocolate. Zander and Rylan didn't add liqueur to theirs. Zander said in faked tones of woe, "It's tough having a cop for a mother."

She made what I suspected was supposed to be a stern face. "You'd better believe it." Her love for her sons was clear in her voice. She didn't spike her hot chocolate, either. She took her mug to the huge front window where Hooligan was looking at ornaments on the tree and drinking from his mug. Her boys followed her.

Leo returned triumphantly, carrying poles in one hand and cross-country ski boots in the other. With skis that looked close to the right length for him, Corey followed Leo. They took the skis and poles outside to the porch and then joined us in the kitchen.

Brent offered them hot chocolate. As I had, Leo chose coffee liqueur.

Corey refused. "Samantha and I can't drink. We have the ambulance."

Samantha had already added almond-flavored liqueur to her hot chocolate. She set her mug firmly on the granite kitchen counter. "We're not on call."

Corey's frown reminded me of the grimace he'd made when he climbed aboard the crashed bus and smelled what must have been bourbon. He repeated, "We have the ambulance."

"It's not on call, either." She explained to the rest of us, "We have another one on loan from Gooseleg, and that one is at our station, along with our second one and the EMTs who are on duty right now. The one we brought here is scheduled for routine maintenance on Monday. Taking that patient to his daughter's was its last trip until it goes into the shop." She offered Corey a smile that didn't quite reach her eyes. "And I knew you don't drink and would drive it back tonight after the party."

"Technically we're not allowed to be in that ambulance with a drop of alcohol in our blood."

"Which is why you said you would drive it back tonight, and I can go home with Hooligan."

Brent had finished ladling hot chocolate into our mugs and was at the stove, stirring chili again. I wasn't sure he'd heard Corey's reprimand or Samantha's tart response.

Corey's gaze took in the rest of us. "Isn't drinking before skiing risky? Especially for those of you who have never been on these trails before?"

Whitney gave him one of her super-wide smiles. "I have. Lots of times."

"Me, too," Leo said.

Whitney added seriously, "Everyone needs to be careful, especially on the first hill. Near the bottom, there's an S curve, first to the right, and then to the left. After that, the trail isn't as steep, but at the bottom of the hill, the trail makes a sharp left. If you're going too fast, you could shoot out onto the lake, and the ice probably isn't thick enough to support anyone, even someone on skis."

Brent warned, "It's not frozen all the way across yet."

Leo grinned. "The lake's far enough from the trail that even if you miss the turn, deep snow will stop you long before you reach the beach, let alone the lake. Whitney is always cautious. Who wants to slow down on a hill?"

Parker hugged Jocelyn to him. "We don't."

Zander had wandered over to join us near the kitchen. He set his empty mug down on the granite countertop. "We don't, either, and we've been around the loop once already. It's not icy, and the conditions are pretty good. If anything, they're a little slow."

Brent cautioned, "Not for everyone."

Whitney glanced at his kitchen clock and announced, "We should get out there. It's two thirty, and it will be getting dark about four thirty."

Everyone brought their mugs to the kitchen. Brent loaded the dishwasher. Detective Gartborg and her sons headed to the guest room for their coats and jackets, followed by Whitney, Leo, and Corey. When they were back in the great room and going out to the porch, Olivia, Ronald, Jocelyn, and Parker went to retrieve their coats. That left only Brent, Samantha, Hooligan, Misty, Scott, and me in the kitchen.

I was about to go get my jacket when I noticed Misty's left hand.

No wonder she'd been glowing during the party.

A diamond sparkled and flashed on her ring finger.

Chapter 33

✣

Pointing at Misty's finger, I squealed, "Samantha! What's that on Misty's hand?" It was almost like we were again in junior high, going into raptures over boys.

Misty waved her hand dramatically, displaying her new ring. "Scott and I are engaged." She said it calmly as if she'd expected this and we had, too. Which was probably true.

Samantha was the first to give both Misty and Scott huge hugs, and I wasn't far behind. Hooligan and Brent hugged Misty and thumped Scott on the back. The three men went off to retrieve their jackets.

Still in the great room with Misty and Samantha, I asked, "Have you set a date?"

Misty adjusted the ring. "Not yet. Or a location, other than somewhere in or near Fallingbrook." She beamed at me. "And it has to be during the summer when your parents will be here."

I placed my hands over my heart. "They'll love that!"

Misty told us, "Also, I hope you two will be my attendants." She said it with a question in her voice.

Samantha and I nearly shouted our acceptance.

Brent, Hooligan, and Scott came out of the bedroom wing and clomped outside in their cross-country ski boots and lightweight outerwear.

Chattering about plans, Samantha, Misty, and I went to the guest room and put on our jackets.

Outside on the front porch, we found Brent, Hooligan, and Scott waiting for us. Hooligan kissed Samantha. "Your skis and things are in my car."

Samantha and I told the other four to go ahead while we retrieved our skis and put them on. I suggested, "We'll probably meet you on your second trip around."

Brent had groomed a trail from his driveway to his porch, and from his porch to the main trail. Detective Gartborg and her sons were already on the far side of the front yard and about to start down that first hill. Nose down, Ivan detoured to a snowdrift, then he took off down the hill after his family.

Samantha and I trotted down the steps and away from the cheerful chaos on the porch. I said, "We'll probably put on our skis before the rest of them untangle their skis and poles from everyone else's."

"Yes." She wasn't laughing.

Striding along the snowy driveway beside her, I glanced at her face. "Is something wrong? You're happy about Misty and Scott, aren't you?"

"I'm thrilled for them." She sounded like she meant it.

I leaped at a guess. "Is it Corey? Back there in Brent's kitchen, he came across as controlling."

Samantha let out a mirthless laugh. "Now you know why I wasn't terribly excited about pairing him off with Olivia. Or anyone else. He micromanages. But Brent had invited Corey, and if Corey and Olivia were interested in each other, I wasn't going to make decisions for them. Besides, Corey promised to drive the ambulance back into town after the party, and I could go home with Hooligan. I decided not to worry that socializing with Corey might erode what little authority I have over him."

"But you're senior on your team, aren't you?"

"He tends to forget that. And that I have years more experience than he does, and I might actually know a thing or two about health care. He can make my life difficult." She opened Hooligan's car. "He resists me. He makes a good show in front of others, but when we're alone or with a patient, he sometimes acts like I don't have authority in the chain of command. I don't think he likes reporting to a woman. Don't get me wrong—he's a good EMT." She toed off her winter boots and slipped on her ski boots. "But in addition to wanting to act like he's the boss, he has this simmering anger about people who drink and drive." She zipped her ski boots and stood up. "I can't blame him. We all have that. We've seen the damage that impaired drivers do, not only to themselves, but to innocent people." She threw her uniform, except for the stocking cap, into the car and put on a jean jacket. She pulled the black knit hat over her red and green streaked curls.

I told her, "I caught a glimpse of that anger when he stepped into the crashed bus and must have caught the smell of bourbon."

She grabbed her skis and poles and locked the car. "Is that what that smell was? It was strong." She snapped her boots into the bindings on her skis. "Luckily, when he encounters what might be a drunk driver, he doesn't let it affect his work. Even if he thinks the injured person caused the accident by drinking or being otherwise impaired, he treats the person as well as he treats everyone else."

I walked toward my SUV. Matching my pace, Samantha skied beside me.

I opened my car, eased onto the edge of the front passenger seat, removed my snow boots, and put on my ski boots. I collected my goggles, gloves, scarf, and hat and shut the car door. Samantha was waiting for me near the back of my car. I joined her, put on my scarf, hat, and goggles, pulled my skis and poles out of the car, and said, "When we were Christmas caroling, the woman with the broken arm, the one who went in the ambulance with Travis on that first trip away from the crashed bus, seemed to be trying to avoid Corey and keep her son away from him."

Samantha was leaning on her poles, a figure in blue denim on the sunlit snow. "I noticed that, too, but I wrote it off to her not wanting her son to run around crashing into people. She rode in the back with Corey and Travis, so she might have witnessed something that I couldn't have known about from the driver's seat."

I locked my car, snapped my boots onto my skis, pulled on my gloves, and looped the poles' straps over my wrists. I could hardly wait to tour Brent's property again, especially the first hill.

"Samantha!" A tiny woman skiing along the trail toward us waved. A huge man was behind her. Whitney and Leo. We waited behind my car. They skied to us on one of Brent's trails connecting the trail to the driveway. Breathing heavily from exertion or emotion, Whitney said, "Samantha, I remembered why your partner looked familiar. He's changed since he was a little boy, but even though it was eighteen years ago, his face from when he was about eight is seared into my memory."

I took a deep breath. I thought I knew what was coming.

Whitney brushed her eyes with the back of her mitten. "It happened up in Gooseleg. A car I was riding in hit a pair of pedestrians—your partner and his father. The man who was murdered Thursday morning—well, we were seventeen then— was driving. Travis Tarriston. I yelled at him to stay at the scene so we could give the man and his boy first aid, but we'd been drinking, and Travis was afraid of losing his license. Other cars were stopping. Travis said those people could pick up the man and child we'd hit, and we didn't need to." Tears glistened in the corners of Whitney's eyes. "I yelled at Travis, but he wouldn't listen to me. He raced away from the scene, drove to his house, got out of the car, and left me to go home and figure out what to do." She took a deep, shuddering breath and went on. "I made a lot of mistakes that night, like drinking—we were both underage—and believing Travis when he said he hadn't drunk too much to drive. And then I waited until the next morning when I was sober before I called the police and confessed to leaving the scene. The police didn't believe me that Travis was driving. It was my parents' car, and his parents lied and said Travis was home with them the entire evening. Even worse, his grandfather was a congressman. I think the grandfather knew who to push and how to push them. My family are only normal people. We couldn't compete." Her mouth thinned with apparent pain. "Your partner was only a boy, Samantha. He couldn't tell the police whether a boy or a girl was driving my parents' car. He just kept crying about eyebrows, and if you think my eyebrows are thick now, you should have seen them when I was seventeen. They were enough, along with the car being my parents' and the lies from Travis's family, to make the police decide I was the driver."

Samantha and I didn't say a thing, and Whitney continued. "I can't help wondering if your partner had something to do with Travis's death, Samantha. I mean, I hate to say it. He's an EMT now, saving people's lives, and he was just an innocent boy then, so . . ."

Behind her, Leo said, "You're shivering, Whitney. We should either go inside or keep moving."

"Let's go around again."

I found my voice. "Be careful."

Whitney pushed off on her skis. "We always are."

Samantha just stood there, watching them ski down the driveway, and, I thought, trying to control her own shivering. When Whitney and Leo were out of earshot, I told Samantha, "Whitney and Leo were seen at the north end of the square around the time that someone used a vehicle to topple our ice sculpture onto Travis. Whitney and Leo were each

driving a pickup truck that night. If one or both of them murdered Travis, Whitney could be trying to shift the blame
away from them by suggesting that Corey was the murderer.
Corey could be innocent. Faces change a lot between the ages
of eight and twenty-six. He might not be the boy who was
hit. He didn't seem to recognize Whitney."

Samantha chewed on her lip for a second and then
squinted toward me. The sun was in her eyes. "I can't help
wondering if Whitney is right. I noticed two strange things
on Thursday morning, but I didn't put them together."

Not wanting to risk catching up with Leo and Whitney, I
stayed where I was and asked, "What were they?"

"After Corey took off his boots at work that morning and
left them on the mat, bigger puddles than usual formed
around them. He walks to and from work, so that wasn't surprising considering that we were still in the midst of a blizzard and the temperature had gone up to almost thirty-two,
and the snow was wet. His boots were soaking as if he'd
walked farther than usual that morning or as if he'd been in
the snow during a lot of the night. Oh, wait, there was another strange thing. He never comes into work before I get
there, but that morning, I gave myself extra time. The roads
were clearer than I'd feared, and I arrived at work earlier
than usual. He was already there. That wasn't very strange. It
made sense that he'd given himself extra time to get there. It's
not like we could have expected everyone to have been out
shoveling their sidewalks at seven in the morning."

I prompted, "And was there a third strange thing?"

"Yes. I maintain our log, keeping track of when we're
called out, where we go, how many people we transport,
when we return, mileage, all those details. The ambulance
seemed to have put on a few extra miles during the night.
When I mentioned it to Corey, he pointed out that my nines
sometimes look like fours. It's true, but maybe the number
that looked like a four really was a four. And I thought I re-

membered writing a four. Maybe after we parked the ambulance, he walked to work in the middle of the night, took the ambulance out again, drove it for almost five miles, and walked back home. That would explain the extra five miles and the wetter-than-usual boots."

The ambulance was parked right behind where we were standing next to my car. Blue sky and sunlit clouds reflected off its windshield, and I couldn't see inside. I asked Samantha, "Is that the ambulance you were using Wednesday night?"

"Yes."

"Does it have a dash cam?"

Chapter 34

❦

Samantha unsnapped a jacket pocket and removed her phone. "The dashcam in the ambulance starts recording when the ignition is turned on. Let's see if Corey took the ambulance out early Thursday morning." She logged on to her dashcam viewer and held the phone where we could both see its screen. I moved my goggles to the top of my hat. Samantha fast-forwarded through Wednesday evening and driving away from the hospital after leaving injured bus passengers in the care of hospital staff. We saw another ambulance inside the garage at Emergency Medical Services, and then the screen went blank. "That's where I turned off the engine," Samantha told me. "If no one took that ambulance out later that night, the next thing we should see is the interior of the garage when we were called out around eight Thursday morning."

But that wasn't what we saw. The video started up again. Samantha pointed at the time stamp at the bottom of the screen. "The ignition was turned on again at one fifty-two a.m." The screen was mostly dark, with a regular pattern of moving lighter spots. "That's strange," she said. "I've never seen the dashcam record a video like that before. It's obvious that the truck is moving, but why is the screen mostly dark except for those moving light spots?"

Having spent time watching the Knitpickers knitting, I guessed, "Those light spots look like the spaces between knit stitches, as if someone covered the dashcam with a knit scarf or hat, like the stocking cap you're wearing right now."

She patted the tight black hat. "Oops. Corey might have something to say about me wearing the hat from my uniform when I'm not on duty. But I think you're right. It could be a hat or scarf flung over the dashcam."

She fast-forwarded the video. The pinpricks of light became brighter and darker as if the ambulance, even with its headlights on during a blizzard, were traveling between streetlights. At one minute after two, the tiny pattern of lights became dim and stopped moving. By five after, it appeared that the ambulance was once again traveling on streets where the light cast by streetlights was blurred by falling snow. At ten after, the tiny lights began jouncing as if the ambulance was on rough ground. Brighter light shined between the knit stitches. The lights stopped moving.

Samantha commented, "The truck stopped, but its ignition was still on." A dark, blurred form came from the right side of the screen, passed between the bright lights and the dashcam, and then disappeared. The blurred form showed up momentarily, again on the right. At two fifteen, the points of light jerked suddenly and then became almost dark. By two seventeen, the ambulance was again jolting over uneven terrain, and then it passed through the intermittent illumination of streetlights. The video went blank again. The time stamp showed that it was two twenty-one.

Samantha stopped the video. "That weird part of that video began at one fifty-two and lasted thirty-nine minutes. That must have been when the ambulance went those five additional miles. My fours are distinguishable from my nines, after all."

"It looked like the ambulance stopped twice before the ignition was turned off. Once in a dimly lit spot, and a second time in a brightly lit spot that became suddenly dark. Can you play it again, from where the lights became very bright?"

She played it at normal speed. After the lights stopped moving, we tried to make out the dark blurry form in the falling snow. When the form came from the right side of the screen, which would have been the passenger side of the ambulance, it moved slowly, but when it returned to the passenger side of the screen, it moved quickly. Both times, it could have been a person crouching down to make himself look shorter.

It could have been someone dragging something heavy and then returning, running while hunched over.

Samantha replayed the lights suddenly zigzagging before going out, and then pointed at the screen. "It was like the ambulance rammed something that was lit, and then the lights went out."

We stared at each other in horror. I said, "Frosty the Donut was lit up at one that morning. It was pushed over onto Travis after that, and I know you would never do something like that."

"I was home with Hooligan, and as I said, I wasn't called out after we dropped off the injured people from the bus, and neither was this truck. We can check something else. This software tracks where the ambulance goes." She tapped the screen. Exclaiming, "Oh, no!" she showed me a map with lines on it. She traced her fingers along the lines. "During those thirty-nine minutes, the ambulance went from its garage to the hospital and from there to the village square where Frosty the Donut was. If this is precise, and it probably is, the ambulance went right into the square. That would explain the way it was bouncing. Then it backed up several feet, went forward, and then backed up again to Wisconsin Street and was driven to our garage."

"Who has keys to that ambulance?"

"They're kept in the station. All of us who work there have access."

"Including Corey."

"Including Corey, but on-duty EMTs might have taken the keys and driven the ambulance that night. . . ." Samantha's voice trailed off into a disconsolate sigh. Staring down at her phone, she whispered, "But Corey's the most likely." She thrust her phone into her pocket and snapped the pocket flap. "He has that angry streak, and he can be a bully, especially around women, but a murderer? I can't believe that."

I asked urgently, "Do you know if Corey has software on his phone like you have, or if he has keys to the ambulance right now? Can he erase the video?"

"He shouldn't have the software or the password for it. He shouldn't know that I have them. He has a key to the ambulance, but even if he could erase the video from the dashcam, copies are automatically archived at county headquarters. He can't access that."

We'd been paying attention to Samantha's phone and not to the ski trail beyond the driveway and the expanse of plowed-up snow. I checked both directions on the trail. Misty must have skied past when we were watching the video. She was already far away, crossing Brent's front yard. I shouted her name, and Samantha let out a deafening whistle, but Misty must not have heard us. She turned the corner and disappeared between trees at the top of the trail's first downward slope.

I suggested, "Maybe Brent or Hooligan or even Detective Gartborg will be along soon."

Now that I was sure that the ambulance in front of us had

toppled Frosty the Donut, I gave the vehicle another look. It had been in bright sun for more than an hour since Samantha parked it. Any snow and ice that had been clinging to the front of the bumper had melted. Samantha and I skied closer. Without touching the bumper, we bent and examined it.

Samantha pointed at a spot near the passenger side and said in a deadened voice, "I don't think that dent was there when I last looked."

She had her back to the trail and couldn't have seen the man expertly gliding along it on skis.

Corey.

His head wasn't turned toward us, but had he seen us looking at the bumper? He continued along the trail toward where I'd last seen Misty.

Trying not to panic, I pointed at him. "What if he did kill Travis, and what if he's trying to catch up to Misty and . . . and harm her somehow? It might not occur to her that he could be dangerous." I tried phoning Brent. I left him a terse message. "Call me." Samantha left Hooligan a similar message, and I called Misty. No answer. I told her to call me, and then frowned at Samantha. "They must not have good reception in the valley."

"Let's go find them." Samantha wore the determined expression I'd seen when she was attending emergency medical calls. We sprinted down the driveway so fast that our skis chittered on the scraped, icy snow.

I heard no voices from the skiers on the hill below me, not even Ivan expressing his joy at being out in the snowy woods with his favorite people.

Nervously, I glanced toward the trail. What if Corey skied the wrong way and came back up the first hill to confront us? Or to do something worse?

Another thought struck me. I hadn't watched him long

enough to know whether he had continued on the trail or gone into Brent's house.

When I could see Brent's front porch, I realized that Corey probably had not gone into the house. Whitney and Leo were on the porch, leaning their skis against the railing. They must have changed their minds about going around the loop again. Trying to sound like a carefree skier, I shouted, "Tell Brent to catch up to me!"

Leo held up a thumb and yelled, "Okay!"

Samantha and I raced along the trail crossing Brent's front yard. At the top of that first slope, Samantha tucked her poles, went into a skier's crouch, and flew down the hill. I gave her a few seconds' start, and then I didn't hold back. I let myself swoop down that hill as fast as smooth snow and gravity let me.

Ahead, I could see that someone in the group must have missed the first part of the S curve. Tracks plowed through deep snow, threading a path between trees.

Samantha was almost at that curve. She slowed. I was gaining on her.

My hat flew off. For a second, I glanced away from the trail in front of me into the woods to my left, but I realized that I couldn't catch the hat and reminded myself that the red, green, and white striped hat would be easy to find, either on my next trip around the loop or during another visit to Brent.

In that blink-of-an-eye moment when I wasn't concentrating on the trail directly down the hill from me, a man in dark clothing had skied out from behind a pine tree on the left, just above the curve and below Samantha. He held a ski pole out straight.

It caught Samantha on the face or neck. Arms, legs, skis, and poles cartwheeling, she tumbled into soft snow to the right of the trail. Snow blew up around her, and then settled, nearly covering her.

Ignoring me barreling toward him, Corey skied across the trail toward Samantha and yelled toward her unmoving body, "What were you doing with that ambulance?" His voice echoed through the snowy forest.

Chapter 35

Focusing on Corey, I didn't slow down.

He raised his pole high above Samantha and aimed the bladelike end at her. He didn't seem to notice that I was speeding toward him.

Maybe he knew.

And intended to silence me after he took care of her.

Closing the distance with lightning speed, I screamed, "No!" I shifted my pole around and aimed it toward him.

His pole slashed down toward Samantha's unmoving form.

My pole knocked his pole out of his hand. I crashed into him. My forehead made a satisfying thud against his shoulder. He cursed. I breezed past him on one ski with my arms and poles out to the sides and threatening the trees crowding the trail. Snow billowed around me.

Clumsily, I controlled my arms and feet, regained my balance, and recentered myself over both skis. My reckless ride took me around the right-turning curve. Avoiding flying off the trail and into the gurgling stream, I scooted around the left-turning curve.

The trail straightened and became less steep. I was slowing, but with every second I was sliding farther from Samantha. I had to go back up the hill and protect her from Corey.

I dragged my poles, forced my skis into the snowplow position, and skidded to a stop only inches before the trail made the sharp turn to the left near the mostly frozen lake.

Enthusiastic barking came nearer. I shouted, "Ivan!" Then more loudly, "Brent! Misty! Hooligan!" And then, hoping that Detective Gartborg and her sons might hear me, I hollered, "Gartborg!"

The trail was wider at the curve. I shuffled around to face the way I'd come. Pushing hard with my poles, I forced myself back up the hill and around the S curve.

Above me on the left, I could see only snow where Samantha had fallen.

Farther down the hill from her, Corey had tumbled into soft snow on the other side of the packed-down trail. His head, shoulders, arms, and the tips of his skis stuck out of the snow. He reached toward a pole on the trail near him.

If he stretched, and if he didn't sink farther into the softer snow, he might grab the pole and lever himself out onto the trail.

Barking furiously, Ivan ran across the tails of my skis. I caught my balance. His tail whipping around like a propeller, he dashed around me and twirled and danced on the fronts of my skis, nearly causing me to slide backward down the hill. I pointed with my pole at Corey and commanded, "Get the stick!" Ivan lunged for my pole. "Not that stick!" I stared hard at Corey's pole. His fingers were scrabbling closer to it. I pretended to throw my pole toward Corey and told Ivan, "*That* stick."

Seeming to float over the snow on his big furry paws, Ivan obligingly galloped up the hill, grabbed the pole away from Corey's reaching fingers, and trotted to me with his prize. I reached for the pole. "Good boy!" The good boy pranced away with the pole in his mouth.

Corey's other pole had slid down the smooth trail and was only a few feet from me. I flung it behind me. Ivan dropped his pole and ran toward the one I'd thrown. Skiing as quickly as I could up the hill toward Samantha, I called Ivan and shouted again for my human friends. Brent's property was big and the trail was long, but lots of people were skiing on it, and although some of them might have stopped to enjoy views, at least one of them should loop around again and come plunging down the hill toward us. I was sure that Brent and Hooligan wouldn't go inside until they met up with Samantha and me.

I skied uphill past Corey. He thrashed as if trying to maneuver his skis underneath him and stand up. "Help me," he demanded.

"No." Sparks of fury were probably shooting from my eyes.

He whined, "I didn't do anything."

Corey, Samantha, Ivan, and I had put major holes and dents in that section of Brent's groomed trail. I maneuvered around them to Samantha. Needing to stay strong for her, I couldn't let myself think about how badly injured she might be. I took off my skis and stuck them and my poles upright in the snow just uphill from her as a warning to anyone skiing down the trail. Calling her name, I knelt on the packed trail beside her. I leaned forward and brushed snow off her still form. The red streaks in her hair shocked me for a second until I remembered that she had put them and the green ones there herself in honor of the season.

She'd ended up on her stomach with her head uphill from her feet and her face turned toward the trail. Her eyes were closed. Her color was good, and she was breathing. My pent-up breath came out in one loud gust.

Ivan must have decided that my newest game was better than the one I'd abandoned. He galumphed to me, poked his head into the snow, and licked Samantha's cheek.

Jocelyn sailed down the slope at full speed and stopped below me in a spray of snow. She leaped, skis first, into the snow downhill from Samantha and sank to her waist. Being Jocelyn, she remained upright.

Parker had been behind her. He also stopped, spraying more snow.

Corey yelled, "Someone, help me!"

Parker headed toward him.

I shouted, "Parker! Don't help him!"

Jocelyn and I lifted Samantha's shoulders until her head was out of the snow, which didn't prevent Ivan from attempting to wash the rest of the snow off her face.

Samantha opened her eyes and laughed.

I let out another breath and asked her, "Any broken bones?"

"I was only stunned. And afraid to move. Corey stuck out his pole. It hit me in the face, and I fell."

I said dryly, "I saw. Can you put your arms around the dog's neck and hold on?"

She did. I stood and felt through that double coat of fur until I grasped Ivan's collar. "Come on, Ivan." He was panting, and his tongue hung out. He looked like he believed he was the luckiest dog on earth. Holding on to him with one hand, I pushed my heels into the snow and led him uphill. Behind Samantha, Jocelyn pushed. Eager to do whatever his human friends wanted him to do, Ivan plodded beside me.

Samantha emerged wearing only one ski. I helped her remove it and sit on the once-groomed trail. She pulled her knees up, encircled them with her arms, and rested her head on her knees. She was trembling. Her jeans and jean jacket were probably soaking up water from the snow, making her even colder.

Jocelyn rolled out of the soft snow, took off her own skis, and added them and her poles to the sort of barricade I'd made with mine to warn skiers away from that side of the trail. Jocelyn sat beside Samantha and put one arm around her. For all the good it would do, I draped my long sweater and lightweight ski jacket over Samantha's shoulders. Like me, she had lost her hat. I hovered over her, bracing myself to protect her from Corey if I needed to.

Letting out another frenzy of joyful barking, Ivan charged away from us down the hill.

Below us, skiing the wrong way up the trail, Zander and Rylan rounded the top of the S curve. Their mother was right behind them.

I had never been happier to see her.

I was even more happy when I heard skis behind me and turned my head. Brent, Misty, Scott, and Hooligan skied full tilt, one after the other, down the slope toward us. They stopped with more grace than Samantha and I had, but they sprayed more snow.

Detective Gartborg, her sons, and their dog joined Parker beside Corey, whose pleas for help had become more polite, maybe because Ivan had switched from being a happy-go-lucky and cooperative young dog to a ferocious, growling beast with his hackles standing up and his mouth, displaying a set of sharp white teeth, close to Corey's face.

I stood and called down the hill, "Detective Gartborg, don't let Corey escape!" Misty took one look at my face and skied to Corey, Detective Gartborg, her sons, and Parker. Scott followed her.

Hooligan took off his skis, sat on the other side of Samantha from Jocelyn, and pulled Samantha close. Whitney, Leo, Olivia, and Ronald skied down the hill. Leo and Olivia stopped near us, but the others joined the crowd around Corey.

Still on skis, Brent asked me, "What happened, Em?"

I quickly summarized.

He repeated, "There's evidence on the ambulance and from its dashcam, and you saw him assault Samantha?"

"He put his pole in front of her. It hit her face, and she fell. He was about to stab her with the end of his pole. He could have killed her." My voice shook. "He must have seen us looking at the dent in the front of the ambulance."

Brent stared into my eyes for a second, then called to Scott. Scott skied up to us. Brent handed him a set of keys and told him where to find his snowmobile. "Bring it down here, please."

"I'll show him," Leo offered. Pushing with their poles, Scott and Leo skied up the trail they'd just skied down.

Olivia stood in front of Samantha, frowning down at her in apparent empathy and blocking any wind that might be coming up from the lake. Samantha still had her phone. She showed it to Hooligan. Holding it, he scrambled to his feet. I caught a glimpse of the phone's screen and the map showing where the ambulance had gone in the wee hours on Thursday morning. Hooligan told Brent, "You and Detective Gartborg need to see this."

He put on his skis, and then he and Brent skied to Misty and Detective Gartborg. The four police officers huddled over the phone.

Corey must have thought it was his chance to escape. He struggled but didn't budge even an inch out of the deep snow before Brent stopped him with a ski pole set gently—too gently, I thought—on his shoulder.

Misty skied up to us and said, "I'm going near the house where reception is better so I can call for uniformed backup." Pushing with her poles, she started up the steeper section of the slope.

Hooligan brought Samantha's phone to her. We helped her stand and replace her damp jean jacket with my warm sweater and nylon jacket. "You'll be cold, Emily," she said.

Olivia offered me her jacket, but I refused. "I'll warm up."

Samantha giggled. "Stop flapping your arms, Emily. Hold them close to your body to retain your warmth."

Hooligan pulled her close again.

Corey was still guarded by the two detectives, the Gartborg twins, Parker, Ronald, and Whitney. And Ivan, display-ing those teeth whenever Corey looked his way. The humans helped Corey stand on the trail. Thanks to my having knocked him into deep snow, he'd lost both of the skis he'd borrowed from Brent.

I didn't hear what Detective Gartborg said, but I caught enough of it to recognize that she was reading him his rights.

He shouted, "I never hurt anyone! I'm the victim here. Samantha and her friend attacked me, threw me into the snow, and took my poles so I couldn't get out."

Whitney spoke in a confident voice that carried through the chilled forest air. "You are the victim, Corey, but not today, and not of this. You were a victim when you were a lit-tle boy. You were only about eight when the car Travis was driving hit you and your father. I'm very sorry that I let Travis drive that night, and I'm sorrier than I ever can say about what happened to your father."

He snarled, "You should be, and you got off too lightly for what you did."

"I know." Whitney apologized again. "But killing Travis doesn't take away your family's suffering or bring your fa-ther's health back." She sounded about to cry. "And it doesn't do you any good."

Corey snapped, "It saves other people. I became an EMT to help people like me and my father. Do you have any idea how many scenes I've attended where people were maimed and worse because of drunk drivers?" Corey must have real-ized that what he'd said amounted to a confession, but he raised his chin and spoke proudly. "I figured out how to stop a drunk driver a long time ago, and I got the perfect storm—an actual storm where even ambulances would be hard to see, and a drunk driver who had not only harmed others that night, but was the very same drunk who turned my dad from a vibrant man into a stranger who could hardly do anything for himself. When I arrived at that bus on Wednesday night,

I recognized the face I'd seen in my nightmares ever since that night, and I was able to carry out the plan I'd dreamed of."

Brent asked mildly, "What plan?"

"While I was attending to that man in the ambulance, I warned him that the police would confiscate his license. I told him I'd take him to my place where he could sleep it off and you wouldn't know where he was until he was sober." Corey glared at Brent. "I know what you're going to say. You tested his blood alcohol almost as soon as he got to the hospital."

Brent merely nodded.

Corey went on. "But he didn't know that was going to happen, and I told him he'd be safer at my place. My plan could have been ruined by the woman with the broken arm who was in the back of the ambulance with him and me, but she didn't say anything. Later, I was afraid she might have heard, though. She sure didn't want her little boy coming near me when we were caroling. But I wouldn't have hurt a child, especially a boy who reminded me of myself when I was that age, and I wouldn't have harmed one of his parents, either."

Brent asked him, "How did you evade surveillance cameras at the hospital?"

Again, although Detective Gartborg was behind Corey and doing something to his hands, which she'd placed behind his back, he sounded proud. "As part of the plan I daydreamed about, I checked around. There are no surveillance cameras at the alley in back of the hospital."

Detective Gartborg had shooed her boys and Ivan farther from the man we all suspected of murder, but they'd gone only a few feet. The boys were listening intently like a pair of future detectives. Intimidating Corey must have been thirsty work for Ivan. He was lapping water out of the stream.

Detective Gartborg asked Corey, "Doesn't the Emergency Medical Services garage have surveillance cameras?"

Corey's smile was arrogant. "Samantha parked the ambulance in the garage after we were done transporting people to the hospital after the bus crash. She left, and the other EMTs were called out. I turned off the station's surveillance cameras and took the remote outside. I went around the corner. Snow covered my tracks and the ambulance tracks in minutes. I turned on the cameras and walked home. Just before two, I walked back to the station. Before I came into the cameras' view, I used the remote to turn them off. The other EMTs were still out. I covered the dashcam with my hat." He pointed at his head. Although the black stocking cap had collected a few white pompoms of snow, it had stayed on. "Then I started the ambulance. When I came back from my errand, the others hadn't returned. I parked in the garage, grabbed my hat, and took the remote around the corner from the surveillance cameras. I waited for the tracks to fill with snow again, and I turned the cameras on. Then all I had to do was make certain I got to work the next morning before Samantha did so I could put the remote back where we keep it."

Gartborg folded her arms. "Tell us about your 'errand.'"

"I wasn't sure he'd leave the hospital like I told him to, and if he hadn't, I would have abandoned the whole plan. But when I drove around to the alley behind the hospital, there he was, with a coat thrown over his shoulders, a cigarette in his hand, and no boots on his feet. He got into the ambulance. I asked him why he didn't bring his clothes and his boots. He said he needed to get away before he got into more trouble, and he knew if he'd worn the boots and carried his duffel bag, a nurse might stop him. Snow was pouring down. That ambulance might as well have been invisible. I drove him to the square, to the first tall ice sculpture I found, and I told him exactly what I thought about drinking and driving. I told him about my dad. He pretended he didn't know what I was talking about, then he said he wasn't driving, that some girl he didn't know had picked him up." He glared at Whitney. "You were his victim, too."

Whitney ducked her head and said something about Travis not deserving to die.

Gartborg asked Corey, "How did the deceased end up underneath the ice sculpture?"

"It's easy to knock someone out and leave a mark that some other blunt object could have made. Don't worry. He never felt a thing. He was unconscious when I dragged him behind the sculpture and rammed it with the ambulance. When I backed the ambulance away, falling snow was covering him and the ice sculpture on top of him. The cold probably finished him off, but he wouldn't have felt it, unlike what my dad has to go through. Travis Tarriston could have killed kids on that bus. Kids! Considering what he did, he got off lucky."

Samantha shuddered. Hooligan pulled her closer. She said, "I'm missing a ski and both poles, but walking up that hill will warm me up, and that's what I'm going to do. And you need to get inside, too, Emily."

Chapter 36

✼

Before we started up the hill, Scott skied down, passed us slowly and carefully, and stopped at the group surrounding Corey. He said loudly enough for all of us to hear, "Leo's bringing the snowmobile around the other way. He said to meet him at the foot of the hill where the trail's wide enough for him to turn around so he can go to the end of the driveway closest to the road. Misty's directing the cruiser there."

Below us and to our left, a snowmobile roared, coming closer along the trail down near the lake.

Brent and Detective Gartborg took off their skis. Each of them holding one of Corey's elbows, they walked him along the trail toward the base of the hill. A plastic tie fastened Corey's wrists together behind his back. Apparently, Detective Gartborg was always prepared to make arrests. Corey walked with his head down. Scott skied behind them.

Samantha turned to Hooligan. "Go help them in case he tries to get away. I'll be fine with Emily, Jocelyn, and everyone else."

Hooligan kissed her forehead, snapped on his skis, and glided gracefully around the holes in the trail to join his colleagues.

Gartborg turned and called to her boys. They yelled, "Okay!" and retrieved Brent's and their mother's skis and poles. Ivan tried to help them carry everything, but despite his eager jaws, they hung on to the skis and the poles plus their own poles. Carrying their ungainly loads, they disappeared around the S curve with apparently no trouble other than interference from their eager dog.

Whitney, Parker, and Ronald had been leaning on their poles close to where they'd helped Corey out of the snow. Ronald followed Hooligan.

Parker and Whitney skied up the hill to us. Whitney asked Samantha how she was.

"Just cold. I landed in soft snow and wasn't sure how to get out. Or whether to get out. But I need to move. I'll walk up the hill. Or maybe I can put my one ski back on and push with one foot while I glide with the other."

Jocelyn looked down at Samantha's feet. "That sounds uncomfortable and difficult, Samantha. Give me a second." Jocelyn scooted into the snow where Samantha had landed after Corey tripped her. Again, Jocelyn stayed upright. With her forehead wrinkled, she moved a foot around in the fluffy stuff. She pulled Samantha's second ski out of the snow and pushed it onto the trail. "It looks fine. Do you have any idea where your poles went, Samantha?"

"No. I might have been accidentally imitating you and turning cartwheels."

I tied the sleeves of her jean jacket around my waist. "You were." I pointed at the woods beside the trail. "I think they flew that direction."

Parker looked up, smiled, reached above his head, and calmly dislodged a pole from a pine bough.

Jocelyn looked doubtfully down the hill toward the trampled snow where Corey had landed after I collided with him. "Corey's a lot taller than Samantha and I are, but Samantha can use one of my poles. I'll borrow one of Corey's."

"Oops," I said. "Ivan and I kind of scattered Corey's poles around Brent's property."

Jocelyn waved dismissively. "No problem. I could make do with no poles, but one might be better than none. Parker will be right behind me. You'll push me if I slow down, right, Parker?"

He grinned and helped her out of the soft snow and up onto the trail beside him. "You, Jocelyn? You, slow down?"

"It could happen." She removed her skis from our temporary barricade.

Down the hill, the snowmobile roared. The sound became quieter as it must have moved off along the trail near the lake.

We all put on our skis again and let Samantha go first. She scooted up that hill as quickly as anyone could. I pushed myself up the hill behind her. Olivia, Whitney, Jocelyn, and Parker followed us.

Gradually, the sound of the snowmobile dwindled in the snowy forest. Chickadees and nuthatches called. A breeze rustled through the pines and blew clots of snow down onto me. I didn't see my hat. We all made it to the top without resorting to herringboning or otherwise destroying more of Brent's careful grooming. I skied across his front yard.

A police cruiser was already at the far end of the driveway. From that distance, I didn't recognize the uniformed officer who shut one of the rear doors and climbed into the front. The cruiser left without sirens wailing or lights flashing.

I asked Samantha, "How are you doing?"

"Physically? A few aches and pains." She patted her mouth. "And my lip is swelling, but I inadvertently started icing it down there. But emotionally?" She shook her head. "I guess if I'd thought about how he sometimes seemed to have rage boiling underneath the surface, I might have expected this. But I never thought he'd erupt like that. Or do what he did, what he admitted doing."

Whitney put an arm around Samantha. "I'm so sorry. A lot of this is my fault. If I hadn't let Travis drive my folks' car that afternoon, I wouldn't have ruined that boy's life. First by contributing to his father's injuries, and now . . ." She looked away from us.

Samantha reminded her gently, "You were a teenager. And you said other people were stopping to help."

Whitney wiped at her tears. "I know, but . . ."

Ivan dashed up the hill with something black and white in his mouth. He dropped it at Samantha's feet and tore down the hill again. That slope was going to need a lot of grooming.

Samantha bent over, picked up Ivan's "gift," and laughed. Straightening, she brushed snow off her black stocking cap. Then she filled it with snow and held it against her lip.

Waving, Brent drove the snowmobile past along the driveway. A pair of skis and poles were strapped to a carrier on one side of the snowmobile. He followed the driveway as it curved behind the house toward the garage.

Ivan charged up the hill again. This time, I recognized the red, white, green, and snowy object in the dog's mouth. I wondered if he knew who it belonged to.

He dropped it at my feet and looked up at me with a huge doggie grin on his face. I picked it up, patted his massive head and told him what a good boy he was.

He went tearing off again, this time down the driveway toward the road. His tail wagged in circles.

He returned with his entire family plus Leo, Ronald, Hooligan, Misty, and Scott. Misty and Scott gave Samantha one-armed hugs, and then Hooligan held her like he never wanted to let her go. Gartborg was again wearing her skis.

Brent returned from the garage. "Let's all go in for chili," he said. "And Zander and Rylan, bring Ivan in, too. I understand he performed some heroics today."

I agreed. "He certainly did."

Samantha added, "He dragged me out of a snowdrift."

I rubbed the dog's head. "And he removed one of Corey's

poles before Corey could use it to help himself out of soft snow." The fur on the top of Ivan's head was surprisingly warm.

We took off our skis and leaned them and our poles against the porch railing.

Inside, Brent started re-warming the chili. The rest of us trooped into the guest room and removed our outer clothing. I also shed my oversized shirt. In my slinky leggings, matching tank top, and cute ballet flats, I joined the party in the great room. Maybe, with my lack of height and the lace trimming my tank top, I wasn't as elegant as the tall, slender detective from the Wisconsin Division of Criminal Investigation, but Brent smiled when he saw me. Beside me, Misty whispered, "You look great!" Most of the others had changed from ski to party clothes, too. Samantha already looked warmer in her long velvet gown with its high neck and long sleeves. Brent gave her an ice pack to replace the rapidly melting snow in her hat.

"Brr! Thanks." She held it against her swollen lip.

I hung her wet hat with her jeans and jacket above the tub in the guest bathroom.

Tom and Cindy arrived with the promised donuts. They frowned when they heard about Corey knocking Samantha down and nearly attacking her. I pretended I'd plowed into Corey accidentally. I probably didn't fool anyone.

I opted for Brent's spicier chili. It was, as always, delicious and satisfying.

After we ate, Detective Gartborg put her bowl and spoon in the dishwasher and told her boys to meet her at the lodge at Lake Cares Away. "Detective Fyne and I need to go question Corey." She turned to Brent. "I'll follow you, Brent."

"Meanwhile," Brent said, "the rest of you stay here for dessert." He looked straight at me. "I'll be back."

Pretending that little thrills of anticipation weren't zinging through me, I merely stared back at him.

Samantha asked him, "What about the ambulance?"

"A flatbed truck is on its way to take it to the lab." He smiled at her. "You can ride home with Hooligan as you originally planned." He and Detective Gartborg left.

I made coffee and boiled water for tea. Whitney heated another pot of hot chocolate, and Scott made mulled cider. Tom had brought a tantalizing array of donuts including apple cider donuts highly flavored with cinnamon, fudge-frosted chocolate donuts with chunks of maraschino cherries and macadamia nuts, gingerbread donuts with tiny bits of candied ginger in them, raised donuts filled with peppermint marshmallow cream, and chocolate-chip lemon donuts. And he'd stacked them up into a Christmas tree. He warned us, "Watch out for toothpicks."

Misty and Hooligan went outside to make certain that the flatbed truck took the right vehicle. "Not that there are a lot of ambulances parked out there," Hooligan joked. "I'll be back in a minute, Samantha."

She smiled back at him. "I'm fine."

Ronald polished off a couple of donuts and said he had to leave for work. Another storm was coming. "Not as bad as Wednesday's." He retrieved his coat, blushed when he smiled at Olivia, called goodbye to the rest of us, and tromped out to the porch.

Misty and Hooligan returned, bringing a drift of cold, fresh air with them. Hooligan told Samantha, "Your ambulance is on its way to the lab."

Zander and Rylan tuned their guitars and started another Christmas sing-along. Misty and Scott cuddled on one end of one couch while Hooligan and Samantha cuddled on the other. Misty kept looking at her left hand. Whitney sat wrapped in Leo's arm on Brent's second couch. Cindy perched at the far end of that couch with Tom beside her on the arm. Parker and Jocelyn weren't good at sitting still. Parker kept the fire going. Jocelyn washed pots and pans and then sat between Olivia and me on the wide stone hearth. Ivan slept next to my feet. I wormed my toes underneath him. Reveling in the heat near my back, I reached forward and stroked him. His legs twitched, but he went on snoring.

Finally, Zander checked the time and looked at his brother. "We'd better go before Mom gets back to our room and calls the cops on us."

They put their guitars away and collected their coats. Ivan seemed to be sound asleep, but as soon as they headed toward the door, he raised his head, stared at them for a second, stood up, stretched, gave himself a shake that jingled the tags on his collar, and pranced outside behind his boys.

That seemed to be the signal for the others. Tom and Cindy left, followed by Parker, Jocelyn, and Olivia. Whitney and Leo gave the doorjamb fond pats as they went out to the porch for their skis and poles. "See you around, Emily!" Leo called.

I was alone. I didn't know when Brent would be back. Everyone had taken their dishes to the kitchen, Jocelyn had put the chili away and washed the pots, and we'd eaten the donuts, so there was no leftover food to put away. I took my time filling the dishwasher and tidying the kitchen.

And then I had a decision to make. Should I wait for Brent? The interrogation could take hours.

Ronald had said a storm was coming.

Dep would be fine at home alone. I sat down with a Christmas magazine. I'd barely turned three pages when I heard footsteps on the porch and then Brent's signature *rat-a-tat-tat* on the door. I stood up. Brent came in and kicked off his boots. "I saw your car, about a mile away on the driveway, so I knew you were still here."

"I . . ." I didn't know what to say. I turned toward the kitchen. "I started the dishwasher."

"Thank you. Are you going to ask how our chat with Corey went?"

I stopped underneath the balcony. "How did it go?" That almost-hidden sprig of mistletoe was above me.

Brent tossed his parka onto the nearest couch. "He confessed."

I nodded toward the dark forest in front of the house. "He more or less did that on the trail this afternoon."

"Now it's signed. Also, Paige emailed us that she was at home. She had emailed a friend who drove up and took her back to Green Bay. I told her we'd made an arrest. She apologized for lying about the things she put in your garbage."

"Thanks for letting me know. You look proud of yourself."

"You helped. Again. And you look . . . like yourself."

Barely aware of what I was doing, I stepped closer to him. I was farther from the mistletoe, but I didn't need mistletoe as an excuse. I took a deep breath, braced my shoulders, and looked up into his face. "That's good to know."

He gazed into my eyes for a couple of seconds and then leaned toward me. Once again, a question lurked in those kind gray eyes.

With my eyes locked on his, I tilted my face up toward his.

"Wait a second," he said. "There's a storm coming, and I'm not on call." He took out his phone and turned off the ringtone.

And then we were in each other's arms. Which was where we belonged.

RECIPES

Gingerbread Donuts

1¾ cups all-purpose flour
1 tablespoon baking powder
2 teaspoons powdered ginger
1 teaspoon ground cinnamon
½ teaspoon ground nutmeg
¼ teaspoon ground cloves
1 tablespoon candied ginger, chopped fine (Note: Candied
    ginger near the outsides of donuts will become crunchy
    during frying.)
2 egg yolks, beaten
¼ cup molasses
¼ cup milk
¼ cup brown sugar, packed
1 tablespoon melted unsalted butter
Vegetable oil with a smoke point of 400° F or higher (or fol-
    low your deep fryer's instruction manual)
Confectioners' or granulated sugar (optional)

Sift the flour, baking powder, ginger, cinnamon, nutmeg, and cloves into one bowl. Stir in candied ginger.

In another bowl, mix the egg, molasses, milk, brown sugar, and melted butter. Stir wet ingredients into dry ingredients until blended. If necessary, add flour by tablespoonfuls until dough is just barely firm enough to handle. Do not overmix. Wrap in plastic wrap and chill several hours or overnight.

Roll dough to ½ inch thick. Cut with donut cutter or one large round cutter with a smaller round cutter to make a hole in the center. Cover with a damp cloth and allow to rest for a half hour.

Heat oil to 360° F. Gently slip the donuts and donut holes, a few at a time, into hot oil. Do not overcrowd. Cook for about two minutes until puffed and browning, turn, and cook for about one minute. Lift and drain on paper towels.

Makes about a half dozen donuts and a half dozen donut holes.

When cool, sprinkle with confectioners' or granulated sugar if desired.

Chocolate-Orange Donuts

1¾ cups all-purpose flour
½ cup unsweetened cocoa powder
1 tablespoon baking powder
2 egg yolks, beaten
½ cup orange juice
½ teaspoon orange extract
zest from one medium orange (reserve 1 teaspoonful for
    glaze)
½ cup sugar
1 tablespoon melted unsalted butter
Vegetable oil with a smoke point of 400° F or higher (or fol-
    low your deep fryer's instruction manual)

Sift the flour, cocoa, and baking powder into one bowl.

In another bowl, mix the egg yolks, orange juice, orange extract, orange zest, sugar, and melted butter. Stir wet ingredients into dry ingredients and stir until thoroughly blended. If necessary, add flour by tablespoonfuls until dough is just barely firm enough to handle. Do not overmix. Wrap and chill several hours or overnight.

Roll dough to ½ inch thick. Cut with donut cutter or one large round cutter with a smaller round cutter to make a hole in the center. Cover with a damp cloth and allow to rest for ½ hour.

Heat oil to 360° F. Gently slip the donuts and donut holes, a few at a time, into hot oil. Do not overcrowd. Cook for about two minutes until puffed up and brown, turn, and cook for about another two minutes. Lift and drain on paper towels.

Makes about a half dozen donuts and a half dozen donut holes.

When cool, frost with chocolate orange frosting or drizzle with orange glaze and then decorate with orange zest, colored sugar, or sprinkles.

For the Chocolate Orange Frosting:
½ cup unsweetened cocoa powder
¼ cup granulated sugar
6 tablespoons orange juice
1 tablespoon unsalted butter
¼ teaspoon orange extract

Sift the cocoa powder or press it through a sieve into a microwavable dish.

Add the sugar. With a fork, blend the sugar and cocoa powder together well.

Add the orange juice, two tablespoons at a time, and stir after each addition until you have created a thickish paste.

Add the butter.

Cover the dish and heat in your microwave oven for approximately two minutes on a medium-low to medium setting.

Stir until the butter has melted completely and is blended well with the paste.

Cool slightly.

Stir in the orange extract.

Spread on donuts while the frosting is still warm.

For the Orange Glaze:
¼ cup orange juice
3 tablespoons sugar

Stir orange juice and sugar together until sugar is dissolved.

Heat in saucepan over medium heat until mixture thickens.

Spoon over donuts while the glaze is still warm.

Connect with U s